THE
JAWBONE
GANG

PENNY GRUBB

ACORN INDEPENDENT PRESS

Praise For The Author

Penny has a way of getting inside the heads and hearts of her characters to bring them to life. Even her villains carry characteristics that make the reader care what happens. But it is Annie who we really empathise with, in spite of her faults, irritabilities, occasional snap judgements and chaotic domestic lifestyle.
Must Mutter Literary Blog

Penny handles scenes of danger particularly well, injecting feelings of fear, anxiety and doubt into the story so that the reader is drawn into the created world.
Stuart Aken, author and reviewer

I particularly enjoy the fact that these books give a real picture of life as a 21st century private investigator, rather than slipping into the hackneyed `amateur sleuth' model.
Susan Alison, author and artist, Bristol

PRAISE FOR THE JAWBONE GANG

Penny deals with real life issues in her detective series, eschewing gloss and glamour to give her readers insights into experiences closer to home. Her descriptions entertain with their detailed vibrancy and her characters leave the page as real people. She builds tension convincingly and the air of menace that prevails on her protagonist at key moments is skilfully contrasted with more basic daily worries assailing Annie as she attempts to modernise the agency in spite of the complacency and indolence of her bosses.
Stuart Aken, author and reviewer

If you haven't read any of Penny's crime novels, I urge you to do so. And, if you have, you'll find The Jawbone Gang as intriguing and enthralling as the others.
Must Mutter Literary Blog

With this new novel featuring PI Annie Raymond, Penny Grubb continues to deliver the high standards of narrative she has shown us with the previous stories.
Angela Dracup, Author and reviewer

Published by Acorn Independent Press Ltd, 2011.
First published in hardback by Robert Hale Ltd in May 2010

Printed and bound by CPI Group (UK) Ltd, Croydon, CR0 4YY

ISBN 978-1-908318-69-5

www.acornindependentpress.com

ABOUT THE AUTHOR

Penny Grubb is a novelist as well as an academic and Chair of the Authors' Licensing and Collecting Society, the largest writers' organisation in the world. Her fiction includes the crime series featuring Private Investigator, Annie Raymond.

Penny won the Crime Writers' Association's Debut Dagger for her novel, the Doll Makers, one of her Annie Raymond series. In 2010, Like False Money, another novel in the series, was nominated for the CWA John Creasey Dagger. A writer all her life, Penny penned her first story at age 4 and won her first writing competition at age 9. She has worked in a variety of jobs and seen the inside of hospitals and pathology labs across Europe. As well as her crime novels, Penny's work has been published as short fiction, non-fiction, textbooks, academic papers, articles and radio broadcasts.

Find out more at:

www.pennygrubb.com

Photograph by Weronika Dziok

Also By The Author

The Doll Makers

Like False Money

Both titles are now available in paperback,
published in 2011 by Acorn Independent Press

Acknowledgements

Thanks to Hornsea Writers for their incisive critiques on the work-in-progress; to Mary for all the stories of Hull, and to B Dziok who created the brilliant artwork for the cover.

To George, of course!

PROLOGUE

Night-time mist lay over the vegetation at the sides of the lane, blurring the contours where the fields melted into darkness.

Peering into a murky landscape that had largely swallowed the light, the woman punctuated the silence with urgent whispers. 'There, Ronnie. What did I tell you? Just look. It's her... No, it's him... Is that a wheelbarrow...? What are they doing, Ron...? Can you see...? Oh God! Keep down. They're coming this way.'

A grumbled response snapped her attention to the man at her side. 'Ronnie!' She grabbed his arm and shook until he jerked awake and glared at her through bleary eyes.

'Uh... Sheryl... for God's sake... what time is it?'

'I don't know... two o'clock. They've seen us, Ron. Quick, get the van started.'

He yawned, infuriatingly calm. 'Where? I can't see anything.'

'Quick, Ron. They disappeared into that shed. And if—' She stopped on a gasp and leant forward to stare hard. 'What if there's a door the other side? Oh my God! They'll see us.'

He laid his hand on her arm. 'Take one of your tablets, Sheryl. You're getting in a state.' He sat up straight and yawned again. 'No one can see us from over there. We're in shadow.'

'But, Ron...'

'I'll start the engine if you want. That'll get their attention. A car out here in the middle of nowhere. D'you want me to try?'

'Don't you dare touch that key!'

'Now tell me what you thought you saw this time.'

'I did see something this time. I saw a shape move out from over there.' She strained forward again to peer out. The low light painted a gleam to the maroon-patterned nail of her index

1

finger as it choreographed her tale. 'Both of them, I'm sure it was. That means he's in it too. And they had something. A wheelbarrow, I think.'

'Sheryl, listen to me. They're tucked up in bed in that house sound asleep. Maybe it was dogs you saw. They probably leave them loose in the yard at nights.'

'It was too big for dogs, Ron. It was people.'

'Then cows or something.'

'Cows! Who has cows walking round their yard at night?'

He turned to look at her and didn't speak until she faced him. 'It's a bloody farm, woman, and you've seen the bloody cattle walking about. Now, let's settle down and get some rest if we can.'

'It wasn't cows,' she muttered.

'All right then, deer.'

'Deer? Come off it. We're in East Yorkshire not Scotland.'

'Plenty of deer round here, Sheryl, you ask anyone. Now for God's sake, get some sleep.'

She threw him a glare as he settled back in his seat. The house and yard lay quiet, but she felt tension in the air as the breeze from the estuary sent ripples through the grass.

'I can't sleep now,' she thought she said, but a moment later realized she had, as she woke with a start, blinking in bright sunlight.

She made no attempt to wake the man by her side who lay head back, mouth half open, his snores reverberating through the vehicle.

Twisting the mirror towards her, she smoothed her hair and brushed down her jacket before clicking open the door of the van and stepping out into a morning that had swept away the landscape's sinister gloss.

From where she stood, the house was almost hidden behind the big shed. Just its roof showed. She wondered if houses learnt to sleep and wake with their owners. If it were a farm, this was the time the house and its inhabitants would be up and awake, bustling about, but she sensed no movement, saw no sign of life.

She pushed her arms out straight, stretching the night-time out of them, bending her hands up and admiring the patterned gleam. Her favourite shade of maroon glinted back at her from her finger ends. For hands approaching their half century, they weren't in bad shape.

'I know what I saw, Ron,' she murmured. 'It wasn't cows. And they're not real farmers.'

CHAPTER ONE

The row of buildings started life as overspill from the big warehouses that held prime positions by the river. Never close enough to the centre of Hull to catch regeneration grants and just too far from the waterway to become fashionable apartments, conversion work had been sporadic and always on a shoestring. The owners of the shabbiest building of all, having converted it to office space, had commandeered the best of it for themselves, which was all the downstairs except for a shared lobby, and rented out the poky upstairs rooms that no amount of effort could make anything other than seedy.

It was late morning as Annie arrived, swapping a 'how do' with the postman who left the building as she entered. He'd left three letters in their tray, which she grabbed before taking the stairs two at a time, relieved to feel the vibration of heavy footfalls from the small upstairs office that signalled her boss's presence.

She pushed the door open, calling out, 'Hi, Pat, I can't hang about. I want to leave some info for Barbara.'

No reply.

Annie felt her insides scrunch tight. Pat would have answered at once. The elephantine tread must be Pat's sister, but the error was irretrievable. Sure enough, Barbara lumbered in from the back office, her bulk filling the doorway, her hand outstretched, her expression thunderous.

'What info? What are you doing interfering in my cases? I don't want you messing things up.'

Annie bit down on a surge of annoyance. 'I'm not. I just stumbled over something. It's important.'

'I'll be the judge of that. What is it? Hand it over.'

'It's something I saw. I was in Mellors' HQ this morning, and—'

'What were you doing there? You've no business visiting them.'

Annie struggled against the temptation to blurt out that she was trying to retrieve something from the mess Barbara was making of the Mellors' case, and said instead, 'Delivering stuff for Pat.'

'Oh... Well, I don't see why she couldn't go herself.'

Annie looked at the woman in front of her. Eighteen stone, she judged, and rising, but able to kid herself she didn't carry too much excess weight because her sister was even bigger. At least Pat made the effort to climb the stairs to the office on a regular basis. Barbara's presence here on a Friday was both unusual and unwelcome.

'Those guys putting the screw on your client,' she told Barbara, 'they claim they knew nothing about the original property deal till everything was well underway?'

Barbara nodded.

'Well, it turns out they knew about it last November. They wrote a letter about it. I have the date and the recipient's address.' Annie pulled a scrap of paper from her back pocket and held it out. 'So you need to write and demand a copy of that exact—'

'Don't tell me how to do my job,' snapped Barbara, grabbing the paper. 'I'm already on to it.'

Annie looked down at the mail in her hand. One letter was addressed personally to her. Without a word, she skimmed the other two on to the desk top, turned on her heel and went back down the stairs. Tell her how to do her job! Someone should. Without that address and date, Barbara would have blundered into a settlement that would make the client wonder why on earth he had wasted his money on a private investigator. Now, with that under her belt, she would close a brilliant deal for a good client and end up with some useful recommendations. And because Pat hadn't been here today, Barbara would take all the credit.

As she stepped back out on to the street, Annie ripped open her letter and ran her eye down the few lines. It was from a woman who ran a riding school out in Holderness, inviting her to come and judge a fancy-dress competition.

Perfect for you as a detective, the scribbled lines ran. *It's a mythical warriors theme. You can bring an advertising banner. Let me know if you can't make it. Otherwise, see you on the day.*

'Oh, for heaven's sake!' Annie fought an urge to scrunch the paper and throw it into the road. A years-old case had forced her to feign a temporary interest in the workings of the riding school and she'd been pestered with these sorts of invitations ever since.

She glanced at the page again. Advertising banner? Even supposing they had such a thing, why would they advertise at a horsey fancy-dress do? With an exasperated sigh, she rammed the letter into her pocket. Another irritation adding to a day that had begun to turn sour. Some risky sleight of hand had gathered that information for Barbara and the world at large wanted to fob her off with fancy-dress shows.

She marched smartly through the streets of Hull, skimming the old town and cutting through Dagger Lane towards the dual carriageway. Castle Street, a fog of exhaust fumes, pulsed with traffic noise. Annie eyed the main road as she emerged from the side street. A block of traffic at the tree-lined roundabout was just revving for the off, so she broke into a run, taking the first triple-laned carriageway in a few swift strides. A single long blare sounded behind her as she vaulted the central fence, but she ignored it. Cars streamed off the wide sweep of Myton Bridge, stopping her briefly, before she saw a gap and was at the other side heading for the quayside pub where she often had lunch.

Speed had taken her away from the poisonous bulk of Pat's elder sister and had calmed her. It solved nothing to risk life and limb on busy roads. She must either confront Pat again over the problems of the business, or she must cut free and strike out on her own. The bits of cases they took on could keep them ticking over forever. The sisters were satisfied with that: Annie wasn't.

She pushed open the door and entered the bar; a dark cave after the brightness of the street, its usually loud music a dull background beat behind the jingle of gaming machines rippling patterns across their square glass faces. As Annie's eyes adjusted, she saw the place was all but empty. She'd beaten the lunchtime rush.

The barman clocked her entrance with a nod of recognition and signalled to a woman at the far end of the counter. Annie ignored the exchange. He was forever telling people she would solve their problems. Stolen car... broken window...? Ask Annie... she's in the business... she'll sort it for you...

And she was forever telling him, 'We don't do that stuff. Tell them to call the police if their car's gone missing.'

She ordered half a pint of smooth and a cheese and onion sandwich which she carried to a table in a corner. The bread was fresh, the cheese chunky and the onion crisp between her teeth. She savoured the sharp taste and watched the place fill up. She was aware of the woman at the bar throwing glances her way, and avoided looking across in case accidental eye contact should be interpreted as an invitation to come over and talk. Then the woman's glances stopped abruptly as a short stocky man came in. Annie watched the mime of conversation between them as the woman drained her glass before linking arms with the man as they made for the door.

They strolled past, looking neither right nor left. Annie heard the woman say, 'Aw, leave it out, Ron,' as she draped her hand over his arm, displaying exquisitely-patterned maroon nails.

For a moment, Annie stared, fascinated at the intricacy of the design, then a familiar face appeared and she felt her mouth curve to a smile of greeting. Jennifer Flanagan came in as the couple left. This was a turn up. Jennifer's shift patterns rarely gave her time for lunch.

'Hi.' Jennifer looked pleased to see her. 'I hoped I'd catch you.'

Annie watched her stroll across to the bar to get herself a sandwich. Jennifer Flanagan had been her first friend when she'd arrived in Hull. Sort of. They'd both been rookies: Jennifer in her police probationer's uniform towering over most of her colleagues; Annie newly arrived to work for Jed Thompson's agency in her first proper PI job. Shared blundering through a case that offered complexities neither of them could have imagined had forged a bond.

'How was your trip home?' Jennifer asked, as she sat down.

'Yeah, good. I stayed with Aunt Marian. She's well.'

'And your father?'

'Busy as usual. A real workaholic. But he was pleased to see me.' *Not.* 'Can't wait for me to get a proper job, of course. So what's up?'

'It's nothing official, but I wanted to run something past you. Is there any chance of you taking on a case for someone who doesn't really have any money?'

Annie looked at Jennifer but kept her expression neutral. 'Not usually, but tell me more.' No one knew the stagnant state of the business. It was one area where she and the two sisters were bang on the same page. Any hint they were an ineffective outfit going nowhere would drive away the custom that kept them afloat. The future's bright, was the official line.

'Have you followed that vigilante case? Yates and Walker.'

Annie nodded. The case had been big news; its major players were from the local area. The court case had been rerun in pubs across the town. The bones of it were that 30-year-old Joshua Yates had killed 33-year-old Michael Walker, a man he didn't know. His only defence was an allegation he could not back up that Walker had abused a young girl and must be stopped. Yates was found guilty of murder and the court awaited psychiatric reports before sentencing.

Annie was puzzled. Jennifer had occasionally passed people on to her, but only a handful and only where there was no question that the case belonged outside official territory. Surely this was on the wrong turf.

'I'd like you to meet a woman called Nicole Perks,' Jennifer said. 'She'll fit in with whatever time you can spare. Just hear her out. Either you can help or you can't, but I know I can rely on you to keep it confidential.'

'Are you going to tell me anything about her?'

'She's a couple of years younger than you, about twenty-four... twenty-five, slim build.'

'No, not the e-fit. What does she want to see me about?'

'Oh... uh... I think you should hear that from her, first.'

So Jennifer wanted to minimize her involvement. This backed up Annie's instinct that this was not a legitimate case for her to pass on. Different angles flashed through Annie's mind as she made a decision.

Nicole Perks? The name was unfamiliar, but she could look up the details of the case before they met. This afternoon had been earmarked for trawling through online files for a case she and Pat were working on, but Barbara might still be lurking in the office, so the excuse of a meeting with a potential new client to keep her in town was welcome. She could do the work just as well at the library. But the biggest question was what was the deal with Jennifer, who usually did everything by the book?

She nodded. 'I can carve out a gap this afternoon, but just to talk to her. No promises about taking the case.'

CHAPTER TWO

When Annie arrived in the library, she found her usual corner writhing with schoolchildren fighting for space at the screens. She took a place at another terminal, resentful of the turbulent atmosphere that made it hard to concentrate.

It took longer than it should have to dig out all she needed for the case she was currently working on with Pat, but once done, she turned her attention to recent media articles on the vigilante trial.

The facts of the murder were not in dispute. Yates had gone to Michael Walker's house and stabbed him several times. He had then walked bloodstained through the streets of Hull to turn in himself and the murder weapon at the central police station, gathering a multitude of witnesses along the way.

Annie shielded the screen as a couple of the schoolchildren pushed by. For all the media coverage, it felt inappropriate to display the lurid headlines for them to see. They settled opposite her, chattering over their notebook. She heard enough to glean that they were part of the annual Young Persons' University scheme. The scheme made a small dent in the local media every year. Annie supposed it was a good thing as the city didn't do well in school league tables, but wished they hadn't chosen her favourite corner of the library to work in. Her mental picture of the supposed victim in the vigilante case put the girl at about the age of the girls across from her – 11 or so – but Yates had never specified.

The partners of both the murderer, Yates, and his victim, Walker, appeared in the news coverage.

VICTIM'S LIVE-IN LOVER PROTESTS HIS INNOCENCE.

MURDERER'S GIRL CLAIMS POLICE INCOMPETENCE.

Reading through the cuttings, what struck Annie was the thinness of Yates's allegations. He claimed he had a witness, but wouldn't name her and no one came forward. His vehement proclamations against Walker were both ghoulishly specific and bizarrely vague. He was quoted as shouting about Walker's 'unspeakable degradations', about him 'forcing unwelcome attentions' on young girls.

Annie wondered how far the police had looked at Walker's background. Enough, surely. The official line remained that Walker was a man of unblemished character and Yates was a madman.

Although aware of the shape of the case and the names of the murderer and victim, this was the first time Annie had paid attention to the detail. Seeing that the girlfriends of each man had spoken up, she expected to see the name Nicole Perks attached to one of them, but it wasn't. Walker's partner, who had come home to find his bloodied body, was called Charlotte Liversedge; the woman fighting Yates's corner was Brittany Booth.

Annie had agreed to the meeting mainly as a favour to Jennifer, but now felt a stab of curiosity about Nicole Perks. Could she be the missing witness?

'Thanks so much for meeting me. I've heard you're really good. We simply have to clear his name.'

Nicole Perks, a slim woman with short mousy hair, was already in the coffee shop where they'd arranged to meet and Annie heard huge expectation in the greeting as the woman leapt forward to shake her hand. Annie smiled back and said, 'Don't get your hopes up. I'm happy to talk it through, but that doesn't mean I'll be able to take the case on. Let's just see how it goes.'

She glanced towards the faraway roof of the open plan shopping mall. The sheer size of the glass panes that made up the walls added to the overall impression of massive space and height. This was not a place to meet when it was packed with shoppers, but the few hundred here now were absorbed easily. The place looked deserted.

She wondered whose name she was being asked to clear.

'Start from the beginning,' she said, as she sat down. 'What's your connection with the case? What exactly do you want me to do?'

'I'm a friend of Charlotte. We're supposed to be business partners but it's all on hold now, of course.'

'Charlotte Liversedge? Michael Walker's girlfriend? Did you know Michael Walker?'

'Yes. Yes, I knew them both. I've known them a long time. They're going to crucify Michael now. We can't let that happen.'

'All I know is what I read in the papers. I know the guy who killed him claimed he had a justification, but I don't know much more than that. I thought it was an open and shut case.'

'Oh, it was dreadful. Yates is a vile man... a madman. He claimed Michael was a paedophile. He said he'd kept a young girl as his sexual slave for years. Kept her imprisoned like that awful Garrido man. As if anyone could have led the life Michael led and hidden something like that. It's absurd.' Nicole's voice rose with a mix of anger and upset. She snatched a tissue from her pocket and blew her nose.

'The police would have checked it all out, anyway.'

'Yes, of course they would. There's no truth in any of it.'

'Who was the young girl supposed to be?'

'Yates wouldn't say. He spouted such garbage from that witness box. We think he insisted on giving evidence; no barrister worth anything would have put him there deliberately. He went on about a witness and how someone would come forward with evidence, but, of course, no one did.'

Annie thought back. Yates's impassioned plea to his witness to come forward sparked memories of overheard comments in a city pub.

'He'd hardly say all that if he didn't have something...'

'If a tenth of that's true...'

But no witness came forward and the tiny swell of sympathy for Yates ebbed.

'Did Yates have any visible support during the trial?' Annie asked.

'Not that we saw. We wondered if there would be because he reckoned to be some sort of a spiritual leader. We were really worried there'd be a gang of nutters in court on his side.'

'What sort of spiritual leader?'

'Some cult thing he founded himself. To do with getting homeless men off the streets. All fantasy by the sound of it. We didn't think he had anyone until that cow started shooting her mouth off. There has to be a way to stop her. She's really going to trash Michael's name.'

'But who is she?'

'She's supposed to be Yates's girlfriend. A vile cow called Brittany Booth. She's talking to people, getting them on her side. She's really scary. It gives you the creeps just to look at her. Making out all kinds of stuff that just isn't true. She's got a campaign to raise money. And what can we do? We can't even afford to hire you properly.'

'Aren't you worrying over nothing? Sure, she might get a few nutters, as you call them, on her side. You just have to say paedophile and some people's brains drop out. But there's never been a scrap of evidence against Michael Walker.'

'Yeah, but now she's saying he was investigated for child abuse six years ago, and that'll get people thinking no smoke without fire.'

Annie thought about the crime Yates attributed to Walker. This wasn't the USA where 11-year-old Jaycee Dugard could be snatched from under her parents' gaze and kept out of sight for eighteen years. The British Isles were too small to hide the crime Yates had described.

'And was there an earlier accusation?' she asked. 'I mean, not that it'll make a difference to the court; Yates is going down for murder.'

'We want him locked away in an institution like the madman he is, but if that Brittany Booth gets things stirred up enough, they might send him to an ordinary prison. He might be out in a few years.'

'I really don't think there's anything Brittany Booth can do that will influence the sentencing. That's going to rest on the psychiatric reports.' Annie struggled to see a useful role for herself. Nicole and her friend would be better off with counsellors. She was surprised Jennifer hadn't eased them that way.

'And what if the doctors believe he was right about Michael? Doesn't that make him less mad?'

'No... I don't know. It's still murder. It doesn't justify what he did. So what story is she peddling?'

'She says he was investigated and got away, that it's down to incompetent policing, that they messed up Ian Huntley's records and now they've let another one through the net.'

'But was there any earlier investigation? Is there anything in her story?'

'No, nothing. It's all garbage. The woman's insane. I mean it. You can see it in her eyes. But it's really got to Charlotte. She's beside herself. She'll barely talk to me about it.'

Annie sat back. She didn't see that Yates's sentence could be influenced by any stories Brittany Booth spread, but it could have a major impact on Charlotte Liversedge if people began to believe the allegations against her partner. Annie could imagine the trial by tabloid that would follow.

... THE LIVE-IN LOVER... MUST HAVE KNOWN...
AS GUILTY AS HE WAS...

And goodbye to any fledgling business venture she and Nicole had going.

'Is there anything you can do? We can pay for a few hours of your time.'

'It's tricky. It's proving a negative. Often it just isn't possible and you could spend thousands trying. If Yates had come out with any names, or where and when, I'd have a starting point. I could look to show that Michael Walker had been nowhere near the supposed victim at the time. But without any specifics, it's difficult.'

Annie paused as she saw Nicole's face fall, as though Annie were the last hope and was pulling the rug from under her. If it meant so much, she could give it a shot.

'There's one handle I can see. This accusation of an investigation six years ago. I can look into that. I can probably show it never happened. It might be useful to talk to Charlotte. Pay me for an hour's time to start with and I'll get to know if it's worth going any further.'

Nicole's expression was fierce with hope. 'Thank you so much. I'll do that. And I'll arrange for you to meet Charlotte.'

Annie's mobile rang as she left the coffee bar.

'How soon can you get back to the office?' Pat's voice said in her ear.

'I'm on my way now. I've got the stuff we need.'

'Good. I'll take over on that. Hurry back. There's another new case for you. Did you pick up any messages this morning?'

'No, why?'

After the ghost of a pause, Pat said, 'Uh... nothing. It wasn't important.'

Annie felt her eyes narrow. What now? What part was she playing this time in the sisters' continual feuding? But this wasn't one to unravel by phone.

'So what's the new case?'

'It's from Vince.'

Annie pulled a face as she heard the tension in Pat's voice. Pat knew what she thought of Vince Sleeman. It had only been a few days ago when Barbara had walked in on one of Annie's attempts to persuade Pat to take things along different lines.

'Dad built this business from nothing and he didn't keep it going by specializing,' Barbara had proclaimed.

'You didn't keep it at all!' Annie had fired back, but neither sister would listen to that sort of criticism. Their late father, Jed

Thompson, was a god to whom they paid homage by keeping his business alive. Except they weren't keeping it alive. All the worthwhile assets, all the business contacts, even the Thompson name now belonged to Vince Sleeman, the trusted business partner who had wrested control from Pat and Barbara within a year of their father's death.

The only chance Annie could see was for the three of them to rebrand themselves as a specialist firm. Investigation of insurance fraud was her favoured route, but Barbara wouldn't hear of it and Annie had to persuade both of them because she had no financial stake to put any clout behind her suggestions. And she was getting weary of the fight.

The cases Vince Sleeman passed on were always dodgy in some respect; often favours for mates he couldn't be bothered with. Pat and Barbara weren't in a position to turn him down, but Annie knew they would have a healthier business if they could. The sisters didn't share her view. Vince had been their father's friend. They felt the connection as a blood bond.

'Vince is very keen to see a result on this one,' Pat went on. 'It'll be good for business if we can pull it off. He's an influential guy.'

As Pat couldn't see her, Annie made no effort to curb her raised-eyebrows expression of incredulity. How could Pat still fall for this?

'Who is it? Have you arranged a meeting?'

'Yes, I've slotted her in for you this evening. You're not doing anything else, are you?'

'Yes, actually. A group of us were going down town.'

'You can get out of it, can't you? This is important and time's tight.'

'Oh, I suppose so, but don't expect me to work all weekend. What's it about anyway?'

'I'll give you the gen when you get here, but you'll have heard of the case. It's a woman called Brittany Booth.'

'Brittany Booth? But we can't. I've just...' Annie paused. Ethical issues wouldn't occur to Pat and sure as hell wouldn't worry Vince. 'That's a coincidence,' she amended. 'I've just picked up the other side.'

'You've picked up what? Hang on, there's someone at the door. Another new client by the look of it. Things are on the up. I'll have to go and let them in. We'll talk when you get here. Don't hang about.'

Annie clicked off the phone and took a quick look back towards the coffee shop. Nicole would be horrified to know her rival had landed up with the same firm, but this might work in her favour. Presumably Brittany Booth wanted exactly the same as Nicole – the truth about Michael Walker. If Annie were to find it, one of her clients wouldn't like the result, but it looked like Brittany Booth was the one with the resources to get the job done.

CHAPTER THREE

Certain sectors become black holes in the network, lying out of easy reach of the city's transport and leisure facilities. Contrasting the burgeoning cafe culture of areas like Spring Bank, these are places where rents bump along the bottom and buildings sport the gloom of decay. Extra money here means a budget for demolition rather than refurbishment. People grumble at the buses but mostly there are plenty of them and they run to time. Where there aren't any at all, people complain at having to bring their cars into town and look without envy at a young woman who jogs up the road, sometimes more than once in a day. They accept that her cardiovascular fitness is better than theirs, but balance that with the assumption she's an obsessive, some kind of weirdo.

Annie ran up the stairs into the office keen both to hear what the message had been that Pat had referred to, and also to get her hands on whatever information Vince Sleeman had passed on about Brittany Booth, but Pat shushed her questions with frantic flapping of her hands and jerked her thumb over her shoulder. Annie's gaze followed the gesture towards the small back office.

'New client,' Pat hissed. 'They just walked in off the street and asked for you by name. They look quite well-to-do so put on a good show in case it's something big.'

'Who are they?'

'A Mr and Mrs Long.'

The name meant nothing, but a trickle of recommendations came through that she was sure could become a flood if they could only focus their resources.

'Any idea what they want?'

'They didn't volunteer, so I didn't push. Go on, don't keep them waiting.'

Pat's hand held a file. Annie's gaze was drawn to the tag where the name Booth was written. It would have to wait.

She opened the door to the back office, put on a smile and stretched out her hand. 'Hello. Mr and Mrs Long? I'm Annie Raymond. I gather you wanted to see me.'

For a fraction of a second surprise threatened her professional welcome. She'd seen these people just a few hours ago in the pub. It looked as though one of the barman's recommendations had at last turned into a real job. The woman with the long maroon fingernails leapt up and grasped her hand.

'Thank you for agreeing to see us so quickly. We need someone investigating. It's urgent.'

'Now, Sheryl,' the man said, 'don't go exaggerating things.' His voice bore the shadow of an East London inflection, which surprised Annie who had expected a gruff Yorkshire tone. He turned to her. 'There's nothing wrong, but it's a case of my wife's nerves. If you can reassure her and it won't cost too much, I'll be well satisfied.'

Won't cost too much? Another worthless bit of a job? Annie held on to the façade of unruffled calm that she used with new clients, but found herself hoping Brittany Booth would not turn out to be the madwoman Nicole Perks described, and that she would have something concrete for her to work on, because out of the three she seemed the only prospect for a job worth doing at the moment.

She sat down in the cramped space and readied her notebook. 'What do you need exactly?'

The woman, Sheryl Long, seemed to Annie to be eager to spill the beans, but her husband was the one to speak.

'We're coming to stay in the area soon, but only for a few weeks,' he said. 'And we've found ourselves a lovely little spot. It's a holiday. We need to relax. We've had a busy year.'

Just a little too much explanation, thought Annie, but it wasn't unusual for people to come through these doors with secrets to hide. It was often the worry of personal agendas coming to light that brought people to firms like theirs. She watched them both closely as the husband explained their problem.

'I took Sheryl out to see the place, just to show her where it was, and she got an idea in her head that she didn't like the neighbours.' Ron Long made a poor attempt at a laugh.

'It might not sound much,' Sheryl broke in, 'but there's something wrong, believe me. We drove past their house and she was just coming out. She gave me this really funny look. You should have seen it. I thought, she's a woman with something to hide. He's in it too.'

A glance speared between the two of them that Annie pretended not to notice.

Mr Long tried again for a jovial laugh. 'See what I mean? There's nothing in it, but Sheryl's highly strung. She needs a rest and for her peace of mind, I'm prepared to let you take a look.'

Annie considered. Her initial assumption had been that they wanted a background check on someone, but didn't want to say why. Now, she wasn't so sure. Something or someone had spooked Sheryl Long. But, providing their personal agendas were outside the job they wanted her to do, she was happy to take it on without knowing more. Ron Long, she judged, cared more about his wife than he would openly admit. He was looking for a concrete solution to make her problem go away. On the little she'd heard, Annie's honest judgement was that this was a case not worth taking on, but their current business model did not allow her to say so.

'What's your contact with this woman? Does she own the place you're going to stay in?'

'No, no. Nothing like that, but she'll be our nearest neighbour.'

'How close? Is she the other side of a semi or are the houses separate?'

'Separate, of course. There must be half a mile between us, but that's not the point. If you'd seen what I'd seen... what we'd seen... you'd know. I couldn't sleep at night with them just down the road.'

'Now, Sheryl, don't get in a state. That's what we're here for. These people are going to prove it's all in your imagination.'

Another negative to have a go at. Annie, seeing that Sheryl did not look at all reassured, added, 'Or find the proof that you're right.'

The comment earned her an indignant look from Mr Long, but Sheryl flashed her a grateful smile.

Pat was right about Mr Long. Well-to-do by the look of him. 'Let's say three hours to start,' she said, tripling the time she thought she would need. 'Now, give me some details. What's this woman's name?'

The two faces in front of her looked blank.

'Her address, then?'

'I don't know as such. I mean we know where it is, of course. It's just across the fields from where we'll be. What would the road be called, Ron?'

'I remember a sign that said Sunk Island.'

'Come through to the main office. You can show me on the map.'

Annie turned the computer screen to face them and pulled up Google maps, zooming in on Hull and dragging the pointer out past Hedon and Paull towards the hamlet of Sunk Island and the skeletal lacework of roads that sewed an agricultural landscape on to the area east of Hull. They must realize how contrived their story sounded.

'Switch to street view,' urged Sheryl. 'You might get to see her.'

Annie laughed. 'I'm sure it won't be long, but it's one of the few places Google hasn't bothered with. Even the satellite pictures aren't that well defined.' She watched the reflection of Ron Long's face in the monitor as she added. 'It's a good place to be if you don't want people watching you closely.'

As soon as they were alone, Annie turned to Pat. 'OK, what message?'

Pat tossed her head irritably. 'It's nothing. I thought Barbara said she'd taken a call from that weird woman, that's all.'

'What weird woman?'

'That one with the stupid name. The one who turned the place upside down that time we did a job for her, remember?'

Annie felt a grin curve her mouth. Pieternel? Of course she remembered. Pieternel had breezed through their lives vibrant, forceful; an investigator working for one of the big insurance firms. She'd made no bones about her frustration at having to liaise with the two sisters, but she and Annie had got along just fine. Both Pat and Barbara persisted with the puerile tactic of mispronouncing, or pretending to forget, Pieternel's name.

'So has she been in touch? Has she more work for us?'

'For heaven's sake, I told you no. There was no message. Don't you want to hear about Brittany Booth?'

Annie couldn't help smiling at Pat's annoyance. Pieternel had really shown them up for the shoddiness of their operation. But instead of prodding them to get their act together, it had united the sisters in their affected disdain for the woman. Annie wished there had been a message. Pieternel had been on the up, looking for opportunities to make it big on her own. She had money behind her and a job that was perfect for grooming future contacts. She'd half hinted to Annie that there might be an opening for her if ever she got a new business off the ground. And Annie had more than half hinted that she would be interested.

She felt herself tighten at the thought of it. Someone striking out on their own, doing just what she wanted to do. She remembered the adrenalin rush right at the start of her partnership with Pat and Barbara; all the ambitions she'd had for the new firm. It could have worked out, but it was too late for if onlys.

'Go on,' she said. 'Tell me what you have on Booth.'

Later that night Annie sat in the deserted office. Brittany Booth was not due for a while, so she decided to make a start on her newest case.

A few mouse clicks gave her the address of the property Sheryl Long had pointed out and the electoral register gave her the name of the couple who lived there.

Tim and Tracey Morgan.

She delved deeper and found they were both 40 years old and had a son and a daughter. Their daughter had been living with them at the time of the previous electoral register but not the latest. On a hunch, Annie trawled Facebook. The daughter had secured her site from prying strangers, but Tracey Morgan had a site of her own where she'd uploaded photographs for all to see. Annie flipped through the evidence of a lavish wedding. She recognized the property the Longs had pointed to on the satellite view. The big yard was enveloped in a wedding marquee.

The Longs surely would have mentioned that expanse of white tarpaulin if they'd seen it. Annie sifted the dates in her mind... date of the wedding... date Sheryl Long saw Tracey Morgan give her a 'really funny look'.

Ron and Sheryl had driven past just a few days before the wedding. Erection of the marquee was incomplete. The bride was hugely pregnant in all the photographs. It must have been a horrendously rushed job to have the yard decked out, not to mention the worry it would become a maternity hospital. To Annie's mind, what Sheryl had seen was the distracted look of someone with masses to do and no time to do it in. She would take a bet that Tracey Morgan hadn't even noticed the car drive past.

The marquee hire company's advertising board was visible in one of the shots. *Caribbean Canvas Yorkshire: bringing the exotic to home shores.* For form's sake, Annie took down the details, then checked the Morgans' credit rating and did a basic finance check. They were neither suspiciously rich, nor desperately poor. The wedding might have stretched their finances but no more than for many people. They were just Mr and Mrs Ordinary. The facts backed Ron Long's assertion there was nothing sinister about the couple.

Annie couldn't bring herself to manufacture more out of the case or insist they paid for a full three hours. It had taken less than thirty minutes to get this far. She would contact the Longs in the morning and see if this was enough to set Sheryl's mind at rest.

The door buzzer sounded.

She pushed the button on the computer, making its screen blank with a luminous flash. Then she went to meet her new client.

Brittany Booth was a tall, well-built woman with compelling eyes and hair an unremitting black as though it welled from a dark inner core. The light of early evening seemed to fade as Brittany walked in, the intensity of her manner matching her stare as she strode forward to greet Annie, then pitched immediately in on a denunciation of 'that monster, Walker'.

Annie held up her hand to stem the flood of Brittany's eloquence. 'Take a seat. I need some general information first. We must be structured if we want a result.'

It was the right thing to say. Brittany, for all the confidence she oozed, looked much younger than her twenty-three years. She needed a prop as much as an investigator, a grown-up to tell her what to do.

'Some basics to start with,' said Annie. 'I need to see the whole picture from all the angles. Now what made you approach Vince Sleeman?'

If Brittany was surprised at the question, she didn't show it, and answered swiftly as Annie probed. She couldn't refuse the case, but Annie needed to know from the start who she was working for and how she should play it. Would this woman report back to Vince? Were they close? Would Vince feel he could wade in and interfere if he didn't like the way things were going? It had happened before. For all her immaturity, there was something unsettling about Brittany, and Annie knew she had to have the upper hand from the off.

Her answers about Vince were reassuring. She seemed to have stumbled on him by chance. Annie could easily imagine Vince ready to assume Walker guilty and to applaud Yates's actions, but he wouldn't want the case. Too messy.

'Now tell me exactly what you're looking for.'

'I want proof about that monster, Walker. I want to see his name in the mud. I want the world to know what he did. And I'd like to see the bitch exposed too.'

'The bitch?'

'The woman he abused all those years. Don't tell me she hasn't seen the case in the Press. She could have come forward for Josh. Look what Josh has done for her.'

'It wouldn't be easy for someone if they'd been abused for years when they were a kid.'

'That's no reason to let an innocent man be locked up. Selfish bitch. I'd show her if I got my hands on her.'

Annie struggled to tell herself that it made no difference whether or not she liked the client, and it mustn't cloud her judgement, but she had taken to Nicole Perks and couldn't help hoping there was nothing in the story Yates had peddled.

'Yates... uh... Joshua was quite specific in his accusations in terms of what Walker did to the girl, but he never said when or where. It makes it very difficult. Do you have anything more for me to go on?'

'Isn't that enough?' Brittany snapped the words out, tossing her shoulders as though Annie were being deliberately obstructive, and looking for a moment as though ready to fly at Annie and attack her for not providing an instant solution.

Annie wanted to shake her, to tell her for heaven's sake stop and think. Don't be so bloody rude to the one person who might be able to help you. She pulled in a deep breath.

'Tell me why you think the police did nothing.'

'God knows. Because they're fools. There's no point talking to them. It's up to us now.' Brittany savoured the word 'us' as though Annie had morphed into a fellow campaigner as fanatic as she to vindicate Yates.

'Can you tell me what was reported to the police about Walker?'

'Does it matter? They did nothing.'

'It matters.' Again, Annie fought down an urge to reach out and shake the girl. She wanted to hear about the supposed complaint from six years ago, but wanted Brittany Booth to be the one to raise it. 'Come on,' she urged. 'If you want me to help, I need to know. What did Joshua have on Walker? Who complained about him? When? Was it Joshua himself who put the complaint in?'

Annie said this more to provoke a response than anything, but as she spoke, she wondered, had Yates known Walker for years and borne some long-standing grudge? Maybe the tale of them being strangers to each other was bullshit.

'No, of course not.' Brittany looked alarmed as though the idea was new to her, too. 'No, he couldn't have. He knew nothing about it back then.'

'Back when?'

'Six years ago.'

Annie leant forward and looked into Brittany's dark eyes. 'Tell me what happened six years ago.'

'The police were told all about that monster, Walker, and they did nothing about it.'

'Told by whom? What were they told? How? When? Come on, Brittany, I'm going to need some facts if you want me to get at the truth. Did Joshua say anything about this in court? I don't remember hearing about it.'

'No, he didn't.'

'Why not?'

Unexpectedly, Brittany slumped forward and put her face in her hands. 'I don't know,' she muttered. 'I just don't know.' She looked up again and Annie read despair in her expression. 'He was waiting for his witness, for the bitch who never came forward. All he told me was that she had the evidence to fill in the gaps. He wouldn't tell me any more; said it was best I didn't know. They should have investigated him, shouldn't they?'

'Of course they should. They probably did. But any case of alleged child abuse is difficult.'

'But surely they shouldn't just have done nothing.'

'Do you know for certain they did nothing?'

'Of course, or that monster wouldn't have been walking the streets. If they did anything, they didn't do it thoroughly. Tell me, what should they have done? Why is it so difficult?'

'Well, OK, in a child abuse case, there are so many things to look out for. You have to protect the child, work with the family, get the relevant professionals on board, make sure the interviews are carried out properly. Then you have to evaluate all the angles. You can't start out with an assumption that the allegations are true, because even if they are, you won't build a solid case if all you're doing is looking from one side. In this case, how could they even try to profile the victim? No one seems to know who she was.'

'Yes, but once they knew about that monster—'

'But they didn't, did they? That's the thing about allegations without evidence and especially in child abuse cases. There's a Chinese whispers effect. The police have to take that into account. Innocent before proven guilty. You can't hang people on allegations. You have to have evidence. That's where Joshua's story fell down. He wouldn't give them anything. Did he tell you anything more than he let out in court, anything concrete that I can use – dates, times, names?'

Brittany shook her head.

'So there is no actual evidence that this complaint was even made.'

'Oh, I didn't say that. Joshua wouldn't tell me anything, but I found this in his things.'

Brittany reached into her bag and pulled out a piece of paper which she held out. Annie took it from her. It was a faded photocopy of a handwritten note. The words remained legible but lines across the paper signified that either it had been folded, or something had been placed to obscure the top and bottom. The writing filled the middle of the page; the rest was blank.

The note was dated 6 May 2004, just over six years ago and addressed to *Police – whoever deals with crimes against children.*

It began with the words, *You must investigate Michael Walker,* and gave Walker's address, age and a brief description. This was someone who knew him or who had done their homework.

Michael Walker kept a young girl as his sexual slave for five years. He frightened her into keeping quiet but now he is planning to abuse another girl and he must be stopped. He must not be allowed to look after children any more.

Annie turned the words over in her mind. Had the original been delivered and if so, where? If it had reached officialdom on that date, it would have sparked a response. May 2004 was uncomfortably soon after the conviction of Ian Huntley for the Soham murders when Humberside Police smarted under vicious criticism for their handling of his earlier records.

'You see. They should have stopped him back then.'

Annie looked up as Brittany spoke and saw in the girl's face the same expectation she had seen in Nicole Perks, but more intense. The weight of it pulled her in opposing directions. The only way I can help either one of you, she thought, is by snuffing out hope for the other.

A glance at her phone showed her that it wasn't that late. If she could get rid of Brittany Booth, there was still time to catch up on Friday night.

CHAPTER FOUR

The weekend ritual starts early in Hull. A buzz vibrates through the last hours of the working day, sending ripples from the city centre out through the estates and villages. Long before dusk paints its first brushstrokes across the sky, brightly coloured creatures flit through the streets, incidental at first amongst sober-clad workers heading for home, but, like the start of a seasonal migration, gathering in ever larger groups.

Beyond the eastern boundary, the town of Hedon witnesses an influx to its marketplace pubs, the jostling crowd in the Queen's Head three-deep at the bar. To the west, the student bars in Cottingham stand prepared with Friday night shifts, extra hands to ease to flow.

Within the city limits, the tide rolls towards focal points: the Goat and Compasses; the Dolphin; the Dairycoates. From Bilton Grange and Greatfield in the east to Gypsyville and Anlaby in the west, the multicoloured horde brings life and money as it surges in towards the centre.

In the old town bars, bright young things rest temporarily cheek by jowl with old men supping their nightly pints; the mood cheerful as the wave flows inward homing in on the cheap drinks deals of the new town where night is an irrelevance to the lights and noise and throbbing beat from outlets designed to attract in a crowd that's on its way regardless, laughing, swaying, priming itself for Friday night.

Around midnight, the tide turns towards the clubs, celebratory cheer still recognizable, but faces glassy-eyed. Come the small hours, it's a baying pack that surges out, wild, robotic, frightening; disintegrating into staggering groups to shout and weave about, arms flailing for taxis, clashing with the weekend shift police to a background wail of sirens.

Annie took herself straight to the new town, estimating where her mates would be by the time she was ready to join them. She loved the buzz of the pounding music, the swell of sound that engulfed her, that made her a component of the crowd. She didn't do drugs, not these days, and automatically turned away the offers that came as she pushed her way into the bars.

Her mates would be well ahead, forging their way into post-working-week euphoria, but she could catch up easily. She fought through a press of bodies, and screamed her order over the cacophony.

A bottle of beer? Momentary glances. Quizzical. But she didn't do vodka shots these days, either. The crowds could make her feel old if she wasn't careful; a staid old matron like Barbara, forever fretting over minutiae, missing the big picture.

The stagnation of the business threatened to creep into her bones even here. The sisters would vegetate forever, earning just enough to kid themselves that good times were around the corner, with more and more work channelled through Vince Sleeman. Was his aim to make them so dependent they couldn't function alone? Then what? Shut them down for good? Or had he another plan?

The hell with it. She would not slide into the trough of acceptance that sucked Pat in. She would complete this case for Jennifer and Nicole Perks, then find a way out. End on a high. That was the key. Never let anyone say she quit because she couldn't hack it. She would get at the truth about Michael Walker before she turned her back on the firm.

And as for the Longs, she would get in touch first thing in the morning and be absolutely honest with them. Pat would disapprove. Barbara too. The sisters would want to milk these clients as dry as they could, just like their father would have done. Ron Long was prepared to shell out money because some woman had given his wife a funny look. Well, more fool him. Annie would bounce the ball right back into their court. The woman Sheryl Long saw had every reason to look harassed by an imminent family wedding, and had probably not even registered the Longs as they'd driven past. If Ron and Sheryl wanted her to continue with the case, then fine, but they would sign up for a full-scale investigation with their eyes open.

She wriggled her way through the mob, straining to find familiar faces to help her make a proper fist of celebrating Friday night.

Saturday, mid morning, found Annie sitting in the office, slightly thick-headed as she stared at the file labelled *Ron Long* without really seeing it. Pat, at the other side of the desk, sat engrossed in paperwork. Annie drummed her fingers on the table wondering how best to tackle Jennifer to persuade her to look out old police files. Michael Walker was the innocent victim of a brutal murder. The court had thrown no doubt on that. They had taken the murderer's accusations against him as the ranting of a madman. But if Annie were to lay these accusations to rest once and for all, she needed to know what was behind this story of Michael having been reported for child abuse six years ago. Maybe Jen had already looked for old files. The problem was that Jen didn't leak this sort of stuff. Not until now anyway.

'Annie! Do you have to do that? I'm trying to concentrate.'

'Sorry.' Annie raised her fingers from the wooden surface and pulled the Longs' case file towards her. Pat had accepted early closure of the case with a tight-lipped 'Hmm', but said nothing more. Annie felt the folder, thin and insubstantial, representing a single hour of paid work. Ron Long, when she'd rung him, had been more than satisfied with what she'd found and happy to pay for a full hour. If she'd charged for three hours, he would have been dissatisfied at paying over the odds. This way they looked good and built a reputation for efficiency. No point saying this to Pat or Barbara who would carp on about the lost two hours' fee and point out with some justification that the Longs were from out of the area and unlikely to be back.

Pat pushed her paperwork aside. 'How did it go with that contact from Vince? What's the Brittany Booth woman like? Is she mad like the other one said?'

'She's incredibly intense. Very troubled and out of her depth. Heaven knows if we can get a result for her and if we do, she might not like it.'

'No big revelation then?'

Annie thought of the note in the file, but said, 'No. Yates sounds like a real head case. I think she just got caught up in the thing. She's very naive, knows no better. But she'll pay us to find the truth so I'll have a go.'

Pat nodded her approval. 'D'you think there's anything in it, Walker – I mean? The police would have sussed it out, wouldn't they?'

'Yeah, that's where I'm going to start. Find out what they looked into and when.'

'You can go to Vince for inside info on this one, you know. After all, he passed it on to us.'

Annie made a face. 'Thanks, but no thanks. I'll see what I can get out of Jen.'

'Strait-laced Flanagan? You'll be lucky.'

'I think she might help me on this one, and at least anything I get out of her will be the truth, not a version that she wants me to hear.'

Pat conceded the point with a wry smile. She knows Vince through and through, thought Annie. Why won't she make the effort to break free?

As Pat heaved herself to her feet, the buzzer sounded from downstairs. Annie got up too and headed for the door. Before she reached the top of the stairs, the buzzer had sounded twice more and whoever was out there kept their finger pressed to it as she descended. Halfway down, she paused. By leaning across on tiptoe it was possible to see the reflection of the person outside.

Sheryl Long. And clearly in a state.

Annie opened the door and Sheryl practically fell into her arms in a move that seemed dramatically staged. 'No, it won't do,' Sheryl blurted out. 'You don't understand. Quick, I need to talk to you.'

'You know your way.' Annie waved Sheryl up the stairs, then put her head outside to look down the street. Sure enough, she could see a hurrying figure in the distance. Ron Long hot on the heels of his wife. She left the door ajar to save herself another trip down and followed Sheryl upstairs.

'You can't leave it,' Sheryl panted, out of breath. 'Ron told me what you said. Wedding... wasn't that...' She flapped her hands ineffectually as though to cool herself.

'Sit down and catch your breath.'

'No, I have to tell you. Ron will guess where I've gone. Can we go in there?' She indicated the back office where they'd first met, and shot a wary glance at Pat.

'Pat's the boss. You can talk in front of her.'

Pat looked across from where she was packing her bag preparatory to leaving, and jerked her thumb towards the door. 'Go in there if you want, but Annie can only give you a minute.'

Annie saw that the same thought was in both their minds. Sheryl would tell them to take the case back, but Ron held the purse strings, and there was nowhere for the case to go. Pat had no inclination to pander to someone who was not a paying client and only temporarily in the neighbourhood. Annie assumed Sheryl was about to come clean about her real reasons for not wanting to come to the area. Hence the urgency for her to get it out before Ron caught up with her.

Sheryl remained in the chair she had slumped into and looked from one to the other of them. Now she had permission to use the back office, she seemed to have lost the energy to get up.

'You have to do more,' she said. 'They're up to no good. I know they are.'

'Is there something you haven't told me? I've found ample reason for the woman you saw to have been looking stressed.'

'Yes, there is, I—'

A clatter of footsteps up the stairs cut the words off. The door burst open and Ron Long threw himself inside. Annie watched him flounder to get words out. He looked with wild eyes from her to Pat to Sheryl, but could only pull in his breath in desperate gasps.

Annie exchanged a raised-eyebrows glance with Pat and pushed a chair towards the man she hoped was not about to have a heart attack in their office.

'Sit down. Catch your breath. I'll get you a drink.'

Sheryl watched her husband sip water as the rise and fall of his chest eased. 'Ron, you've got to let them carry on investigating. You won't want to stay anywhere near those people once you know what they're up to.'

'Now, Sheryl, they're up to nothing. You've got to stop this.'

'There's no point in an investigation into nothing,' Annie pointed out.

Sheryl turned to her. 'I wanted you to find out without me having to say anything, but if you need a reason, I'll give you a reason.'

'Sheryl!' A clear warning accompanied the look of alarm Ron Long shot at his wife.

'It's nothing to do with *that*, Ron' she hissed back, as though lowering her voice might allow the words to reach her husband's ears whilst bypassing Annie and Pat.

She turned back to Annie, who felt she could read the swift calculations behind Sheryl Long's eyes. What story would Sheryl come out with?

'They're murderers,' Sheryl burst out, her gaze bouncing from Pat to Annie to Ron as though to gauge their reactions, to see if she'd done enough. Annie felt only curiosity to see how on earth Sheryl would back this up.

'They're both in on it,' Sheryl went on earnestly, when no one else spoke. 'I don't know which of them does the killing. They bludgeon them to death, hit them over the head. I didn't want to have to say that. I warn you, I won't be a witness in any trial. I'll deny it. I wanted you to find it out for yourself. I'm not staying anywhere near them. You didn't see that look she gave me. She wasn't worried about any wedding: she was worried that we'd find the bodies.'

Annie glanced sideways at Ron, who was staring at his wife, open-mouthed. She lifted her eyes to meet Pat's and they exchanged the ghost of a sceptical look. Ron gaped as though fearful his wife had flipped over some mental edge.

'But, Sheryl, what can you mean? Murderers? They're just an ordinary couple.'

'You read about it all the time in the papers.' She appealed to Pat. 'Some ordinary person keeping body parts in their fridge, killing all the neighbours, don't you?'

Pat zipped her bag with an air of finality. 'Not in the papers I read. Don't keep Annie too long or we'll have to charge you for another hour. See you on Monday.' With that, she went out leaving the three of them to listen to the grunts that accompanied Pat's lumbering footsteps down the stairs. The outer door slammed.

Annie pulled a third chair forward and sat down. She was curious to see how Sheryl would work her way out of the tale she had begun to spin. The Morgans, she knew, were incidental. Sheryl had fastened on them as a reason not to stay because something in the hidden agenda scared her half to death. Maybe she aimed at a story Ron couldn't dismiss and Annie wouldn't be able to prove. If so, she should have gone for something more subtle.

'OK,' said Annie. 'Tell me everything.'

'We went to watch them one night, didn't we, Ron?'

Ron looked shamefaced and nodded. 'I wanted to still Sheryl's fears. She said this woman had given her a look.'

'If you'd seen it, Ron, you wouldn't doubt me.'

'I thought if we go out there at night, it'll be obvious nothing's going on. See, it's night that worries her. I'll have to be away sometimes while we're down here. But we didn't see anything out of the ordinary.'

'How can you say that? We saw them both with a wheelbarrow in the small hours. Is that what you call normal behaviour?'

'I'd dozed off, Sheryl. I didn't actually see—'

'The wedding would only have been days away,' Annie pointed out. 'They must have had a lot on their mind.'

'Wedding nothing! There's something I haven't told you... either of you. I went into the yard, Ron. The next morning when you were still asleep.'

Annie read the disbelief on Ron Long's face, hastily smothered into a look of concern.

'I went into that shed we saw them go in,' Sheryl went on. 'I found the wheelbarrow. It was under a big heavy sheet. I saw what was in it.'

Annie watched the byplay between them: Ron, desperate not to upset his wife and tip her into any indiscretions; Sheryl, desperate to find a way to make him change his mind about this trip. Sheryl's gaze swung briefly to meet Annie's then returned to rest on her husband's face.

'What was in it?' he asked.

'A body, Ron. We saw them wheel a body across that yard.'

Ron Long's eyes briefly met Annie's. Sheryl looked with growing desperation from one to the other of them, then burst into theatrical tears and put her face in her hands, the intricately patterned purple of her nails making her fingers a flower closing around her head.

CHAPTER FIVE

Annie saw no point in contacting Pat over the weekend to tell her she'd reopened the Longs' file. Pat would be fine with it, because they were paying clients again. Sheryl had accused the Longs of murder. On paper that made it a police matter, and Annie had considered telling them she would have to treat it that way, but Sheryl's tale was too thin, too clearly fabricated. And she would receive no thanks for kick-starting the paraphernalia of a murder enquiry when she knew the evidence didn't stack up. Instead, she would complete the job they wanted her to do. It would mean a trip out into the wilds of rural South Holderness to see the place the Longs planned to spend their few weeks in the area; their allegedly casual break for which they'd come all this way to case out the holiday home. Even Ron Long had looked uncomfortable spinning that line. No, the truth of it was that Ron wanted them both to drop out of sight for a while, and Sheryl didn't.

But the Longs could wait. She'd said she could do nothing for a few days and they'd accepted that. Annie thought that anyone who had really seen a body might protest that it could be moved and hidden in that time, but Sheryl hadn't said a word. Maybe she realized that a disappearance could be quite convenient. If she held to the fiction she'd seen it in the first place, Annie would be left to prove another negative.

She shrugged the Longs out of her mind, not ready to let them cut into what was left of her weekend.

Saturday afternoon found her slouching round the supermarket in the St Stephen's mall annoyed at herself for shopping in amongst the crowds again. She'd left a message on Jennifer's phone, inviting her round for a meal on Sunday so had to have some food in. She wanted Jen on her own so they could chat privately about Michael Walker; whether he had really been reported to the police six years ago and if so, what sort of enquiries had been made.

She paused in the fresh veg section. The aubergines had beautifully smooth dark skins, their colour reminiscent of the deep intensity of Brittany Booth's hair. Annie had had flatmates in the past who did wonders with this sort of stuff; Jen herself could knock up an impressive meal from real ingredients, but it required such an array of specialist equipment, knives and chopping boards and so on, that Annie always did what she did now – ran out of motivation before her thoughts were beyond an embryo idea and left the fresh veg section empty-handed.

Automatically, she dropped tins into her basket, tuna, sardines, baked beans; things that could be tipped in a bowl and microwaved, or eaten straight from the tin. Jen had developed a liking for pink wine which Annie found sickly, but she grabbed a bottle along with a few cans of beer.

The weight of the basket cut uncomfortably into her arm, so she balanced it along the edge of the freezer cabinet as she peered in, reading the labels on the boxes.

A frozen honey mustard chicken dish caught her eye and she scanned the directions. The picture on the box looked succulent and tempting and it could be microwaved without the bother of thawing. She played with a mental image of sitting Jen down with her pink wine and bringing the honey mustard chicken out of the kitchen in a fancy dish as though she'd cooked it herself. It was almost worth a detour back to the kitchen aisle to buy a serving dish, but she'd had enough of the crush of the big shop with its regimented aisles decked out to tempt shoppers as though they worked on nothing but an instinctive, magnetic draw to the bright colours.

As she waited in the baskets-only queue, the things Annie had read about the murderer, Joshua Yates, and the way Brittany Booth had repeated them played in her mind. It wasn't just the potency of the belief she saw in Brittany, nor the detail of Yates's allegations, nor even the confidence with which they both claimed the existence of a witness, but some combination of all these things added to an anonymous note that might or might not be for real. Something inside Annie made it impossible to reject Yates out of hand. The story held together in a weird way she couldn't dismiss.

She would very much like to meet Joshua Yates to assess him face to face, eye to eye. She had floated the idea with Brittany who said she would arrange it.

The queue shuffled forward and Annie could at last put her shopping down. She rubbed at the red lines across her forearm where the handles of the basket had bitten and wondered where all this left Nicole. She and Charlotte were equally convincing in their confidence of their guy's innocence and the law was behind them. How much behind them? Annie hoped to find out tomorrow from Jen.

Annie's instinct was to believe both sides, but that left a gaping chasm in the middle where the two truths would not mesh. The only explanation was that Yates had targeted the wrong man. And yet Brittany was right when she said the witness couldn't have missed the publicity of the trial. Yates's descriptions were too detailed for any real victim not to know them and surely there was more motivation to come forward if the wrong man were in the dock.

Michael Walker was not in the dock, he was dead. Annie pulled herself up. It bothered her that she kept thinking of this the wrong way round.

'Sorry, how much?' She was jolted out of her reverie by the total now showing on the cash register. Either the pink wine or the honey mustard chicken cost a sight more than she'd anticipated.

As she'd said to Brittany, trauma could have been the reason for the victim not to come forward to save Joshua Yates, but why wouldn't the woman come forward, even if anonymously, to say that Yates had targeted the wrong man?

Wouldn't or couldn't? She played with uncomfortable thoughts all the way home. If Yates's story were true, but Michael

Walker wasn't the perpetrator, then perhaps the victim couldn't come forward because her story was live and her enslavement continued.

Just as Annie unlocked the outer door to the shared house where she rented a flat, her phone sang out. The screen told her it was Jennifer, so she sat on the stairs, bags balanced beside her, and took the call.

'Sorry, I can't do Sunday,' Jennifer said. 'We've been called in for overtime. There's a flap on at the prison.'

'No sweat.' Annie smiled to herself. It was a measure of how much Jennifer had come to trust her that she mentioned anything about her work. A year ago, she might have said she had to work an extra shift but no more than that. 'How about Monday evening? I'm planning to cook honey mustard chicken.'

'Uh... yes, that sounds lovely.'

After she'd ended the call, Annie had to laugh at the ill-concealed surprise in Jennifer's tone. *I'm planning to cook...* She wondered if she could pull it off. Jennifer would be on the alert for some subterfuge. A serving dish was a must now. And some of that garlic bread that went in the oven for ten minutes. That would provide authentic cooking smells and the fan would mask the sound of the microwave.

Her phone beeped a new message as she pushed her way into the flat. She dumped her carrier bags on the coffee table, seeing that two new voice mails had arrived while she spoke to Jennifer, and wondered what made people ring at the same time.

The first was Brittany Booth.

'Joshua won't see you. He's annoyed that you asked. He wants me to drop the case, but of course I won't. I'm determined to see justice done and I won't see him sent to an institution like he's a madman. He's worried for me. That's the sort of person he is. You mustn't ask to see him again. I'll get in touch next week.'

The tone was imperious, chiding Annie as though she'd done wrong. It irritated her, but she was relieved Brittany had not chosen to drop the case. The staccato tone could have been interpreted to mean that Joshua Yates did not want anyone digging too deeply into his story, with its gruesome detail and no hard facts, but Annie knew better than to read too much into a second-hand account.

The other message was Nicole Perks, saying much the same. Charlotte Liversedge didn't want to see her either, but Nicole's tone, unlike Brittany's, was not at all accusatory.

'I'm sorry to mess you about. I'll try again, but she's upset. She'll come round. I'm sure she will.'

Three people had turned her down in the space of a few minutes, but that was how these things went. As she pulled the honey mustard chicken free of its carrier bag and took it to cram into the freezer compartment, she wondered if Yates had been as vehement in not wanting to see her as Brittany's message implied, and if so, why? It was all very noble of him to declare, as he had in court, that it must be for the woman's conscience to say whether or not she came forward, but that suggested a level of empathy between two people who knew each other. Could he know her as well as that and still have targeted the wrong man? She wasn't too worried about Charlotte refusing to see her, but she might have another go at Brittany, because surely Yates himself was the key to this.

Realistically now it looked as though progress on this case from either side rested on next week's meal with Jennifer.

Annie pulled the crumpled letter from her pocket and smoothed it out. Her invitation to judge a fancy-dress mythical warriors competition. It might have some interest as a new experience, but it would mean getting up close to a crowd of ponies with their ever-ready weapons of iron-clad feet and snapping teeth. She felt along the top of the cork board that hung beside the TV and found the oversized red pin that rested there. It was a process she termed 'red-pinning' to fix a reminder to the board using this. The pin itself had been a present from her aunt. Too fancy to throw away, but of no practical use that Annie had ever worked out. As a means of holding things to the cork board, it was inefficient and unwieldy. Its sole advantage was that it stood out as a reminder, getting in her way when she leant across to turn the plugs on or off. She paused. Red-pinning was for important stuff. Why not just ring now?

As she reached for the phone, she answered her own question. It was too late in the day. The woman might be in. Far better to give her refusal to an answer-phone that couldn't waste her time in pushing for a change of mind. She'd call up during the day tomorrow when the house would be empty. Her memories of the livery yard were of constant noise and bustle during all daylight hours.

Action scheduled, she put the red pin back on top of the board, shoved the letter in a drawer and turned her mind to the important issues. She cleared a place on her small settee and sat down, fidgeting at the uncomfortable feel of anonymous stuff under the cushions. One day soon she would have a clear out. The evening sun shone through the window, highlighting the columns of dust that sparkled in the air. In one corner, a stack of borrowed DVDs had slid in an untidy avalanche to tangle with the wires from the TV. One of those would provide all the entertainment she needed for tonight, but first she intended getting a head start on her latest bit of a case. Ron Long's patience would run out soon, but before then she would take a trip out into the country at his expense and gaze at an isolated property, cast an eye over the place the Longs were taking so much trouble to check out, see if anything of their hidden agenda showed.

To make things run smoothly, she should go out there as an expected visitor, rather than cold calling the people at the farm. She flipped through her notebook to find the number for the marquee hire company.

'Hello. I'm ringing on behalf of a client. We're organizing an event and I'm making enquiries about marquees.'

'What size were you after, flower? And how soon's your event?'

'Fairly big.' Annie thought back to the photographs of the Morgans' daughter's wedding. 'Sixty odd.'

The man at the end of the phone laughed. 'That's not big, love. You can lose sixty-odd in one of our cosies.'

'What do you call big?'

'We can have the whole of Hull under canvas for you if you want.'

Annie laughed. 'OK, not that big. But before I take things further, I'd like to talk to someone who's used you for a wedding. You have a marquee out Sunk Island way and I'm in that area next week, so I wondered if I'd be able to call in.'

'Oh right, yeah, I know where you mean. Yeah, it's been up a while, that one. So it's had a bit of hammer. You wouldn't normally have it up as long as they have. They look brand spanking new when they go up, and they stay that way if you don't keep them up weeks somewhere that gets battered right off the Humber. I'll have to ring them, of course, but it shouldn't be no bother. When d'you want to go?'

'I can fit in with them. But did you say it's still up? I'd have thought you'd have had it down by now.'

'Yeah, you'd think. But it's still there.'

His tone alerted Annie that he wasn't happy about it. He took her details and promised to get back to her.

As she clicked off the phone, she reflected that there was something slightly odd about the marquee still being up, and about the hint of prickliness in the man's tone when she queried it.

Ten minutes later he rang back.

'I'm real sorry, love, but they don't want anyone round. I can find you someone else no bother, but I can't send you to the one you saw. I can only give out their details with their say-so. Data protection and all that.'

'No worries,' said Annie. 'I'll drive out there and take a look from the road. I know where it is. That's where I saw your board.'

'I wish you wouldn't. They was adamant. They've a lot on and they don't want strangers prying.'

Annie sat back after she'd ended the call and thought through what the man had said. No reason Tim and Tracey Morgan should invite strangers into their home, but the vehemence with which they'd denied her access had clearly rattled the man.

CHAPTER SIX

Converted buildings, for the most part residential, lined the streets. Flats and bedsits nestled around small print shops with thick glass in their front bay windows, and upmarket clinics offering alternatives to conventional medicine. The imposing Victorian architecture frayed at the edges, where the long terraces tapered off into run-down houses and shops with mismatched paintwork and leaky gutters. Conversions creatively called flats squeezed the necessities of living into tiny spaces.

By Sunday evening, Annie was bored with the uneven walls of the space she called home. She'd done the paperwork she felt inclined to do; watched the DVDs she fancied watching, and had flicked through the TV guide without finding anything to spark her interest.

She grabbed her thin jacket from the back of the door, shoved some money in her pocket and headed out.

After the excesses of Friday night, all she wanted was good beer and bright surroundings, somewhere to relax and drain tensions away. She walked briskly, turning off the main thoroughfare that led to the town centre, and followed the course of the river Hull. Dark buildings grew from the roadside, without benefit of gardens or greenery, in an area caught between an industrial past generated by the loading and unloading of thousands of ships and a potential future of expensive riverside apartments. With deliberately heightened awareness, she skirted an old cemetery, unafraid of the dead, but wary of anyone living who chose to lurk there at this hour.

Cutting her ties with Pat and Barbara would mean moving away, having to get to know a new city. That wasn't a problem. Exploring new territory held excitement and adventure. But no doubt she would miss this place with its contradictions and unexpected corners of history. Her target tonight was an unassuming building that straddled the corner at the convergence of several roads.

When she'd first stumbled on it some years before, late one night, and seen the word Whalebone spelt out in dark letters above the street, she'd tried the door without much hope, assuming it to be no more than a relic of a long-dead trade waiting for demolition or conversion. But the door had opened on to a bright space, buzzing with talk, and busy with photographs and pictures tracking 200 years of history. Better still, she'd found an enthusiasm for good beer that extended to a micro-brewery on the premises. It was a long walk from home but quite handy for the office and had become something of a sanctuary for her. A place to reflect, to be anonymous amongst a cheerful crowd.

She took her beer to one end of the narrow space that curved round the bar and sat back to watch the leisurely groups of Sunday drinkers. Her shoulders relaxed as she sipped the well-kept ale, anonymity cushioning her from the need to interact with anyone.

Then the far door swung open and Scott Kerridge walked in with his new fiancée, Kate. At once, her shoulders tightened and her face prickled with the knowledge her shell was about to be breached. She tracked the couple's steps as they headed for the bar. What chance they wouldn't spot her? Slim, although they might go to the far corner round the curve of the room. Her best hope was to slope out now through the other door. She sat up preparatory to rising, but then stopped. Why the hell should she leave a good pint just to avoid Scott Kerridge?

She and Scott had conducted an on-off relationship almost from the moment she arrived in Hull. Jennifer had originally introduced them. PC Kerridge, her senior colleague, the guy with the nice smile. He and Annie had fallen into bed pretty quickly, but that was the only part of their liaison that ever really worked. Scott wanted a serious relationship; to settle down and get a semi with a garage, a couple of kids. He tried not to hate Annie's job, but couldn't hide his feelings and couldn't stop trying to ease her away from it.

During the five years they had devoured each other physically, whilst finding little other common ground, both she and Scott had dallied with other partners, Annie just for the companionship of someone who didn't take life so seriously; Scott seeking a soul mate to share his life. And now he seemed to have found one. Kate was a stocky woman, Annie's age, a detective constable from West Yorkshire who had transferred in to Hull and now worked with both Jennifer and Scott.

Annie would have liked Kate in another context, but Kate had taken against her from the start, insisting upon seeing her as a rival for Scott's affections. Left to her, Annie knew she could have quashed Kate's fears and probably made a friend of her, but Scott's heavy-handed attempts simply stoked Kate's jealousy.

Now they turned with drinks in hand, looking for somewhere to sit. Watching the double-take, the tightening of stance, the narrowing of eyes, Annie resented that she was made to feel self-conscious, but it was absurd to ignore them so she looked up and gave a half-wave and semi-smile.

Kate wrinkled her nose as though she smelt something nasty. Scott mouthed, 'Hi,' and gave her a proper smile. She wished he wouldn't. It was his smile that reminded her how good they could be together.

Kate stalked to a table at the far side of the room. Scott gave Annie a hunted glance and followed. Annie watched from the corner of her eye the tense, teeth-gritted exchange between them that culminated in Kate tipping her head back and emptying her glass in one go. Annie saw the suppressed flinch that showed whatever she'd ordered had had a kick in it. Scott was left to flounder over his pint. He hated being rushed over his beer. Annie made a point of turning her head away so as not to add to their discomfort. Her own beer had lost the power to relax her.

A movement caught her eye. Kate was marching off to the Ladies leaving Scott staring morosely into a full glass. As she disappeared through the door, he stood up and came towards Annie.

'Hi. You OK?' he said.

'Fine. You?'

'Yeah.' He pulled a face, taking quick look over his shoulder. 'I don't know why she's like this around you.'

'It's not rocket science, Scott. And you won't help things if she comes out and finds you talking to me.'

'Yeah, I know. I just wanted to give you this.' He put the full pint down in front of her. 'I'm not tipping it down my throat just because she won't stay here for five minutes.'

'Maybe I should go.'

'That's hardly fair. You were here first. You meeting someone?'

'No, just relaxing, getting rid of life's tensions, you know.'

'That's what I told Kate. I mean, you weren't to know we'd be here.'

'Scott, you're not helping by telling me this stuff. Just go back and... Uh... too late.'

Kate had come out of the Ladies and stopped dead when she saw Scott talking to Annie. Annie resigned herself to becoming the centre of a scene to entertain the punters. Kate would berate her and Scott would flap and make hopeless, inflammatory interjections like, 'Annie's not like that, Kate...' Annie had a sinking feeling that it would end in a fist fight one day that would lose Kate her job.

Maybe Kate had similar thoughts. Her face suffused with rage, she stalked past with a growled, 'Outside, now!' to Scott, and marched from the bar.

Annie blew out a sigh as she saw anger rush to Scott's face. Kate's comment had been loud enough to draw interest from others in the room. 'Go on,' she urged him. 'Go after her. Don't make things worse.'

'She's no right to speak to me like that. Who does she think she is?'

'Yeah, well, you go and tell her that. For Chris'sakes don't leave her hanging about outside while you're talking to me.'

'Might do her good to have to hang about a bit.'

'Scott, go after her. If you want to have a fight, have a fight, but leave me out of it.'

'I've a good mind to stay and finish my beer, first.'

'In that case, I'm going. You can drink mine, too.'

She made to stand up, but he put his hand on her shoulder to stop her. 'Sit down, Annie. I'll go. I'm sorry about all this.'

'No problem. You go and repair the damage.'

She smiled at him as he turned to go. He smiled back. Again she wished he wouldn't, as their eyes met and gazes locked for just a fraction too long.

Once Scott had gone, interest from the others in the bar waned and Annie was able to sit back and regain the composure she'd lost. She didn't hurry over her two pints. It was more than she'd planned to drink, but that was no penance when the beer was this good.

When she stood up to leave, she found herself slightly light-headed. Darkness was closing in on the city. She hadn't meant to stay this late, and yawned expansively as she headed up the road.

'Hi, Annie.' A voice pulled her up.

She looked at Scott, standing in the shadow of a doorway, his voice not slurred but with a hint of a drink too many. She made no effort to hide the exasperation in her tone. 'How long have you been there?'

'Not long. I had a couple in a bar down the road. Didn't want to disturb your peace.'

'Where's Kate?'

He shrugged. 'Dunno. Silly cow was gone when I came out. I went for a beer on my own.'

'I can tell.' She set off again up the road. Let him follow or not as he chose.

'I'm not chasing over town for her,' he said, as he dropped in beside her.

'Why? Don't you want to marry her now?'

'Oh sure, we're gonna get married, but I'm not chasing after her all the time.'

'Well, you should, you idiot, if she's the one you want. I don't want to be the reason you wrecked your life.'

'Why wouldn't you marry me, Annie?'

'You know why. How drunk are you? You know full well we'd never last five minutes.'

'We could have tried. Why would you never come and meet my family? They thought it was strange. We'd been seeing each other for years.'

'Scott, we've had all this out. It was never that serious. I'm not having this conversation. I'm going home.' She snapped at him because he had a point. She could easily have gone to meet his family without committing herself to their relationship. The real reason was the unspoken assumption that he would then have a right to come home with her, and she could never explain to him why no one could come to meet her family, because she couldn't develop a lucid reason for herself.

They walked in silence up the dark road. As they passed by the office where Annie spent much of her working days, he looked up at its windows, dark reflective eyes on to the city. 'It must be a good view from up there.'

'It's crap. We look over the back.'

He smiled. 'We might have worked it out between us.'

'Not in a million years.' She spoke lightly, because he no longer seemed to be serious.

'We had some good times.'

'Yeah, that's true.'

'You don't want me to walk all the way back with you, do you?'

'No, I'm fine. You get on your way.'

He smiled into her eyes and leant forward to kiss her goodbye. No harm in friends exchanging a brief embrace, she told herself, knowing it was nothing so innocent. His lips brushed her cheek, but she couldn't have said which of them turned first to find the other's mouth. She pressed her body on to his, as his tongue pushed its way against hers and his hands circled her waist to pull her closer.

A passing thought for Kate – stupid cow, shouldn't have run off like that in a pet if she wanted to keep them apart. And anyway, Annie didn't want Kate's man in any permanent sense, she just needed to keep clear of him when they'd both been drinking because sex was the one area where they were a perfect match. And it was hard to turn down a really satisfying conclusion to the weekend.

They were in the shelter of the office doorway now, her hands under his shirt, fingers slipping inside the waistband of his trousers. She felt him pull the material of her T-shirt out of the way so his hands could feel her skin.

'Wait. Not here.' She scrabbled in her bag for her keys. The street was quiet, but not that quiet and there was an empty office above them.

Once upstairs, he pulled her to him, kissing her uncomfortably hard almost as though to punish her for what was more his indiscretion than hers. She put her hands under his shirt and ripped it open, feeling at least one button fly adrift. Would the petulant Kate be the one to sew it on again?

She twisted free of his lips and ducked her head, snaking her tongue down his naked chest and over his belly, feeling him shudder as his hands found the sides of her head and gripped hard as though to suffocate her against his flesh. This must be the last time they did this, and because of that she vowed to make it count.

Afterwards, they lay on the floor, semi naked still, clothes and papers strewn around them, fingers entwined but otherwise not touching. Annie felt the cool breeze cut across the drying sweat on her skin and laughed softly.

Scott half turned his head, smiled. 'What is it?'

'If this floor was carpeted I might fall asleep. I was imagining Pat walking in on us tomorrow morning.'

'She never did like me much.'

'She wouldn't be overjoyed with me. I— Shh, what's that?' She stopped; her laughter smothered by the click of the latch downstairs.

She and Scott exchanged a glance, but she held up her hand to signal that he must keep quiet. Sound raced through this old building, especially at night.

The clatter of someone moving about came up to them clearly. Annie turned to Scott. 'It's Pat,' she mouthed. 'Quiet.'

Pat's lumbering tread was not yet on the stairs. Whatever she was here for, she had things to do in the shared lobby first. Priority was to get all trace of her and Scott out of the main office. They could crouch in the back while Pat came in and did whatever she'd come to do.

With as much speed as was consistent with absolute quiet, Scott bundled up their discarded clothes and Annie lifted the fallen papers back on to the desk.

Again, she stopped to listen. Movement from downstairs but as yet no one coming up. Could it be someone from one of the downstairs offices? But Pat's heavy tread was unmistakable.

They stood frozen, Annie not wanting to risk creeping across squeaky floorboards to the back office unless they had to. Scott, their clothes balled in his arms, waiting for her lead.

Again the heavy tramp of footsteps. And then the click of the latch.

Annie put a finger to her lips, and tiptoed carefully towards the door. Was Pat leaving or was someone else coming in?

Leaving.

Annie ran lightly down the stairs to the halfway point to strain to see out through the frosted pane with its eerie reflection of the outside door.

She saw Pat's rear view lumbering away and formed the thought that the distortion of the glass took several stone off her, before realizing that it wasn't Pat at all.

Scott appeared at the top of the stairs.

'It's OK,' she whispered up. 'It was Barbara, but she's gone. I'm just going to see what she was doing.'

'Here.' He threw her clothes down to her.

She stopped to pull on her jeans as she looked round the lobby. What on earth had Barbara been up to?

Scott was downstairs beside her now. 'So why was she here?'

'She must have been putting something in the post, but heaven knows why it couldn't have waited till tomorrow. It won't go till then, anyway.' Annie looked at the envelope in the tray, but didn't take it out, not wanting to let Scott into any secrets. 'You should get away home, Scott. I'm going to stay behind and make sure it's all ship-shape upstairs.'

He protested a bit and offered to walk her back, but it took little persuasion to get him to leave her.

'Just tell me, Annie, I'm curious, that's all. Why wouldn't you let me meet your father? Were you ashamed of me?'

'Of course not. What a silly thing to say.'

'Well, are you ashamed of him?'

'No. You're being stupid. Argyll's a long way to go. I don't see much of him, anyway. It's just hassle, that's all.'

'Yeah, all right.' He raised his hands in mock surrender. 'You take care getting home.'

This time they exchanged a chaste kiss that anyone could have witnessed and he went out into the night.

Before Annie returned upstairs, she went back to the post trays.

Barbara didn't come in on Mondays ever, so she would normally have given a letter to Pat for posting. But Pat wouldn't dream of taking the two metre diversion to put it in the tray before she came upstairs. She would carry it up and give it to Annie. Thus, Annie would get to see who Barbara was writing to.

She lifted the letter free and squinted at it in the dim light from the streetlamps outside, curious to see what Barbara had wanted to hide from her. Annie recognized the address. It looked like Barbara had taken her advice and written for a copy of that document. Thank heavens for that at any rate, but why hadn't she just slapped on a stamp and put it in a post-box? Maybe she wanted it franked as coming from the office.

Upstairs she made sure there was no trace left of her encounter with Scott. All this harping on about family, she thought irritably. Like everyone had to play happy families just because he did.

She could ignore him like she always had, except she knew there was something in what he said. She should devote some time to repairing the breach in her family. Well, maybe one day, but not now.

CHAPTER SEVEN

Annie couldn't stop herself rushing in far too early on Monday morning just in case she'd left any trace of the previous night's activity. Because that left her on her own, she nipped downstairs, pulled Barbara's letter out of the post tray and opened it. Then she felt ashamed because Barbara had not made a hash of it, but had written a good and tight request for the information, as good a job as Annie could have made of it. She re-sealed the envelope but would suffer agonies until the post was collected in case Barbara herself should come in and see it had been tampered with.

Why the clandestine late-night visit? It was possible she just happened to be passing, but unlikely.

At last, Pat's heavy step sounded on the stairs and Annie listened intently to hear how it was different from Barbara's. They couldn't sound the same; Pat had the weight advantage by many kilos, but twice now Annie had mistaken them.

'Paperwork to get straight today,' Pat said as she pushed through the door. 'Any messages?'

'No. Were you expecting anything in particular?'

'Why would I be expecting anything in particular? I was only asking.' Pat barked out a sharp laugh as she spoke and Annie looked at her surprised. What was that about?

'I have the case files out.'

'Let's hope we get a clear run at it. It's to be done before we leave tonight, no matter how late that makes us.'

'Jennifer's coming round for a meal tonight. I'd like to be away in time to cook.'

Pat threw her head back and laughed loudly. 'Yeah, right. How long can it take to heat a tin of beans?'

'Scoff all you like. I might have been going to cook something. I'll surprise you one of these days. She is coming round though so let's try and finish at a reasonable hour.'

'Suits me. I'm off out too.'

'Yeah? Where're you going?'

'Pole-dancing classes.' Pat surrendered to another burst of hilarity and added, 'It's as likely as you cooking.'

The papers were a tangled mess, but they cleared all the desk space and gradually pulled together what was needed to pass on to the client's legal team. Their part of the job was done. It was up to the courts now.

It was just on six o'clock when everything was packed away.

Annie hurried back to the flat to prepare for Jennifer's arrival. Ridiculous to feel this rush of apprehension, especially that it was connected less to the information she wanted to prise from her friend than to the challenge of persuading her that she could cook.

Almost an hour. It should be enough time. The honey mustard chicken needed nine minutes in the microwave, the garlic bread ten in the oven. As soon as she reached home, Annie turned on the oven to heat up and then tugged the box out of the freezer compartment, bringing a shower of ice crystals and a small avalanche of frozen peas that bounced across the floor. She put the box unopened on the surface by the sink. The garlic bread could go straight on an oven shelf and the honey mustard chicken would cook in its own dish, but what about serving it?

She spun round in the small kitchen. Somewhere in here there had to be a large enough receptacle. When had she last used anything like that? Of course! With a crow of triumph, she leant across the sink to the crowded window sill. Under the clutter was a beautiful, shimmery-blue, oval plate that she used to store oddments. She upended it into the sink, looking with some dismay at the array of artefacts that poured out. Paperclips, batteries, pencil stubs, her driving licence and rental agreement, a serrated metal disc that she couldn't identify. She scooped everything out into a supermarket carrier bag and hung it on the back of the door.

The blue dish, now empty, looked an unlikely vessel for food. Grime covered the base; a strange stain discoloured it in an untidy gash. Annie wondered if poison from the batteries might have seeped through the surface of the material. She let hot water into the sink and smothered the dish in washing-up liquid. Relentless scrubbing buffed it up nicely round the edges, the bits that would show, and she let the ache in her arm convince her that anything the dish might leak out must have been removed.

She carried cutlery to the table only to find it cluttered with magazines and papers and, now she looked at the surface, thick with dust. Clearing and cleaning left her flattened and with a sweat starting to form, almost as though she'd been out for a run.

Three minutes to go. She shot back to the kitchen and shoved the garlic bread into the oven, swearing as her finger brushed the hot shelf, then ripped the packaging off the honey mustard chicken, racing through a last read of the instructions, before ramming the giveaway outer paper with its succulent picture into the bin. A few stabs with a fork pierced the film lid and the microwave began to work its magic.

Just time to grab a glass for the pink wine and a tumbler for her beer before the doorbell chimed.

'Wow,' said Jennifer. 'Something smells good.'

'I thought I'd push the boat out for once. Come and have a drink. What's with the gaol thing, anything serious?'

'More of the usual really. Hints of a breakout plan, but with it being high security, they don't take chances.'

'It sounds such an old-fashioned crime, a gaolbreak.'

'Happens all the time, though. Not usually high profile stuff, but there are some high risk guys in Hull.'

It suited Annie perfectly to have Jen so relaxed. It was a real measure of the trust there was between them that Jen treated her more like a colleague these days than someone to be ultra cautious around.

A loud ping from the kitchen signalled that the honey mustard chicken was ready.

'The oven timer,' murmured Annie. 'Help yourself to another drink. I'll go and dish up.'

Manhandling the hot food out of the microwave with a tea towel to protect her hands gave Annie the idea of carrying it through in the blue dish using the towel as though it had come this way straight from the oven.

Jennifer stared and then laughed. 'It looks good, Annie. When did you learn to cook?'

Annie waved the comment aside, saying, 'Help yourself,' as she placed the dish and returned for the bread. Instinct said to go straight for the point while Jennifer was in this relaxed mood so as soon as she was seated, she said, 'Jen, I need some info for the business with Nicole Perks. Brittany Booth is spreading rumours that Michael Walker was reported for child abuse six years ago. Do you know anything about it?'

Jennifer paused and reached forward for a piece of garlic bread which she turned in her hand before nodding slowly. 'Yes, I do.' She broke the crust from the bread and dipped it in the sauce on her plate without looking up.

They both knew she had crossed a line.

'I heard the rumour and I asked around.'

'And?'

'For starters, none of this is coming from me. That's understood, isn't it?'

Annie nodded.

'Yes, there was a complaint. It wasn't specific, but it was looked into. There was nothing in it.'

'What was it, an anonymous note type thing?'

'I don't know how it was first reported. It was all before my time. You should ask Scott. He'd know more. That's if you're on speaking terms at the moment. I never know with you two.'

Annie laughed uncomfortably. 'Kind of. But is there anything you can tell me about what they looked into, what enquiries were made, that sort of thing?'

'May I get more sauce?' Jennifer indicated the dish and anticipated Annie's affirmative by pulling it towards her as she spoke.

'Mind it isn't still hot,' Annie said, instinctively still playing cook.

Jennifer threw back her head and laughed. 'Come off it, Annie. It's delicious, but I'll lay money you didn't cook it yourself. And even if you did, it sure as hell wasn't in this dish.'

'How do you know?'

'It's plastic, you idiot. You gave the game away when you carried it in with a tea towel. Microwave?'

'I did the garlic bread in the oven,' Annie countered.

Annie raised her fork to her lips. Jennifer was right. The honey mustard sauce both smelt and tasted delicious. She'd overplayed her hand. No way could she have created this from scratch.

'I asked what they'd done,' Jennifer went on, 'when they had the complaint in. Of course I did, with the timing of it, Soham and all that. They found nothing against Michael, but they thought the person who reported him probably held a grudge.'

'They knew who reported him?' Annie clocked Jennifer's use of Michael Walker's first name, almost as though she'd known him, but pushed it aside in her surprise that the complainant might not be anonymous.

'Oh yes, they knew. It was a woman called Donna Lambit.'

Jennifer looked up, her gaze meeting Annie's as she took another mouthful of chicken.

'Who?' The name meant nothing to her.

'She went back to her maiden name when she divorced. Her married name was Liversedge.'

Annie felt her eyebrows lift in surprise. Liversedge was Charlotte's name. Michael Walker's partner. The one who'd found him dead after Yates's attack. She looked the question at Jennifer.

'Michael had just moved in with Charlotte at the time. Donna Lambit is her mother.'

'Charlotte Liversedge's mother reported Michael Walker to the police six years ago?' Annie sat completely still, trying to fit this piece into the jigsaw. Nicole Perks had been so certain there was nothing in the complaint story. Annie said this to Jennifer.

'I know. I couldn't tell her. I presumed Charlotte had her own reasons for keeping it quiet. I mean, wouldn't you keep quiet if your mother had done something like that?'

Annie shrugged. She had no landmarks when it came to assessing normal interactions between mother and daughter. 'And the victim? Yates's supposed witness? Did this Donna woman say who he was supposed to have abused?'

Jennifer nodded. 'It's been difficult. I haven't pressed too hard. I don't want it to look like I have a particular interest in the case.'

What is your interest in the case? Annie couldn't bring herself to ask the question aloud.

'But Charlotte's mother named someone? Do you have any idea who?'

'Well, yes.' Jennifer paused as though not sure how to frame the words. 'It seems ridiculous, but she named Charlotte as the victim.'

'But Charlotte Liversedge is not a child. Was she saying he'd abused Charlotte when she was young?'

Jennifer shook her head. 'I don't think they knew each other when they were kids. And anyway, he'd have been a child too.'

Annie sat forward, elbows resting on the table, fingers steepled in front of her. Talking to Charlotte Liversedge had suddenly become more important than seeing Joshua Yates. But there were several reasons not to enlist Nicole. It didn't matter. Now she had a name, it would be the work of a moment to track down Charlotte's mother, the obvious intermediary to bring about a meeting.

CHAPTER EIGHT

A neat, pale-brick house, with a good-sized garden and a car on the drive, stood beneath pristine pantiles that shone in the mid-morning light, displaying a military precision carried down through curtains hung just-so, to a garden with set-square corners and trimmed beds. One house amongst several dozen, part of a pattern of avenues, closes, walks and boulevards, making up what was considered to be a good corner of this estate.

Annie studied the house as she approached. Cold-calling this time, just as she must with Tim and Tracey Morgan later in the week, but they were the Longs' case and this visit belonged to the file labelled Nicole Perks. Strictly speaking, it belonged to Brittany Booth because it was she Annie would bill the time to.

The house itself belonged to Donna Lambit.

This was the woman who had reported her daughter's lover as a child abuser. And Charlotte as the abused child? That couldn't be right. Jennifer must be wrong about that. After all, she'd been diffident in her enquiries, not wanting to be connected with the case.

Annie was determined to get to the bottom of this story, and do it quickly, because once the court reconvened for sentencing, Brittany Booth would pull her resources out and the case would be left hanging.

Donna Lambit must have had serious concerns for her daughter's safety to do what she did, but in the bright light of mid-morning, Annie's plan to play on these fears and to offer a sympathetic ear did not seem so solid.

She pressed the bell and heard it chime inside the house. At once, the shadow of a hurrying figure shimmering in the pattern of the smoky glass came towards her from the back of the house.

The door opened on a woman a few inches taller than Annie. Neat brown hair topped a smart, severe outfit of skirt and blouse in browns and reds.

Annie smiled. 'Mrs Lambit?'

Even before the woman spoke, Annie knew she had been mistaken for someone else. 'Yes, yes. Do come through. You're on the ball. I thought I had ten minutes yet.' Donna Lambit's gaze flitted here and there, never once meeting Annie's eye as, with a nervy laugh, she ushered her in.

Annie let herself be led into a small sitting room, neat as a showroom. The surfaces gleamed and the tang of polish hung in the air, ingrained in the fabric of the house. She turned and spoke, as though the thought had only just occurred to her. 'But you can't have been expecting me, Mrs Lambit. I was going to ring, but I couldn't find your number.'

'I'm not in the book. But aren't you from the council?'

In the flurry of explanations, Annie saw suspicion and antagonism play around Donna's face.

'You're Press, aren't you?' Donna accused, still not looking her in the eye. 'If you are, I'm calling your editor. And the police.'

'No, I'm not.' Annie held out her card, which Donna looked at but didn't attempt to take. 'Really, I understand how hard it must have been for you. I'm here because I want to find the truth. I want to make things easier for Charlotte.'

'You know Charlotte? How is she? When did you last see her?'

'No, I haven't met her yet, but I'm hoping to be able to talk to her soon. I've been looking into her partner's murder.'

'Huh,' Donna snorted. 'You're another one out to whitewash him. She's better off without him. She knows it, and she'll admit it before long, whatever lies you feed her.'

'I'm not after feeding lies to anyone, Mrs Lambit. It isn't Charlotte who's paying me. I'm working for someone who wants me to get at the truth, pure and simple.'

This seemed to give Donna pause for thought. Eventually, she said, 'Did you know Michael Walker?'

'No, I didn't.'

Annie looked at Donna, reading real hatred for Michael Walker, and wondered what secrets the dead man had hidden. Her time was leaking away. She must get to the point.

'It must have caused serious friction between you and Charlotte when you reported Michael six years ago.'

'How did you know about that? Well, of course it did. The police were hopeless. They had him and they let him go.'

'But after all this time... I mean, he and Charlotte lived together for six years. Did he abuse her?'

'I hope to God not. He knew someone was on to him. That stopped him.'

'I meant did he abuse her when she was a child?'

'Of course not! What are you saying? She didn't know him then.'

'But Charlotte was an adult when you reported Michael. You referred to a young girl in your complaint.'

'Charlotte was a young girl six years ago. She was barely eighteen.'

'Had there been other victims?'

'Of course there had. A man like that!'

'But who were they?'

'It's not for me to say.'

'But do you know?' Annie pushed. 'I'm not asking for names, but do you know who they were?'

Donna remained stony faced and repeated, 'It's not for me to say.'

'But can you tell me—?'

'No,' Donna cut across her. 'I don't want to talk to you any more. You push your way into my house, with all your questions, pretending to be someone else. You know nothing about Michael Walker, do you?'

'Not yet, but I'll get at the truth before I'm done.'

Donna, mouth open to speak, stopped as though weighing Annie's words. 'The truth,' she murmured, then she looked Annie in the eye for the first time and said, 'You want to see Charlotte, don't you?'

'Yes, I would like to.'

'Give me your details again. I want to know exactly who you are. My daughter's happiness is important to me.'

Annie passed her card across. 'I'm just looking for the truth,' she said again. 'A lot of pain has been caused in all this. The people who've taken the brunt of it deserve to have the truth known.'

'I want to have all the detail for Charlotte when I speak to her.' Donna studied Annie's card, and as she spoke, she stood up and walked across to the door, still turning the card in her hand. She paused at the doorway and looked back at Annie, signalling with a small smile and inclination of her head that the interview was at an end.

Annie rose. 'Thank you—' she began, but Donna interrupted, her tone even.

'I want to have all your details for Charlotte so I can warn her off. I don't want you anywhere near my daughter.' Her voice hardened. 'Now get out of my house.'

CHAPTER NINE

Annie lost the best part of an hour racing back to the office to pick up Pat's car, inwardly raging all the way at another absurdity of this job. She had a car of her own and tried to kid herself it was her choice not to drive anywhere when she could avoid it, but the reality of the last year or two was that she couldn't afford to run it. The tacit understanding held that if she needed a vehicle for work, she could use Pat's, but when the unexpected cropped up and she needed to be somewhere fast, that plan fell apart. Donna Lambit had had ample time to warn her daughter.

She climbed out of the car now and looked around her. A soft breeze feathered her face and neck. She took in the intimacy of the street, recognized the house in front of her as a poor relation of the one she'd just left. It was smaller, bundled close to its neighbours in a terrace, no front garden. The ambience was not so neat, nor so prosperous, yet warmer. It wasn't hard to imagine wartime housewives in a grainy black and white film, out on these front steps, swapping gossip, living each other's lives.

Donna's about-face sat in her mind; an irritant; something she should have seen coming. She had no plan of action, just a need to grab at the information before it flew from her grasp. This was where she should have come in the first place. Striding forward, she knocked at the door.

The young woman who answered was a softer, rounder version of Donna, her wispy fair hair escaping an elaborate hairclip in strands that she batted ineffectually aside as they wafted round her face.

Annie didn't try to dissemble but held out her card. 'I'm Annie Raymond. I've been working for Nicole Perks. I'm sorry to drop in unannounced, but I need to talk to you.'

'Oh right.' Charlotte Liversedge was not at all hostile. 'Nicole's told me all about you. I'm glad to meet you. Do come in.'

Charlotte seemed genuinely pleased to see her, but Annie knew she must get her cards on the table if she wanted a useful interview.

'I should tell you I've just seen your mother. She didn't want me to talk to you.'

'Oh, take no notice of her.' Charlotte laughed without warmth and led Annie inside.

The door let straight into a cheerless living room where an over-large settee piled high with clothes and magazines dominated the space. Charlotte led the way past an open staircase that divided the downstairs space and waved Annie to sit at a small kitchen table.

'If I'm to get anywhere with this enquiry for Nicole,' Annie said, 'it's important I ask you some questions. I don't want to intrude; things must have been very difficult.'

'No, no, don't worry. I told Nicole I wasn't ready to talk to you, but the truth is, I wanted to talk to you without her around. There are things I don't want her to know. Will you have tea while you're here? I've just made a pot.'

So there were secrets between Charlotte and Nicole.

'Thanks... uh... any chance of a coffee?'

'Yes, of course. We don't drink coffee much but there's some in. Michael drank coffee. Nicole said you're from down south.'

'Further north than here originally, but yes, I worked in London before I came to Hull.'

It was months since Michael's death. Annie watched as Charlotte rummaged through a cupboard and wondered if it were too late to change her mind about having a drink at all when she saw the dusty jar, with its lid not properly closed, a bold label proclaiming it as value coffee powder. But shared drinks made for greater intimacy, more productive talk and the stale coffee that Charlotte was hacking out of the bottom of the jar with a knife was the price she must pay to get the best out of her.

'I realize that Nicole doesn't know about your mother reporting Michael, but I need to know more about it.'

'Nicole's told me about you. She makes you sound like the sort of person I could trust. You will keep quiet about stuff, won't you?'

'Yes, of course. It goes with the territory. But you must appreciate that I've been asked to get evidence of the truth about Michael and I have to report back to my clients, the people who pay.'

'Oh yes, I don't mean that stuff. I just mean stuff that it's better Nicole doesn't know. They sent me to a counsellor after it happened, but I couldn't talk to him.'

Annie felt awkward. Charlotte didn't seem to appreciate that the details of the six-year-old allegation fell into the category of things Nicole would have a right to know. She looked at the pale liquid in the cup Charlotte put in front of her. No hint of coffee lingered in the stale aroma that reached her nostrils. She hoped she'd be able to stomach enough of it not to seem to reject the friendship Charlotte was trying to offer. She knew if she had time, she could play Charlotte into revealing everything she knew, but time was scarce. Pat had asked around. The word was that they wouldn't delay a second longer than necessary to get Joshua Yates safely sentenced and locked away, and once that happened, Brittany Booth would pull out and there would be no money to carry on.

'Charlotte, what happened six years ago? Why did your mother do it? I gather she didn't like Michael, but why... I mean, did she believe it?'

Charlotte plumped herself down in a chair at the table and picked up the teapot. 'My mother never liked Michael. She never liked any of my guys. But things got serious quite quickly with Michael. We bought this house together. That's as big a commitment as anyone makes these days, isn't it?'

Annie smiled and nodded as she raised her cup to her lips, bracing herself not to react as the insipid liquid seeped over her tongue in a sickly trickle.

'But I'd had enough. She'd broken up every one of my relationships and I wasn't having it anymore. I thought she'd come round; learnt her lesson to stop treating me like a little girl, but as soon as we got the house, she was at it again. See, I fell over a paint pot while we were decorating and she turned round and accused Michael of hitting me. Well, next thing we know, there's been a complaint and Michael's hauled in by the police.'

'But they didn't find anything in it, as far as I heard.'

'No, of course not. But you wouldn't have thought it when they first took him in. They had him in most of the night. They accused him of some dreadful stuff, said he was like the guy that killed those two little girls. He was in a terrible state when he got back. But they let him out without charge and we thought that was it. Then, next thing, they've hauled him off again. They said sorry later, well, one of them did, but they said they couldn't take chances with something like that.'

'And did you know it was your mother who'd reported him?'

'Not at first. It was after they came back to take him the second time, that's when I went to her. I went for help. That was stupid of me. She told me, then. She said it was her, that she was protecting me. You see, she thought because they'd come back, they must have found something.'

'But why? What made her do it? Why that allegation? Not just to get at Michael, surely.'

'Oh, she'd have jumped at anything to get me away from him, but I'll tell you what was behind it. Senile old women gossiping.'

Annie felt surprise. Without knowing what she'd expected Charlotte to say, she knew it hadn't been that. 'Tell me more.'

'You know my mother's a carer. She's with an agency. They go round and look after people in their homes. Old people mostly.'

Annie hadn't known, but she nodded as she put the cup to her lips and let a drop of liquid seep into her mouth, before murmuring, 'It's shift work, isn't it?' automatically trawling for information about someone she might need to question again.

Despite being at loggerheads with her mother most of her life, Annie guessed that constant battles were a necessary spice

70

to both their lives. This estrangement, though inevitable after Donna's action and its appalling sequel, was sapping the life from them. Annie's connection with Charlotte was borne out of the woman's current isolation, but would snap at the least thing.

'One of my mother's clients was a woman called May Gow. You know the sort, an old busybody, been around Hull forever. So she reckoned to know Michael's family and all about him, that's what my mother said. I didn't believe her. She'd been going to that woman on and off all the time I was with Michael. Why would she suddenly remember it just when Michael and I got serious? She hadn't said a word before.'

Annie could think of several reasons. Donna might have mentioned that her daughter and boyfriend were buying a house. Michael's name would have cropped up. She imagined a bent old woman, with fluffy white hair and beady eyes. *Michael Walker?* she could almost hear the words. *Now, is that the family from... isn't he the one who...?* and she thought of the detail in the note sent to the police.

To Charlotte, she just said, 'Where does May Gow live?'

'She had a house up my mother's way, but she died a year ago.'

No information to be had from that source. 'How long was your mother with her?'

'Six or seven years.'

'She knew her well, then?' Annie made the words into a question, but noted that the timing was tight. Six or seven years? Donna probably didn't know her well at the time she reported Michael.

'No, not really,' Charlotte said. 'May Gow was never one of her principal clients. My mum's often first stand-in when people are away or off sick. See, they're always short-staffed. Young kids go into caring because there are no other jobs, but they soon move on. My mum's one of the few who keeps the job on.'

For the first time, Annie heard a hint of warmth for her mother in Charlotte's voice.

'What exactly did May Gow say about Michael?'

'That's the thing. I don't think she said anything, really. From what I heard, she was a stuck up old cow and I think all she said was that she didn't think much of Michael's family. Listen, about me keeping all this from Nicole; the complaint and it being my mum. I'll tell her, next chance I have. She'll get to know because of that cow, Brittany Booth. I wanted to talk to you first, but I'd like to tell her before she hears it from anyone else. She'll go apeshit.'

A warning bell rang in Annie's head. It hadn't occurred to her that Charlotte was keeping anything from Nicole other than the six-year-old allegation, but there was wariness in her voice. She ran through a mental list of possibilities. The big connection between the two women was the business venture Nicole had alluded to. She gave Charlotte an encouraging smile as she lifted her cup, putting her lips to the rim. The liquid left a repellent aftertaste in her mouth. Each small sip was torture and didn't seem to diminish the volume left in the cup at all.

'Tell me about your business. Nicole explained it's all on hold, but business opportunities don't hang around, so I can understand Nicole wanting to get a move on with things.'

'Is that what she said? Oh, I'd love to get it all up and running. I've held back because of Nicole.'

'Really, why's that?' Annie gave Charlotte an encouraging smile, confident she'd found the right territory to uncover this mini-mystery.

'Nicole's more upset about all this than I am. I mean it was awful to come back and find him like I did, but... well... she sort of expects me to be really upset all the time, and I'm not. Well, I am, of course. I want Michael's name cleared. Of course, I do. The thing is that we wouldn't have lasted much longer, me and Michael. For heaven's sake, don't breathe a word of this to Nicole, but I was holding back before, because if we'd started up the business with Michael in the driving seat and then we'd split up, it would have scuppered it. I wanted to do it differently without Michael, but Nicole wanted him on board. She really believed in him.'

'Why would it have been Michael in the driving seat?'

'Oh... Money and things,' Charlotte said vaguely, tipping her cup towards her and staring into its depths. Then she looked across at Annie. 'D'you want a refill?'

'No, no. I'm fine. So what happened?'

'We still hadn't committed to anything when Michael was killed. I can't tell Nicole why I was holding back before, it seems so heartless. See, we hadn't talked about splitting up; I just knew we were close to it. And Nicole was ready to put everything into the business. And just imagine if me and Michael had split up and Nicole had lost everything. How was I going to feel when I'd seen it coming? Now, without him around, we could really make a go of it, but it sounds so callous to say it. I'll do anything I can to prove that madman was wrong about him. He didn't deserve any of that, but the thing is, business-wise, I'm better off now he's dead.'

Annie toyed with warning Charlotte against that sort of talk. She was close to giving herself a motive for her partner's murder, but she said nothing. The identity of Michael's killer was not in doubt. Instead, she asked Charlotte about the embryo business and whilst listening to her talk, took a gulp of her drink and swallowed the mouthful straight down, because she wanted to leave an empty cup, and she would have to go soon.

The detail of Charlotte's proposed business did not interest Annie. It revolved around life-coaching in which apparently both she and Nicole held relevant qualifications. She half listened as Charlotte talked about the needs of the corporate world and how she intended to take advantage to build an enterprise that would ultimately pull in huge sums of money from the work of others. What caught Annie's attention was Charlotte's account of the creative way in which she, Michael Walker and Nicole Perks had gone about raising capital. There were ideas here she could explore for herself.

But this was not relevant to the case. It was time to make a move. Charlotte had given Annie a push forward on the allegations against Michael Walker, but the real story was back with Donna Lambit. It was not an easy option, but Annie hoped Donna had more to tell, because otherwise the truth was likely to be in the grave with May Gow.

CHAPTER TEN

Annie mulled things over as she left Charlotte's house. Donna was the key to this, but her next approach must be just right. She headed for a general-purpose store, its open door angled at the corner of the street, and bought a flat, dry-looking cheese sandwich and a can of lemonade, an antidote to the pallid fake coffee taste that hung in her mouth.

She and Pat had well-practised tactics for awkward people. Good cop, bad cop; one of them fake-apologizing for the other's behaviour; appearing to take sides, any ploy that would extract the information they needed. They were a good team. Annie would miss it when she broke free. But this job needed speed, not haste. She would touch base with Pat later this afternoon and work out tactics for a new assault on Donna tomorrow morning.

Chewing on her sandwich, Annie considered her options, and decided that as she had Pat's car, the best use of her time right now was to drive out to the Morgans and wrap up the case for Ron and Sheryl Long. Her discarded sandwich wrapper bounced down into the foot well in front of the passenger seat as she set off, winding the car through the back roads, cutting as direct a path as she could towards the dual carriageway that ran from one side of the city to the other, following the course of the Humber.

If not Donna, what other options had she to find out what May Gow had said? Tracking down May's family and friends would take time, and they might know nothing when she found them.

It was a smooth run through the town centre, and across the river Hull. She slowed the car a fraction as she passed the prison and looked across curiously. Sturdy high walls faced her, their bulbous roll-topped peaks with high-tech alarms that heavy-footed pigeons could set off. They looked impossible to climb, although she supposed it had been done in the prison's history. And anyway, twenty-first-century breakouts must be more sophisticated than makeshift ladders slung over walls. It was grim and packed to overflowing, she'd heard. High security. High risk guys. She wondered if the flap Jennifer had mentioned was over.

This had been a regular journey once, when they first started up and worked from Pat's place by the river. As she left the city behind, Annie clocked the road that went northwards, up towards the coast around Hornsea. That, too, had become a familiar drive when she'd been new to the area floundering to find her feet in her first proper case, the case that had brought her up close to the world of the Pony Club. It reminded her she hadn't yet rung to decline the invitation to judge that fancy-dress competition. She'd do that later.

For today's journey, she turned the other way, towards the village of Paull, screwing up her eyes against the iridescent sheen of the Humber as she drove through. But the lane out of the village didn't turn as she expected and she cursed herself for not taking the trouble to make sure of the directions.

No choice but to follow the tarmac ribbon in a loop back towards the Withernsea Road. Sheryl had spoken with irritation about the circuitous route they had followed after missing their way. It was all too easy to do in this sparse network of lanes that accommodated the abrupt turns of the field edges, no concessions to vehicles that couldn't bump their way across ploughed land.

Charlotte's words played in her mind. The business she and Nicole planned resonated with her own situation and her relationship with Pat. Charlotte, like Pat, had some capital behind her. Nicole hadn't, but had collateral enough to borrow her way into the deal. Nicole was where Annie should have been, with a real stake in the business, a right to determine its future direction. She supposed Nicole had family to back her, and wondered if the two women would make it; wondered, too, what Michael Walker would have brought to the venture. Nicole had seen value in his contribution, but Charlotte seemed to view him the way Annie saw Barbara, a millstone, a drag that would pull the whole thing to its knees.

On the right road at last, Annie saw the square shapes in the distance that made up the isolated dwelling that must be the Morgans'. But where on earth could the Longs be planning to stay? Within half a mile, they'd said. Did they intend to camp at the side of the road?

The property sat inside a tall boundary; the protection of a stout fence allowing a thick hedge to grow. This close to the sea, the branches could not grow tall and although the wooden gate was closed, there remained a clear view into the yard. She peered in curiously, taking in every detail as she drove by. She knew Sheryl had lied for her own ends, but the woman's words floated through her mind.

They're murderers. They bludgeon them to death.

She stopped the car on a grass verge and looked again at the house. Because of the alignment of the outbuildings, the marquee didn't show from the road so her story was thinner than she'd realized.

As she walked towards the entrance, she replayed fragments from Ron Long... *coming to stay in the area... a lovely little spot... a holiday... need to relax...* Their own agendas had shone out from the moment they opened their mouths. This was nothing whatever to do with the Morgans.

She paused before trying the gate and ran her gaze over the walls and paths inside the yard, looking for wires, conduits or insulated boxes. No obvious sign of security lights overlooking the place. Then she pulled at the latch and, as though she'd pressed an 'on' button, a cacophony of barking rang out, followed at once by a river of dogs that flooded round the corner of the big barn and headed for the gate.

Annie pulled it shut and took a step back. Dogs, all shapes and sizes, crowded the gate, making her suddenly aware of the flimsiness of the barrier between them. Some of the animals immediately lost interest, two of them diverted into a circular chase that raised dust from the gravel path, a couple more pushing their noses into the dirt at the hedge bottom following invisible scent trails. But the smallest three bounced up and down as though on springs, barking frantically and non-stop, their stares never leaving her face. Two outsize hounds stood foursquare, barking in intermittent deep-throated woofs.

As the immediate alarm for her safety subsided, Annie took in a mental image of Sheryl Long, teetering on spindly heels, making her way into this yard unobserved, and thought that if Sheryl hadn't made it up, then she'd dreamt it.

She heard a shout and saw a man striding towards her across the gravel. He wore a grimy blue overall, smeared with dirt and carried a pitchfork.

They bludgeon them...

He yelled again, an indeterminate cry that caused the small dogs to stop bouncing and to race towards him.

'Geddown, dog!' He waved the pitchfork at them, and they immediately turned and flew back to the gate to bark in Annie's face.

The harassed and dishevelled figure was barely recognizable as the neat and suited father-of-the-bride she had seen in his daughter's wedding photos, but when he came closer, Annie could see it was Tim Morgan.

'Can I help you?'

'Mr Morgan? Sorry to trouble you, but I wondered if I could take a look at your marquee. The man from the company said...' It wasn't difficult to let the sentence fade away under the ear-splitting assault from the canine pack.

Tim Morgan, apparently unaware of the furore around his legs, frowned. 'But we told him no.' He shot her a glance through narrowed eyes. 'He told us you'd seen it driving past. You don't see it from the road. How did you know it was there?'

Annie was thankful she'd clocked this when she arrived, because now her subconscious was ready with an answer, and the fact he asked the question was reassuring. It was a legitimate reason for them to refuse her access. It strengthened her certainty that they were no more than innocent bystanders in Sheryl Long's private agenda.

'I saw it on Facebook in the wedding photos your wife put up there. The guy I spoke to must have just assumed I'd seen it from the road.'

Tim Morgan's frown smoothed. 'Oh right. Bloody Internet.'

'I've come quite a long way,' she went on quickly, before it occurred to him to ask how she'd found the site. 'Any chance I could just come in for a quick look?' Annie had to ask the question twice as one of the smaller dogs, a wirehaired terrier, grew suddenly hysterical in its frantic yapping and bouncing.

'The wife's out.' Tim was unsure, and Annie had an idea that if she'd been a man he would have invited her in without a qualm, but after a moment he stretched out his hand to unlatch the gate.

Annie fought down a surge of alarm. This man seemed completely unconscious of the danger his pack of dogs might pose to her, but she had to take on trust that he knew what he was doing as he swung the gate wide.

Tim's irritable, 'Geddown dog,' had little effect and, as they crossed the gravel expanse, Annie had to bat her hand at the bouncing trio and fend off acres of soggy tongue from the bigger dogs who barely had to raise their front feet from the ground to be on a level with her face. She waded through the pack, trying to match step with Tim Morgan, who strode on oblivious to the mayhem. It was largely boisterous play, but several times Annie whipped her fingers away from white teeth that flashed too close.

The marquee flapped noisily in the breeze from the estuary and Annie had to strain to listen to Tim Morgan's commentary and she trudged around it with him. The dogs stopped at the entrance. The small ones hung about and made little darts towards the canvas, without venturing in. Annie assumed someone – surely Tracey and not Tim – seeing the effect of their muddy feet on the white material had instilled discipline with a few serious thrashings.

They'd had the marquee for the wedding, Tim explained, but with a christening on the way, they'd asked to keep it up, because where else would they have the second do? Had she any idea how much it cost? He turned his cheerless gaze on her for a moment and answered his own question, 'No, you won't. Too young for kids that age. And all the bother of having it set up. Banging about, upsetting the animals. We weren't going through that twice over.'

Annie nodded and murmured and took every chance to look through the gaps in the canvas at the house and buildings, particularly the one Sheryl had identified. She ought to find a way to get inside that one to do the job properly.

'Take no mind of that,' Tim said, seeing her lift a flap of torn canvas to look through into the yard. 'They're all fully repaired and cleaned up for proper customers.'

'Aren't you proper customers?'

'Not really.' He explained that the marquee company belonged to Tracey's brother-in-law. They'd traded a less than perfect set-up for a good rate, and then traded further on the family connection to keep the whole thing up for the forthcoming christening.

'Thank you,' Annie said, as he led her back into the yard. 'That's been really helpful.'

She meant her words. All the tiny anomalies smoothed out as the pieces fell into place. Their original mistrust of her was already explained by her claim to have seen the marquee from the road. And now she understood the marquee man's irritation at them keeping the canvas construction beyond the agreed time. They'd played on family links and were probably costing the company money.

The three small dogs bounded up to join them as they headed back towards the gate. The rest of the pack was nowhere to be seen. She looked across at the big shed, but couldn't construct any subtle way to push Tim Morgan into inviting her inside. It was a full frontal assault or nothing.

'Oh look!' she cried, pointing at the big wooden doors. 'That's just like the barn where...' She exclaimed with bouncy, ersatz enthusiasm, allowing her words to be smothered by the trio of yapping dogs. 'Can I just have a quick look inside?' She tossed the words behind her as she darted across the yard.

Tim Morgan was at the doors ahead of her. His expression hadn't changed. She found herself struck by the immobility of his face, uncomfortably close to hers. Her hand rested on the metal catch; his was flat against the wood. The pitchfork in his other hand stood out in her peripheral vision. She became aware of the small dogs at her feet, their yapping silenced, as from behind her, a larger canine throat let out a low growl that ran shivers up her spine.

'Best if you just leave now.'

Annie dropped her hand from the door, her gaze from his and murmured, 'Yes, OK,' as she turned and walked to the gate.

Whispers in the gravel surface told her the pack was right behind her, stalking her departure.

CHAPTER ELEVEN

Half an hour's drive took Annie back to the office, where she found Pat leafing through files.

Tim Morgan's face shimmered in her memory.

Best if you just leave...

Damn Tim Morgan and his lined, harassed face. It was too frayed a loose end to leave, but she shook him out of her head. The Michael Walker case was priority, and her first goal to find out what Donna Lambit knew.

She told Pat about Donna: about how the woman had warned her off, about her subsequent conversation with Charlotte and what she'd learnt of the six-year-old complaint and May Gow.

Pat digested the story, then said, 'Sounds like I should go in heavy-handed. Apologize for the young kid overstepping the mark, but with a threat underneath it. What can I use?'

'She complained about the guy without any evidence. Six years later he was killed. At some level she might blame herself.'

'Did she know Yates?'

'I didn't ask outright.'

'Worth a shot. I'm only after a veiled threat. And you reckon we're on the clock?'

'Of course we are. Once the court reconvenes for sentencing, that's it. Brittany Booth will call it off and Nicole Perks doesn't have the resources to keep us on.'

'I'll call in on her tomorrow,' Pat said. 'What's the best time?'

'She does early morning shifts. She's back at home by about ten.'

'OK, I'll go straight round from home. See you back here when I've done.'

Annie nodded. 'Anything new come in?'

'No, but the files we did yesterday were well received. We'll get more work from them. And Barbara's put in an official request for a rather interesting document on the Mellors' case.'

Annie listened, stony-faced, to Pat tell Barbara's version, which was to take all the credit for ferreting out the existence of the document Annie had tipped her off about.

'When did she send the request in?'

'It must have gone in Friday morning's post.'

Annie said nothing. If she knew no better, she might believe it. Barbara hadn't been in the office since last Friday, and the post had been collected before she and Annie had spoken. By sneaking in late Sunday night, Barbara aimed to show that at worst her letter had lain in the post tray overlooked since Friday morning. Thoughts tumbled in of previous occasions when Barbara seemed to have pipped her at the post. Letters ready, documents in apple-pie order, notes on files showing – apparently – that Barbara had been more on the ball than Annie had given her credit for. Not only was Barbara stifling Annie's ideas for the business, she also clung on her coat-tails, using the sleight of hand of her late-night visits to make herself look good at Annie's expense.

She would regret leaving Pat, for all her prickliness, but this evidence of Barbara's duplicity hardened her resolve to find a way out.

Nicole gasped as she recognized Annie's voice on the phone. 'What's happened? What have you found? What's so urgent?'

Annie hastened to reassure her. 'We're short of time,' she said, 'and it would help to iron out some background details before we meet tomorrow. I won't bill you for the time. Come round to my place.'

She'd broken a cardinal rule – never let the client into your personal space – but told herself it didn't matter because she was moving on. And she had her own reasons to quiz Nicole. Charlotte had been practical and grounded as she'd explained their business venture to Annie. It would be a partnership between equals and it would work. Now, Annie wanted to hear it from Nicole's side because Nicole was the one whose situation was closest to her own.

When she reached home, Annie rushed about, pulling cushions off the sofa and dragging out the accumulated bits and pieces from underneath. She raised a cloud of dust that stung her eyes and caught in her throat before rushing upstairs to an elderly neighbour who had helped out before with household appliances.

'My vacuum's broken again, would you mind?'

He chuckled. 'You mean the bag's full and you've forgotten how to change it. Use mine tonight, but you bring it round at the weekend and I'll sort it for you.'

'Deal.' She smiled and hurried back.

The noise filled the small space and the machine left a track across the thin carpet that changed its colour. Annie raced it over the floor, pushing chairs out of the way to get into the corners, gritting her teeth at every metallic clank that signalled something other than dust sucked into the innards of the machine, but it was robust and kept running. She wrestled free the tube and ran it over the sofa, the cushions, the table top. Every surface she cleaned highlighted another thick with grime.

She was on hands and knees reaching under the cupboard unit when she spotted the time and clicked the vacuum off. Standing up, she brushed down her trousers and went to detach the cord from the wall. Now she noticed them, lines of dust thrust themselves forward from every angle, but the air was fresher and the space shone in a way it hadn't for weeks.

Nicole was far from relaxed when she arrived. 'Tell me if you've found anything. I'd rather know the truth.'

'No, really, it's nothing like that. It's just that if I don't get to the bottom of it before the court reconvenes, certain doors are going to close.'

'Official sources who won't talk to you once the madman's put away, you mean?'

'Something like that. The thing is, Nicole, I need to look at all the angles, all the possible motives for anyone involved in wanting to blacken Michael's name. This business you, he and Charlotte were about to set up. I want to know more about it.'

'But what could that possibly have to do with his murder?'

'I've no idea, but business interests are a classic motive for getting someone out of the way.'

'That madman wasn't interested in the business.'

'But suppose someone else was. Suppose they wound up Yates with their allegations. It could be a perfect crime. Yates insane enough to believe in what he was doing and tied into saying nothing to bring anyone else into the frame by whatever tale he was fed.'

Nicole looked startled, digesting this new angle. And well she might, thought Annie, who had constructed the theory as a viable way to ask the questions she wanted, without seriously considering it as a motive for murder. Now, hearing herself tell it for the first time, she experienced a moment's doubt. It put a different complexion on the stories she'd heard from several people, Nicole herself being one of them.

Nicole, however, was reassuringly willing to talk about the details of the business and its proposed finances. Annie listened intently.

'So Charlotte would have a far bigger financial stake than you. Would that have been a problem?'

'Oh, no. If we go ahead, we'll be equal partners. It's Michael who would have had the greater share.'

'He'd have been the senior partner then? Wouldn't that have made you feel at a disadvantage? Michael and Charlotte between them would have had control.'

'No, it wouldn't have worked like that. It would have been a partnership of equals, but Michael would have had the biggest financial stake. And he had such ideas...' Nicole's voice thickened as her words faded away.

Charlotte hadn't thought much of Michael's ideas, but Annie wasn't about to say so.

'The damage people cause!' Nicole burst out. 'And they've no idea.'

'That's vigilantes,' Annie murmured. 'No due process. Where will you get the money to cover Michael's share?'

'Charlotte can raise it on the house once things are sorted out.'

'Won't that leave you the minority partner?'

'I'm raising more too. From family.'

'That's lucky,' said Annie, trying to keep the acid out of her voice. 'Having family with funds to spare.'

'It's not that.' Nicole laughed. 'Far from it. None of them has a bean to spare. But they have assets and they're willing to lend me the money they can borrow. I've convinced them it's a good investment.'

'That's quite a risk for them.'

'Oh yes, if we go under, we'll take them all down with us. But it's not going to happen, not even now we've lost Michael.'

'Explain to me exactly how it'll work.'

Later that night, Annie sat mulling over what Nicole had said. Even after all that had happened, Nicole was ready to make the leap. What reason could Annie possibly have for any doubts on her own account? For the sake of tying loose ends, and for no other reason, she would wrap up this case. And then she was off. It didn't matter what she was going to: what mattered was what she was getting away from.

Chapter Twelve

Morning sun over the estuary speared its light across the city making Annie shade her eyes against the brightness, making a dark cave of the office when she arrived, blinking to adjust to the dim light before climbing the stairs.

First in today, because Pat was to head straight to Donna Lambit's, the empty rooms echoed the insistent beep from the phone signalling a new message. As she pushed the door open, footsteps hurried from one of the downstairs offices and a voice called out, 'Is that you, Annie? Can you come down? I've coffee brewing.'

She smiled. The guy downstairs had taken to buying really good coffee once he found she liked it. There wasn't much interaction between the floors, but they'd fallen into an easy relationship, something else she would miss.

'We've had reports, Annie,' he told her as he poured the coffee. 'People have been seen in the building at nights.'

Annie felt the blood rush to her face and ducked her head. Please God, don't let anyone have seen her creeping half-naked down the stairs, followed by an equally dishevelled Scott. 'Uh... when? Who's seen people?'

'The woman across the road. You know they sometimes work round the clock over there.'

Annie didn't, but she nodded.

'She happened to mention it. People in and out of the door. Well, one person anyway... in the small hours. I just want to be sure it's legitimate key-holders. From the description, it might have been one of your colleagues. A... uh... larger lady.'

'Ah, right. It's Barbara. She drops stuff off at odd times.'

'On a regular basis? In the small hours? You're sure?'

'Yes, I know she pops in out of hours, but I'll mention it. Do you have dates?'

Annie smiled. She looked forward to dropping this into the conversation in front of both sisters.

Half an hour, more gossip and two coffees later, she climbed the stairs, and was met again by the beep-beep of the waiting message. With the speaker-phone on, she pressed the button to retrieve it, whilst opening e-mail on the nearest of the PCs.

'This is for Ms Raymond,' a voice rapped out. Annie's eyes snapped wide in surprise. Donna Lambit. 'I've had time to think. I'm prepared to talk to you. But on my terms, not yours.'

Donna's voice rattled out her conditions. She would listen to questions, but there must be no pressure on her to answer; no threats; no police; no contact with Joshua Yates; any funny business and that would be it.

Annie smiled as she clicked out Pat's number to let her know there was no need for heavy tactics now.

'I'll go back this morning,' she told her boss. 'No time like the present. And I'll let you know if she's on the level.'

As she arrived within sight of the neat house she'd been thrown out of the day before, Annie's curiosity welled up. What did Donna know? How much would she tell?

This time Annie felt she had the upper hand, arriving as invited guest, and Donna showed no surprise at seeing her on the doorstep.

'Come through.' She held the door wide and waved her hand towards the small living room.

She pointed at a chair. Annie sat.

'I was overwrought the other day... worried for my daughter. For her sake, I'll co-operate.'

Annie recognized a prepared opening speech, badly executed.

'But before I listen to your questions, I've some of my own.'

'Go ahead.'

'What do you know about Michael Walker?' Donna betrayed her nervousness by obsessively picking at her nails.

'Over and above what anyone could have read in the papers,

very little. He and your daughter planned to set up as business partners. That's about it.'

'And you're out to prove he didn't do any of the things he was accused of?'

'No, that's not my brief.' Annie chose her words with care. 'I'm after the truth.'

'And what if the truth shows he was guilty of all those things?'

Annie looked her in the eye. 'Then so be it.'

'And you'd tell my daughter?'

'No, she's not the one employing me. But she'll get to know, I'm sure.'

'Who is employing you?'

'I'm not allowed to say. Client confidentiality.'

Donna stared hard at her for a moment. Annie read the message, *don't think I trust you yet,* but Donna sat back a little, so Annie mirrored the move by sitting forward, and said, 'Tell me about May Gow.'

Donna's lips pursed, 'I slaved for that cow and she left me nothing.'

Both the words and the tone surprised Annie. Charlotte had implied that her mother and May were not close.

'Why would she leave anything to you?' She watched closely trying to catch a glimpse of the real story.

'Don't get me wrong. I'm not saying I had any rights over Susan, but there was some stuff she promised me.'

'What stuff?'

'It doesn't matter. It has no bearing on this.'

'But what was it?'

'I said it doesn't matter.'

'OK. Who's Susan?'

'May's daughter, but you'll get nothing from her. She kept herself well out of the way until the time came to pick over her mother's things.'

'Does she live locally?'

'I haven't a clue. I only spoke to her a couple of times.'

Scraps of information. Annie tried to build them in her mind, to work out which direction to go. May Gow promised something to Donna, but didn't deliver. No love lost between Donna and May Gow's daughter. Despite her previous decision that it was unlikely to be worthwhile tracing May Gow's family, Annie knew she would have to trace Susan.

'What's Susan's surname?'

'Gow. Same as her mother.'

'Never married?'

Donna shrugged a don't know.

'What did May Gow tell you about Michael?'

'Nothing.'

'I thought she talked to you before you put in the complaint.'

'No.'

The bald negatives nonplussed Annie. 'So what did you find out about Michael Walker, and where from?'

'You know what I found out. You know what he did. It all came out in court.'

Annie bit back the obvious comment, that the court had discounted everything Yates had said, and asked again, 'Who told you?'

'I know you've spoken to Charlotte. You needn't try to hide it. She tries to believe anything that'll make that man look innocent, but I can assure you, May Gow told me nothing at all about Michael Walker.'

'Then who was it?'

'No one,' said Donna, her voice rising a little. 'No one told me. But it's all true.'

Annie looked across at her, knowing she'd had all that Donna would give her for now, but wanting to leave the way open once she'd worked it out. 'Do you want to know what I find out about Michael Walker?'

Donna's gaze snapped up to meet hers. 'Would you be allowed to tell me?'

'If I choose to, yes.'

'Then yes, I would.'

'And if I have more questions, you'll answer them?'

Seeing Donna frame an instinctive refusal, Annie added quickly, 'Not now... maybe later on.'

Donna hesitated, then nodded.

Annie stood up, wanting to be the one to end the visit this time, to be in control. She looked into the woman's eyes which were hard as flint, staring back, radiating hostility, but deep down showing something else, something that Annie couldn't read.

That afternoon, Nicole arrived at the office twenty minutes early and apologetic.

'Sorry, I wasn't sure how long it would take me to walk up here. I thought better early than late. I can just sit and wait till you're ready for me.'

Annie smiled and pushed forward one of the office chairs, wondering if Nicole had expected a comfortable waiting room with low tables and magazines.

'I'll wait for Pat before I debrief you. She's the boss. She wants to hear how things are going.'

They chatted desultorily and Annie eased the conversation again towards Nicole and the details of how she raised finance from a family who had no money. If Nicole thought the questions intrusive, she didn't show it, and spoke openly. Annie was intrigued by the diligence Nicole and her family had put into exploring their options. The solution they'd settled on wasn't something Annie could duplicate, but she saw avenues open up that she had never properly considered. She was weighing the pros and cons when familiar sounds reached her. Pat's grunts and laboured breathing matched the thudding of her footfalls as she hauled herself up the stairs. That's the difference, Annie realized: Barbara doesn't grunt and groan on her way up.

Once Pat was settled and introductions made, Annie outlined where she'd got to. She could tell from Nicole's pursed lips that Donna's role in the six-year-old complaint wasn't news. Charlotte must have broken it to her.

'What's next?' Pat prompted, when Annie had finished her account.

'There was nothing in the complaint itself,' Annie said, with more confidence than she felt, 'or something would have come to light at the time. So I want to get to the bottom of what

Donna said and where she heard it from. If I can nail that and discredit it, then that takes the rug from under the stories that are going about.'

'You haven't forgotten,' Nicole said, 'that we can't pay for much more of your time?'

'No, I hadn't forgotten, but we're all right at the moment. And there is something you and Charlotte could help with. Can you get anything out of Donna? I know she and Charlotte haven't spoken for a while, but she could probably get the gen from her far quicker than I can.'

'I'd like to kill that cow!'

'That won't help,' Pat said. 'Annie's right. If you could persuade Charlotte to dig out the detail, you could save us some time and yourselves some money. It might be the difference between getting the job done or not.'

Annie looked at Nicole. Her outburst against Donna was still visible in the tension in her jaw. If Nicole chased her instincts, she would wreck the chances of anyone finding the truth.

'Your job,' Annie told her, 'is to persuade Charlotte to go and talk to her mother, to find out who told her what before she reported Michael. There's no point in you trying to force it out of her. She'll just clam up.'

Nicole nodded. Annie could see she was itching to lay into the woman she saw as the root of the trouble, but she wanted a result and would curb her baser instincts to achieve it.

A discordant jangle of both door buzzers pressed simultaneously cut through their conversation. It was followed by the murmur of voices, then the tramp of footsteps up the stairs. Annie and Pat exchanged a glance. It was unusual for the guy downstairs to let someone up without announcing them. Annie got to her feet, stepped across to the door and swung it open.

Three faces were in her line of sight as she looked down. The guy from the office looked worriedly at the two people on their way up. Annie felt a sudden shock to see Scott and Kate on the stairs. Scott, face grim, did not look at her. Kate stared with cold hatred, and marched in as Annie retreated from her advance.

'Pat Thompson? Ann Raymond?' Kate rapped out.

Annie, aware of Nicole's gaping mouth, thought for a surreal moment that she and Pat were about to be arrested.

Pat looked Kate up and down coldly and said, 'Ah, PC Ronsen. To what do we owe the pleasure?'

'DC,' Kate snapped. 'We have intelligence that someone we're interested in has made contact with a local PI. It's probably a man, and he's from outside the area. We need to know if it's you he's contacted.'

'As you can see,' Pat said, in measured tones. 'We're with a client at the moment. Perhaps you'd like to wait and speak to us privately.'

Kate matched the ghost of a nod to a slight curl of her lip and planted herself firmly where she stood, making clear that if she were to wait, it would be right here in the middle of them all. Annie looked at Scott whose face was blank. He knew this wasn't the way to get co-operation from her and Pat.

'And you know you'll have to give me more than that,' Pat said. 'Assuming you're looking for co-operation.'

'Oh, you'll co-operate, all right.'

'Are you suggesting we've not been co-operative in the past?'

'Of course not,' Scott broke in. 'We know you'll help us if you can.'

Annie eased back. This was one for Pat to deal with. She shot a look at Nicole, who stared from Kate to Pat and back again, clearly excited to be in the middle of this drama.

Kate's stance was confrontational, Pat's was to stonewall and Scott tried to go softly-softly whilst backing up his colleague. Watching them, Annie lost the drift of what was being said, until jolted back to attention when Kate turned to Nicole.

'And what's your business here?'

Outraged, Annie pulled in a gasp. 'You've no right—'

But Nicole, looking scared, launched at once into an explanation.

Kate smiled at her, and spoke gently. 'You want to unearth the truth about Michael Walker?'

'Oh yes,' said Nicole, looking up at Kate with sudden hope.

Annie too, found her protests stilled. How odd that Kate

should have a smile that so completely transformed her face, just like Scott. And was she going to give Nicole something they could use?

The thought had barely formed when Kate turned to look at Annie. Her mouth still curved to a smile, but her eyes had hardened, making her expression more sly than pleasant. Her stare remained on Annie, but she spoke to Pat.

'Be sure and get in touch, Ms Thompson, should anything come to light.' She then looked back at Nicole, her expression softening. 'You must be fed up with that girlfriend of his and her campaigning.'

'Oh, you mean Brittany Booth? Yes, I wish there was a way to lock her up along with Yates. She's every bit as dangerous.'

'Interesting you should have chosen to work with Annie Raymond,' Kate said. 'You know she's working for Brittany Booth's campaign, don't you?'

Nicole's eyes snapped open. Shock leached the colour from her skin. 'No... that's impossible.'

'Oh yes. They've been with Booth from the start.'

Nicole swung round to Annie. 'It's not true. Tell me it's not true.'

'Nicole, listen, it's not like it sounds. It—'

'Are you working for Brittany Booth?'

'Nicole, I can't tell you who else we are or aren't working for. We have to respect—'

'My God! You are! How could you?' With a cry that was half a sob, Nicole leapt to her feet and flew out, leaving the four of them to listen to her footsteps clattering down the stairs.

'Right,' said Kate, pleasantly, 'just a few routine questions and we'll be on our way. Both of you,' she added sharply, as Annie took a step towards the door.

Opening her mouth to protest, Annie caught a brief movement from Pat. Her boss was signalling her to leave it. She felt anger, clamped her teeth together and clenched her fists, but sat back down. Nicole wasn't the only one who would need explanations. This would get back to Jennifer.

CHAPTER THIRTEEN

By the following morning, the heat of anger within Annie had become a hard knot. If Kate wanted war, then war it was. She determined she would get to the bottom of this case, money or no money, if she had to stay in Hull forever to do it.

Her immediate objective was to find Nicole, but she'd been trying since yesterday and had no luck. Nicole's phone remained off.

Annie stood now outside Nicole's flat, but the place lay empty. She clambered round the narrow outside space to peer into the windows, and toyed with the idea of breaking in, on the off-chance Nicole had seen her and was hiding inside, but crushed the idea as it was born, seeing in her mind's eye a picture of Nicole calling the police and Kate arriving.

If Nicole weren't here, the obvious place to look was Charlotte's.

Charlotte opened the door to her knock, looking dishevelled as though she hadn't been up long.

'Hi, come through. I wasn't expecting you. Has anything happened?'

Annie hesitated a moment but then stepped inside. Better that Charlotte heard this from her than from Nicole. They sat at the table in the kitchen. Glossing over the exact timings, Annie explained that Brittany Booth had approached the firm for help after they had already taken on the job for Nicole.

'And now Nicole's found out about it from a third party. She's very upset. I need to find her.'

'Are you allowed to work for different sides like that?' Charlotte seemed surprised, but not angry, just interested.

'Well, it's unusual,' Annie murmured. 'But...'

97

'I suppose you have different people working on each bit.'

'Um...'

'Oh, and it could be good, couldn't it? Your colleagues would tell you if they found anything that was useful for us, so you wouldn't have to find it all again. It could save us some money.'

Annie laughed uneasily. The situation was far from a model of good practice and could harm their reputation.

'She doesn't know, does she? The Brittany woman? That you're working for us?'

'No, no. Client confidentiality. I wouldn't have told you about her except for Nicole finding out. It's Nicole who signed us up and I'm not sure she wants us to carry on with it.'

'Don't worry about her. She'll come round. She gets emotionally tied up in things, but I'll talk to her. You carry on.' Charlotte looked into Annie's eyes and gave her a grin. 'And I'll expect to see a nice light touch on our invoice.'

Annie made herself smile back, but wasn't sure it reached further than the curve of her lips. Before she could speak, Charlotte said, 'Ah, yes!' and jumped to her feet. 'I have something for you. I was going to ring.'

Charlotte walked across the kitchen to rummage in a large floppy handbag that sat on the work surface. Annie watched her, reflecting that she hadn't wasted a moment worrying about divided loyalties, just homed in razor-sharp on the unethical aspect and used it to her own advantage.

'I went round to Mum's last night.'

'Oh right. That's good. Did Nicole tell you what we said?' Annie spoke lightly, but kept her eyes on Charlotte, who wasn't supposed to have spoken to Nicole since the meeting in Annie and Pat's office.

'I haven't seen Nicole. I told you. What was she supposed to have said?' Charlotte sounded surprised and Annie relaxed. Mustn't look for conspiracies where none existed.

'With time being tight, we thought it would be quicker for you to talk to your mother. She's not too keen on talking to us. And we need to know more about what happened six years ago.'

'I didn't think you'd get anything out of her.'

'So did she tell you why she made the complaint?'

'Hell, no, we didn't talk about that. We'd have ended up scrapping.' Charlotte pulled a sheaf of papers from the bag.

'What did you talk about?' Annie asked.

'This and that. Nothing much.'

Annie saw Charlotte's gaze slide away as she made a pretence of rummaging through her bag again. She became more like her mother on every visit.

'I brought you these. When she nipped up to the loo, I went through her work files.'

Charlotte handed Annie a crumpled wad of papers. Annie smoothed them out on the table top. The page in front of her was printed with a grid of about thirty rows. Each row was initialled and each recorded a date, a time and a short commentary. Several different pens and hands had written in the narrow boxes.

Gave May her dinner, steak pie and peas...

May says her water tablets don't agree with her...

Supper and COT...

'C-O-T?' Annie queried.

'Cup of tea. But it's the info page you want. I just grabbed the lot to be sure I had it.'

Annie riffled through the sheets. The info page was headed with a smudged logo that made no obvious sense. She hoped the care agency put its money into training its carers. It didn't spend much on its stationery. She recalled Charlotte's remarks from her earlier visit.

They're always short-staffed. My mum's one of the few who keeps the job on.

The grid on this sheet was a different shape and had some pre-printed captions, starting with name, address and date of birth.

Annie read down the list. May Gow had been born 14th April, 1919 and seven years ago had signed up for the Gold Care Package, which entitled her to four visits every day. Hadn't Charlotte told her Donna was not her prime carer? But at four visits a day, a number of people could have come to know

May. Annie flipped back through the other pages and checked down the edge of the lists, deciphering the scrawled initials. The overall pattern was a dozen the same, then a few different. Annie surmised days off for the regular carers. Donna's initials, DL, appeared several times across the half-dozen pages in short blocks of two, three or four. It fitted with Donna covering someone else's time off.

'Who's this?' Annie held the sheet out to Charlotte and pointed at the initials that occurred oftenest.

'I've no idea. Those sheets are years old. I'll bet every one of those people have left bar my Mum.'

Annie turned back to the front page and read down the list. May's GP was logged, along with a detailed record of medication.

'Shouldn't this stuff be at the agency?'

Charlotte shrugged. 'You'd be surprised how careless people can be. It stays at the client's house while they're live on the books, but you get relatives shoving it away into drawers and cupboards and no one knowing where it is. It's not unusual for the carers to keep it with them if they happen to be doing a long stint with the same person.'

'But shouldn't this have gone back to the agency when May Gow died?'

'I suppose, but I guess no one asked.'

It all seemed far too casual, but if Charlotte had a better explanation, she wouldn't give it to Annie, who concentrated on the page in front of her. She reached the bottom without finding anything of particular interest. She noted May's GP's name but knew that medical records confidentiality would bar her from anything useful from that source.

'Can I take these away with me?'

'No. I need to put them back in Mum's file before she notices.'

At least she had May Gow's address. She could try the neighbours and see what they could tell her. As the thought formed, she flipped the page and there at last was something useful.

Next of kin: Susan Gow, and a mobile phone number.

Annie wrote the number down, not knowing if it would still be current, or if Susan Gow would be able or willing to shed any light on what had happened six years ago.

As she said her goodbyes, the difficult conversations she had to face with Nicole and Jennifer sat at the back of Annie's mind, but she felt a growing curiosity about Susan Gow and what she might have to say about her mother's carers. She'd had no hint that mother and daughter had been close, so maybe the best she could hope for would be something she could use to loosen Donna's tongue.

On the way back to the office, Annie's mind buzzed with plans for a lightning background search on Susan Gow prior to ringing her. Thankfully, her name wasn't Smith or Jones, but it wasn't unusual enough to make for an easy search. Sometimes mobile phone numbers could be matched up to their owner's personal information and sometimes they couldn't. It might not even be Susan's phone any more. And maybe there would be a link back to Susan from her mother's address in one or other of the databases to which they had easy access.

A police patrol car cruised by. Annie watched it as she rehearsed different opening comments. It was always harder to cold call by phone than face to face. No body language to use to modify an approach or tailor opening questions.

The distinctive livery of the patrol car was swallowed up in the busy road ahead, and, as it disappeared, she realized she hadn't given Kate a thought since she'd arrived at Charlotte's. Instinctively, she pursed her lips to try to re-stoke her resentment, not wanting to let the foolish woman off the hook by allowing her anger to subside so soon, but it was gone. Kate had become an annoying distraction to the real business of the day.

She would curse Kate anew if things went sour between her and Jennifer, but she was confident Jennifer would give her a hearing and would understand. She must make clear that Brittany Booth came to them after she'd first seen Nicole, and explain to Jen how Vince had sent her. Jen knew the deal with Vince Sleeman and the Thompson sisters. She and Annie had had occasional conversations over the years where they'd shared oblique references to Sleeman, neither quite getting to the point. Annie, who had never got to the bottom of where Sleeman's real business interests lay, had wondered what the police knew, but eventually came to the conclusion that neither she nor Jen knew more than the other.

The thoughts of Jen, about the constant dance around people to prise out the information that they sometimes didn't know they held, became the catalyst that took her mind back to Kate and Scott's clumsy intrusion. Words she hadn't registered at the time now began to make sense. Kate had given away little detail, but she'd mentioned a few snippets. They had been after someone from outside the area.

On this flimsiest of evidence, Annie became certain that the person Kate was after was Ron Long.

Ron, uncomfortable with his stilted tale of a quiet holiday, but needing to reassure his wife. Sheryl, with her very real desire not to be involved in whatever was planned, and with her ridiculous story about murderers and bodies in wheelbarrows. Annie's musings stalled for a moment as Tim Morgan's face came to her mind, but she dismissed it. He was a bit part in the Longs' drama, nothing more.

If Kate hadn't behaved so badly, Annie would probably have contacted someone, maybe Scott, to have a quiet word. But the reality was that Kate had allowed her dislike for Annie to get in the way of a constructive exchange. She had not given Pat enough information for her to draw any useful conclusion. Instinct told Annie it was Ron Long they were looking for, but it was all supposition, and she decided she would keep her options open and say nothing.

CHAPTER FOURTEEN

As Annie ran lightly up the stairs to the office, she could hear Pat moving about. She paused. Was it Pat? Yes, the telltale huffing and puffing was audible over the creaking of the floorboards under the heavy footfalls. As the outer door swung shut with a bang, she had a sudden sense of a conversation cut off above her. Pat must have been on the phone.

But when Annie entered, Pat was at the far side of the office nowhere near the phone. Her boss nodded an acknowledgement and said, 'What's new?'

Annie explained about her meeting with Charlotte and her plan to contact Susan Gow. 'I want to see how much background I can get on her before I ring.'

Pat glanced at her watch. 'We've nearly an hour before lunch. Let's see what we can dig out. Did you get that, Babs?'

Annie looked across in surprise as Barbara came out from the back office. Was it her imagination, or had Barbara been around a lot more lately. It couldn't be pressure of work that was the cause. She saw the briefest of glances flash between the sisters.

'Yes,' said Barbara. 'Susan Gow, May's daughter. That case for Vince.' She rubbed her hands together. 'Where to start?'

Annie felt a stab of resentment. Case for Vince! She watched as the sisters wedged themselves at one side of the desk. It surprised her that Barbara had even agreed to help out.

Without Barbara, she and Pat could talk each other through what they were doing and what they found. But with Barbara in the game, it was best just to keep quiet and work alone or it would become a competition, where Barbara argued against any suggestion Annie made and they ended up working against each other.

She started with the quick basic searches that could cut out hours of work when they struck gold, but although Google turned up a couple of thousand entries for Susan Gow, the list shrank to nothing when she added geographic information. She tried Susan and May together with no success. It was no surprise that May did not turn up on any social networking sites, and a disappointment that Susan too seemed to have no web presence.

One of Annie's tenuous leads seemed to link with May Gow's family in the late 1940s. She couldn't be sure, but followed the electronic tracks across the decades. Could May have married and moved abroad? That could explain why there was no trace of Susan in the area. The gentle clatter of keyboards overlay the background sounds of the city. Occasionally, one or other of the sisters threw out a question.

'What was May Gow's maiden name?'

'Don't know.'

'Did she marry in Hull?'

'Don't know, but I'm wondering if she married and moved abroad.'

'Is Susan Gow married?'

'She was down as Gow on that form, so maybe not, but I don't know.'

Then, after quarter of an hour, it was Pat who murmured, 'Ah ha! Got her.'

Both Annie and Barbara stopped what they were doing and looked at Pat, who carried on pecking at her keyboard and peering at the screen for some moments before raising her glance to meet theirs. 'That's interesting,' she said. 'Gow was May's maiden name.'

'May? The mother?'

'Yup.'

'Why is that interesting...?' Barbara began.

Pat shot her a glance. 'Think about it, Babs. Annie, how old's Susan?'

'I can't be exact, but she must be in her fifties minimum. So she'd have been born in the early 1960s.'

'Oh right, child out of wedlock. Big deal back then.'

Using the link Pat had found, Annie followed a different route to pick up another trail.

'May went to Spain by the looks of it.' She studied the information on the screen in front of her. 'She might have married abroad but I can't find anything. She came back to live in Hull when she retired.'

'Retired from what?'

'I don't know. And I don't know if Susan came back with her. She might still live over there.'

'Have you enough to have a go at her?' Barbara asked.

Annie nodded. It was precious little for a cold call, but there was no time for a full search. And it had been a long time since the three of them had worked together without tangible friction.

When the sisters left for lunch, she picked up the phone. It was answered on the third ring.

'Hello. I'm not sure I have the correct number, but I'm trying to trace Susan Gow.'

'Yes, I'm Susan Gow.'

The voice was precise and clipped, with no shade of curiosity underlying it. Annie imagined Susan Gow as a tallish, angular woman, standing or sitting very upright.

'My name's Annie Raymond. I'm a private investigator based in Hull.' Reacting to Susan Gow's tone, Annie stripped all emotional cover from her words.

She left out any mention of Michael Walker, Joshua Yates and the real detail of the case. If Susan lived in Spain, she was unlikely even to have heard of it. She implied that her work involved heir hunting and was only peripherally connected with Susan's mother. And without spelling it out, she eased in an implication that she was investigating the care agency. She would drop Michael's name in later as the conversation progressed.

Annie read out May's address and date of birth and asked if Susan could confirm these as correct. Using the information she, Pat and Barbara had found, she followed up with a series of ostensibly routine questions aimed at adding credibility to the legitimacy of her enquiry.

Once satisfied that Susan was comfortable with her as someone with a right to ask questions, she moved on to May's legacy. 'I understand that some of your mother's effects went outside the family.'

'Yes, two of the neighbours had been good to her over the years. Helped out in times of crisis. I offered them the better pieces of mother's furniture. Frankly, there was nothing of real value.'

'Had she left anything to them in her will?'

'No. The will was very simple. All she had came to me. There was very little. It barely covered the costs of my trips to sort it all out, but that was as I expected. Mother and I were frank with each other over the years. Spend what you have while you're here. That was her motto and mine too. Her only asset was her house and the care package took that. I'm only thankful the equity lasted out.'

'Did she have contact with a family called Walker? Specifically, a Michael Walker?'

'Not that I know of.'

'Or a Joshua Yates?'

'No, the name isn't familiar.'

Annie wished she and Susan were face to face so she could be sure, but she heard no hesitation, no wariness, nothing to suggest Susan was not being straight with her. She thought of Press comments that had associated Yates with some kind of oddball spiritual sect.

'Was your mother a member of any religious group?'

Susan Gow barked out a short laugh. 'Not Mother. She was a committed atheist. Always had been, though she was brought up in a strict chapel-going family.'

'I understand that something of hers went to one of her carers.'

'Oh, that? Yes, you're right. Mother had been insistent about who should have it.'

'What was it, exactly?'

'An old box. Mother had had it all her life. It wasn't a valuable antique or anything like that. Of course, I wouldn't have let anything like that go without making full enquiries.'

'But this wasn't mentioned in her will?'

'No, the will had been drawn up years ago. But Mother made clear who she wanted the box to go to. To be frank, I forgot all about it until the woman got in touch.'

'That would be Mrs Lambit?'

'Not a pleasant woman. I had to tell her I assumed the box had been thrown out.'

'So she never actually got it.'

'Oh, she did. It turned up soon afterwards. I had a man in to clear the house and he found it tucked away under the stairs, hidden almost. But that wasn't unusual. That box was always hidden away wherever we lived. Mother's locked box.' Susan gave a short laugh, as though recalling the behaviour of a wayward child.

'What was in it?'

'It was empty. Mother used to keep papers in there years ago, but there was nothing there when we found it.'

'Are you sure? I mean could the man who found it have taken anything out?'

'No, I was there when he pulled it out. He handed it to me and I got it open. The key was long gone but the hasp had rusted shut. I had to take a screwdriver to it.'

'What had she kept in there? Years ago, I mean.'

'I don't know. I was never allowed in it.'

This was heading down another cul-de-sac, and Annie was running out of things to ask. 'About Donna Lambit,' she said, 'wasn't it out of order for her to have something from one of her clients? They have strict codes of practice, surely?'

'Yes, I was frank with the agency about her. I didn't like her tone when she contacted me. Quite inappropriate.'

'But you allowed her to have it?'

'Oh yes. Mother had been clear about it. I wouldn't have gone against her wishes without good reason. And it was only an old box.'

'Mrs Lambit must have wanted it badly to contact you directly. She could have lost her job.'

'Yes, I understand she did get into trouble over it. She contacted me again later, a very emotional phone call. I couldn't make any sense out of it. I told her not to ring again or it would be an official complaint. I believe there was a warning issued, but I was told she had been an exemplary worker to that point, with a good record. I expect she would have been for the high jump though, had the box been for her personally.'

'I'm sorry?' Surprise snapped Annie's eyes wide open. 'How do you mean, for her personally? Wasn't it for her?'

'No, no. It wasn't for Mrs Lambit: it was for her daughter, Charlotte. Mother was most insistent about that.'

CHAPTER FIFTEEN

Pat's car was in the street outside. Annie plucked the spare key from the drawer, clicking out a text to Pat as she headed out. *Taken your car. Won't be long.* Then she turned her phone off so Pat couldn't say no.

Minutes later she was back on Charlotte's doorstep.

'You again?' said Charlotte. 'You can't keep away.'

'Can I come in?' Was it her imagination or was the flinty core within Charlotte suddenly visible these last couple of visits. Certainly, there was a hard glint in her eye. 'Something's cropped up.'

Charlotte held the door open.

As she walked through to the kitchen, something made Annie ask, 'Have you spoken to Nicole?'

'Yeah. She's livid.'

'Where is she? Do you think she'll talk to me yet?'

'Give her a day or two to simmer down. She'll come round. I told her I didn't think you were after doing a cover-up job for Brittany Booth. I'll be bloody livid with you if I find out you are.'

Annie waved this aside. 'Of course I'm not. It's just unfortunate the way it panned out.'

'Do you see much of Booth? Nicole wanted to know.'

'No, I only met her once and I've spoken to her a couple of times on the phone. I haven't needed to see her. She's just a patsy in all this. Yates might have something useful to say, but as he wouldn't tell the court, he's not likely to tell me. And anyway, he refused to see me. My best chance at the moment is to get to the bottom of what your mother did six years ago.'

'Oh right,' said Charlotte, and there was no mistaking the steel underlying her tone. 'So you are working for both sides? You personally, I mean. But don't worry, I won't make a fuss about it.'

Annie could have kicked herself. She'd been unforgivably careless. The only consolation was that she was pretty sure Charlotte's motive was a simple financial one. She was prepared to play along. 'Well, it'll work out well for you and Nicole. You get your result at a bargain price.'

Charlotte gave her a smile that said I'm glad we understand each other, and went on, 'So what's this thing you want to ask me about?'

No offer of a drink this time, Annie noted. 'The old woman your mother worked for, May Gow. How well did you know her?'

'Me?' Charlotte looked surprised. 'I never met her.'

'Then you wouldn't expect her to leave you anything when she died.'

'Of course not. Why would she?'

'That's what I'm trying to find out. According to her daughter, she wanted you to have an old box of hers.'

Charlotte's mouth hung slightly open. 'What? What old box? I don't know what you're talking about.'

Annie watched closely. If it weren't genuine surprise, it was a good act.

'You never had anything from May Gow?'

'Never. I told you, I never even met her. Why would she leave anything to me?'

Why indeed? Annie looked at Charlotte. There was a hint of worry and confusion in her face now.

'I don't know,' Annie said. 'But I intend to find out.'

Annie drove away from Charlotte's house. If Charlotte was on the level, it was Donna she needed to see. There had been some prickliness, the edges of a personal agenda showing through, but Annie judged that the May Gow business had come out of left field for Charlotte.

But Donna must have known. Annie glanced at the time as she drove across town. With luck, she would catch Donna in.

The street with its neat houses looked subtly different at this time of day. More people milled about, cars sat out on driveways and on the street, not hidden away in their garages. Donna's house looked the same. Neat, surgically scrubbed, turning a blank face to the road.

There was no surprise on Donna's face when she opened the door and saw Annie on her step. Annie wondered if Charlotte had been in touch, and thought probably not. Charlotte played her cards close. She wondered if Nicole knew how close. The more she saw of them, the less confidence she had in the two so-called friends as a business team.

Donna radiated unease as she greeted Annie with, 'What have you found out?'

Annie let her gaze rest on Donna until the woman's eyes rose to meet it. The first time she'd called, Donna had been dressed up to the nines and had mistaken Annie for someone else. This time, the woman was still in her work clothes, an unbuttoned overall hanging open to show a shabby and slightly stained suit.

'Shall we go inside?' Annie said.

They went into the neat sitting room, where Annie sat on a hard-backed chair in the window with the light behind her, and barely let Donna follow her in before she spoke.

'Tell me about May Gow's locked box.'

Donna's hand shot to her mouth and she sank into a chair. 'Oh my God, how did you find out?'

'I've spoken to her daughter, Susan.'

'Yes... well... what would she know about—?'

Annie saw Donna starting to frame a clumsy lie and cut across her. 'Susan Gow told me she'd given you the box.'

'OK, she did,' Donna muttered. 'What of it? It was only a lousy old box.'

'And Susan Gow also told me that her mother had left it to Charlotte, not to you.'

'Stupid cow!'

Annie watched Donna squirm, saw her wring her hands, shift in her seat. She was close to breaking, but Annie wanted everything she had to give, not just hysteria, and not grudging half-truths.

'I'm not here to judge,' she said. She felt no sympathy for Donna, but allowed her tone to soften. 'And I'm not trying to find out things about you that I can tell the world. I just need to get at the truth so I can find out what happened and why.'

'Yes, she gave it me,' Donna said, without looking up. 'God knows why the old cow left it to Charlotte. What was she trying to do? It should have been for me.'

Annie watched closely, taking in the compulsive twitch of Donna's finger and thumb rubbing at the moquette of the chair arm.

'But why?' she asked. 'Why would she leave it to you?'

'She told me she would.'

'Do you still have it?'

After a pause, Donna nodded.

'Can I see it?'

Giving her the briefest of glances, Donna pulled herself to her feet and left the room. Annie heard her footsteps go up the stairs and into the room above. She heard the click of a cupboard door.

Annie felt some surprise. She hadn't expected Donna to admit to having received anything from Susan, let alone produce it, and wasn't confident she would until she reappeared in the doorway cradling a wooden box in her hands. Annie reached out for it as Donna passed it across.

The box was plain, but sturdy, and rested comfortably on Annie's lap. She looked it over. It was rectangular, half as high as it was wide and would have held A5 paper comfortably, but not A4. The remains of a rusty hasp were set into the lid and front panel. The wood had a bumpy feel. The box had been made from scraps of rough timber and must have pushed many splinters under May Gow's skin before she'd polished the sharp edges to smooth rounded bumps over the years. There was no doubting its age, nor that it held no intrinsic value. She wondered though at Susan Gow not feeling any sentimental attachment to a box that her mother had had all her life. She turned it upside down and stroked the bottom panel. It was the same smooth but uneven surface as the rest.

'Don't bother looking for hidden compartments.' Donna's voice came from across the room. 'Believe me, if there'd been anything to find, I'd have found it.'

Annie heard the resentment in Donna's tone and asked, 'Do you think Susan took something out of it?'

'Of course she did. She'll have just emptied it all on to the fire, or into the bin.'

'So you don't think she knew what it was?'

'No, she'll have no idea what she did.'

'And what exactly was it that was in there?'

'The proof,' Donna said, looking up at Annie in surprise. 'I thought you'd worked it out. May said the proof was in there. I mean, it was. I didn't just take her word. I saw it with my own eyes. A whole stack of papers.'

'Oh my God!' Annie slapped her hand to her head. 'All that stuff about not knowing Yates. That was garbage, wasn't it? You're the one Yates was calling for. You're the missing witness.'

CHAPTER SIXTEEN

'I never said I didn't know him.' Donna spoke defensively.

'No, you didn't, not in so many words. And I was fool enough not to ask. But you do know him. You're his witness. The woman who's supposed to come forward to vindicate him.' Annie spoke authoritatively, consolidating her position. Donna could simply order her out of the house, but she was upset enough not to realize it.

Donna lowered her head so Annie couldn't see her face.

'You are, aren't you?' Annie kept up the pressure, determined to hear the woman admit it. 'You're Yates's witness.'

'Yes.' It was a whisper.

'But what does it mean? The witness was supposed to be the victim. Did Walker assault you?'

'Of course not,' Donna snapped, then burst out, 'Yates is a fool, a madman. I never told him to go out and do murder.'

'Why did he believe you were one of Walker's victims?'

'He didn't. That was all made up by the Press. Joshua Yates never said that.'

Annie thought back to the reports and documents she'd read. It was true, she couldn't pinpoint a specific quote from Yates that identified the unnamed witness as one of Walker's supposed victims.

'His girlfriend believes it. She thinks the mystery witness was someone Walker abused.'

'She's a fool, too. Not that I've ever met her. I haven't. That's the truth. I don't believe she's his girlfriend. She's just a hanger-on, a follower.'

'A follower?'

'Yates is... was some sort of lay preacher. One of those pretend religious groups that go round thinking they're it, trying to pull people in. They did gardens for free for old people who couldn't manage any more. That's what he told people, anyway. I think he picked men off the streets, down and outs, bribed them with the promise of work and stuff. He talked to me about organizing people to go and cut lawns for some of my clients.'

'Shouldn't he have gone direct to the agency for that?'

'He didn't want to be bothered with all the red tape.'

Annie felt her eyebrows rise, but let the comment pass. Donna saw no anomaly in a dodgy character like Yates given access to vulnerable people without any safeguards.

Yates's background was one side of this case that Annie had yet to research beyond what she'd read in the Press reports. There hadn't been the time to chase into every corner and she'd had more pressing leads to follow. Had she made a mistake? Should she have spent more time on him? Brittany Booth was due to meet her on Friday. She would decide after that.

'How big was this movement? How many followers did he have?'

Donna laughed. 'None now, I should think. It was never serious. He picked on wasters and persuaded them to try something new. But one go with a lawnmower was enough to drive most of them away. I never saw one of his lot come back to the same house twice, that's if they came at all. And Joshua did nothing himself, though he talked a good day's work.'

'How did you come to talk to him about Michael Walker?'

'One time he brought a guy round and set him on clipping a hedge. I made him a drink of tea. We just got talking.'

'This was at May Gow's house?'

'No, one of my regular clients.'

'It's a big step from inviting a stranger in for tea to telling him your daughter's partner is a paedophile.'

Donna tossed her head in a defensive gesture. 'He could see I had something on my mind. Who else was I to talk to? The police had been neither use nor ornament.'

'What did you tell him?'

'I told him there was proof in the locked box, that I'd seen it. The trouble was I couldn't find it. May wouldn't say where it was. She was a bit senile by then. But she knew I was the only person prepared to do anything about it. She said she'd leave it to me when she died.'

'When did she tell you she'd leave it to you?'

Donna looked uncomfortable. 'I overheard her telling someone else.'

Annie questioned Donna about what exactly she'd overheard, but she either couldn't or wouldn't say. In any case, it matched what Susan had told her. She must tie down the times, so quizzed Donna on when she'd spoken to Yates, when she'd seen May's so-called evidence.

'It was not so-called! It was for real. It was everything he said in court and more.'

'What was it, though?'

'Documents showing what Michael Walker had done.'

'What sort of documents?'

'What does it matter? Just documents.'

'It matters. What were they? Where had they come from? Who'd written them?'

'I don't know. I can't remember. I heard what was in them. That's all I could think about at the time. I wanted to go and snatch those papers out of her hand, believe me. But they'd have just made a fuss. I held back. See, I knew where she kept them and I was going to get them out later and have a proper look for myself.'

'So when did this happen? When did you find out about them?'

With Donna half defensive, half upset, it was a while before Annie had the timeline clear. Six years ago, Donna claimed to have seen evidence of Michael Walker's guilt. She'd taken her suspicions to the police. They'd looked into it and found nothing. Then some eighteen months ago, she had met and confided in Joshua Yates who had set his pseudo-religious zeal on to getting justice for the supposed crime. Soon after May Gow's death, he had stabbed Michael Walker.

'Why didn't you tell the police about the evidence in the box six years ago? They could have found it if it was there to find.'

'Oh yeah, and how long would I have kept my job if I'd done something like that? I nearly lost it through that cow as it is.'

'You never liked Michael Walker, did you?'

'No, I didn't. And I was proved right.'

'What you learnt from May Gow's papers, was it new or did it confirm what you already suspected?'

'I hadn't a clue what he'd done... what he was. If I had, do you think I'd have let Charlotte go off with him? I knew I didn't like him. I told Charlotte time and again not to trust him, but she wouldn't listen.'

'How soon did you get the box after May Gow died?'

'I didn't think I'd ever see it again, frankly. I contacted her daughter, but she was very stand-offish. Then out of the blue I had this call and she turned up with it.'

'What did she say?'

'Nothing much. Snooty cow. Just that it had been found. She wanted to honour her mother's wishes and she handed it over.'

'How did May Gow know Michael Walker?'

Donna shrugged. 'I've no idea.'

'Why didn't she go to the authorities herself?'

'It's that old-fashioned thing, letting sleeping dogs lie. Only Michael Walker wasn't a sleeping dog. He was wide awake and my daughter was in danger.'

'So you thought you had the evidence when Susan handed over the box.'

Donna, who had become quite animated, now dropped her head as she spoke. 'Yes.' Her voice was almost too low to be heard.

Annie thought back to Susan Gow telling her about the hasp being rusted shut; how she'd forced it open with a screwdriver. She looked at the box in her lap, flipped the old hasp back and forth. It was a tight fit, even now. Suppose Susan Gow had pushed it closed again and it had stuck. Annie lifted the box, weighing it in her hand. Could she tell, simply from the feel, whether there was anything inside? The wood made it heavy.

'You didn't know it was empty, did you?'

Donna leant further forward, her hair falling to obscure her face as she shook her head.

'What happened? Did you tell Yates you had the proof before you'd managed to open it? What did you do when you found it was empty? Did you try to tell him?'

'He's a madman.' Donna's voice thickened and Annie saw a tear splash down on to her hand. 'Susan Gow must have burnt the papers. I tried to get back on to her to find out. See, she stayed in May's house while she was seeing to everything, but she'd left. I took copies of May's records from the agency so I could get back in touch, but she wouldn't speak to me. And then the next I know...' She stopped on a sob and gulped in a breath. 'Then my daughter went home and found Michael's body. Can you imagine what it did to her, finding someone like that? And then Joshua's calling for me to come forward with proof and I have none.'

Annie sat in silence for a minute, giving Donna space to compose herself. Then she said, 'Tell me about the time you saw this proof?'

'I was there when May got it out to show to a friend. It was a few days after her eightieth birthday. If I'd just known. I'd shifted that box I don't know how many times, going in the cupboard for her medicines, but after that, when I looked for it, it was gone.'

'Who was it she showed it to?'

Donna shook her head. 'Some old cow. I don't know. I wasn't her regular carer. I didn't know her friends. I tell you when I got that call, when she told me she'd found May's box and she was bringing it, I thought, that's it. I've got him now. I'll have my Charlotte back off him.'

Annie heard grim satisfaction as the woman in front of her talked of the events that had led to a brutal murder, and thought that in her own way, Donna was as guilty as Yates.

Chapter Seventeen

Early evening found Annie back in the upstairs office, the box on the desk in front of her. There was a forlorn quality to it. It had been hugely important to an old woman who had kept it all her life. *Mother's locked box.* What had been in it? Why on earth would she leave it to Charlotte, a woman she'd never met? If she wanted someone to act on the evidence held there, why not her own daughter? Susan Gow struck her as the sort not to quail if action were needed.

The wood was thick with grime, the hasp covered in rust. When she pushed it home, it jammed shut and was hard to wrench open. Annie's hands were grey and sticky from handling it. Again, she ran her fingers over the surface and felt the years of effort smoothing such rough hewn timber; hours of polishing, inside and out. It could only have been May Gow.

On impulse, she went to the tiny kitchen they shared with the downstairs office and raked through the cupboards, returning with a bowl of steaming hot water, a cloth and scourer and a bottle of abrasive floor cleaner. She laid them out on the desk and set to work. The cream cleaner took the grime from the wood in a gloopy grey mass that turned the water black. She worked carefully, not quite sure why she was doing it. It seemed an inappropriate tribute to the late May Gow, an atheist whose motto was to spend what you have while you're here.

A locked box kept for years, lovingly cared for. It felt wrong just to leave it to rot. She held out no hope of finding the hidden compartments Donna had searched for, indeed she began to nurse a worry that her cleaning efforts would dissolve the timber, and she rubbed the surfaces more gently.

Rubbing at the wood with the damp cloth infused with white paste was soothing work. Annie relaxed into a rhythm and allowed her thoughts to roam over the case. Joshua Yates... Donna Lambit... the bloody murder of Michael Walker. Charlotte with her air of calm despite her being the one who had walked in to find her lover's body after Yates's frenzied attack. Nicole Perks, Jennifer's friend, more edgy than Charlotte, more openly driven to lift the slur from Michael.

The lid was done. Annie looked at the portion of the hasp she had cleaned. It shone out, a triumphant vindication of her efforts, and a sign the floor cleaner she'd used was a good metal polish. It struck her then that metal polish might not be ideal for cleaning old timber, but May Gow had laboured over this box for decades, and Annie felt obliged to finish the job she'd started.

The phone rang. She glanced at the time, saw she could legitimately claim to be gone, and let it ring through to voice mail. After a minute, the beep-beep of a new message began to sound. Annie reached across, set it to speaker-phone and pressed the button to retrieve the messages.

As she heard Charlotte's voice, she paused.

'Charlotte Liversedge here. Nicole's gone out to the Nag's Head. I said I might go too, but it's a trek and I probably won't. She's still pissed off with you but she's ready to listen if you want to go and find her.'

Annie's cloth resumed its movement, rubbing back and forth across the surface of the wood as she digested this message. The Nag's Head? A trek for Charlotte? She must mean the pub out in Preston village. Nothing to lose by giving it a go. Yes, she might head out there.

She looked down at the box, knowing now she wasn't going to clean it all, it would take too long, and thinking that if the wood could express an opinion, it would probably be relieved. But for the moment, she continued with her polishing, concentrating on an awkward area inside the box, below the hinge. As she worked, she saw her efforts uncover a tiny circle carved into the wood.

Lethargy gone, Annie pulled the desk lamp across and looked closely. The real value of this box, the reason it had been treasured for decades, had been known only to May Gow, and she was gone forever. Yet maybe the box had held on to a tiny secret of its own, something to reveal from across the decades.

She worked gently on the wood. The mark that looked at first like a tiny circle, became a letter e. Now she was looking for it, she could see an indistinct inscription across the inner surface close to the hinge. Next to the e, she uncovered an h, then a t. She had pulled the word backwards from years of grime. T-h-e. She looked at the neat, childish shapes of the letters and then set to work on the rest of it.

Someone, a long time ago, had etched something into the surface of the wood. Slowly she uncovered it until the inscription was clear. It was written in the neat, round hand of a child. It meant nothing to her. It probably meant nothing to anyone still living.

She reached out with her finger and traced along the words. *The Jawbone Gang.*

Chapter Eighteen

Annie climbed the stairs to her flat, the box in her arms. Two of her neighbours came down as she went up. They exchanged hellos and glanced at what she carried, probably wondering what on earth she had in the battered wooden box.

Once inside, she stood it on the table, its lid propped open so she could see the words carved into its inner surface, then she pulled a chair in front of it and sat down.

'Who wrote that?' She felt foolish speaking the words aloud, but she wanted all the information this box had to give, and could think of no better way than to interrogate it. And at least there was no one to hear.

The answer to her question, she had to assume, was May Gow.

'When did she do it?'

The letters were neat but childish in form. How old would May have been? Weren't children taught to write in a neat uniform script when May was at school? Somewhere between eight and twelve, Annie guessed. That would mean it had been written between 1927 and 1931.

'Why did she write it?'

There was no way to help the box with an answer to that one.

'Does it have any bearing on what she kept in there as an adult?'

Almost certainly not, Annie decided. The box had been a treasured possession from childhood. Once she'd grown up, it would be natural for May to put it to use to keep confidential papers safe.

The question she had to answer remained the same as when she'd talked to Donna. What had May kept in there?

She walked through to the shower room, pulling off her top and scrunching it into a ball to lob across towards the heap of clothes waiting for the launderette.

Who had the answer? May, Donna and who else? Maybe Susan, maybe not.

As she washed and changed, she reran the story Donna had given her. Six years ago, so she claimed, she'd seen the contents of the box, but had taken no note of what sort of papers they were. Was that credible? Had she been so shocked at what they revealed about Michael Walker that she hadn't taken anything else in? Of course, she said she'd planned to look later, to check it out at her leisure, but the box had vanished.

As Annie set off in her car to look for Nicole, she imagined Donna in May's house and reran the words Donna had told her.

May wouldn't say where it was. She might not have known. She was a bit senile by then.

The words, and the tone in which Donna said them, painted a disturbing picture. Donna alone in the house with May. Donna with the power in the relationship. Maybe May's encroaching senility was the only weapon she had against her carer.

Could she trust Donna's account? The story of the locked box was a bizarre one to have made up.

Annie headed east along Holderness Road, its bumpy surface a legacy of the floods that had devastated the city in 2007, and a reminder of cases that had bubbled up out of the foul water as it receded back to the drains and sewers. She turned off at the village of Bilton and drove past the out-of-town supermarket, still busy with shoppers. Bilton merged into Wyton, the route carrying her beyond the streetlights and on to the dark country road. The last vestiges of daylight leached away into the landscape, an overcast sky obscured the moon, even the glow from the Saltend chemical works, usually a sparkly landmark from across the fields, was dimmed.

She slowed as the lights marking the outskirts of Preston village appeared, and drove towards the Nag's Head pub. It sat on a corner site, where the road from Sproatley met the main road through the village. She drove slowly past the pub. It was a chilly night and most people were inside, but half-a-dozen or so sat round the tables outside, smoke from their cigarettes curling up into the night.

Sitting alone, well-wrapped in a thick coat, was Nicole, staring into the middle distance as she raised her hand to her mouth to draw on her cigarette, making the end glow red.

Annie drove to the back entrance where Nicole would not see her arrive and made her way through the pub where she picked up a glass of lemonade and ran her eye down the bar snacks menu before going outside.

Nicole jumped when Annie walked up and sat down at her table. Then her face hardened.

'What do you want?'

'To talk. To reassure you we're not working for the other side against you. To find a way forward.'

'Huh.' Nicole spat out the syllable and stared stonily into the distance.

'I've spoken to Charlotte. She understands that—'

'Yes,' Nicole snapped, speaking over her. 'Obviously you've spoken to Charlotte. How long did it take you to badger her into telling you where I'd be?'

'I didn't mean that. She left me a message telling me where you'd be. She wants us back working together.'

Nicole tossed her head as though irritated. 'What have you told the Booth woman about us? I suppose you've had a good laugh with her.'

'Of course not. I haven't spoken to her about you. The same as I didn't talk to you about her. I'm not allowed to. Our clients are entitled to confidentiality. We have a code.'

'Yeah, and this code lets you work for both sides, I suppose.'

'It's unusual certainly, but there's nothing says we can't.'

'PC Ronsen said you could lose your licence.'

'She's wrong, of course,' Annie said, wishing she had as much confidence as her words implied. 'And it's DC. She's precious about that.'

Nicole sniffed. 'Not that I care. All I wanted was a good job doing.'

'And that's what you'll get if you let me do it. You'll get nothing from the police, you know that. It isn't something they'd touch. You trust Jennifer, don't you? She wouldn't have recommended me if she didn't have confidence.'

'I bet she didn't know you were working for that cow.'

'We weren't when we took your case on.' Annie wasn't sure that was strictly true, but certainly she hadn't known about it when she'd first met Nicole.

'Weren't you? PC Ronsen said...' Doubt clouded Nicole's face. 'Well then, shouldn't you have turned Brittany Booth down when she asked you?'

'The thing is, she didn't ask me. She approached another side of the firm and they took her on.'

'What do you mean, another side of the firm? There's only two of you.'

'Three,' Annie corrected, though noting silently they would be all the better for just being two. 'Both contracts were signed before any of us realized. And after all, it works in your favour. You're the ones short of money. We're not going to duplicate work. Anything we find out for her is a result for you.'

'That's what you meant when you said that doors would close once that murdering git's sentenced. She'll stop paying you.'

Annie opened her hands in a gesture of admission.

'But when you find the proof that Michael's innocent, she won't want to pay you, anyway.'

'There are lots of things I don't want to pay for. It doesn't mean I don't have to. And anyway...' Annie thought back to the fracas in the office. She didn't remember any talk about licences. 'When did Kate Ronsen say all that about licences and when we took the cases on?'

'I bumped into her that evening.'

'Oh, right.' Annie kept her voice even. So Kate had engineered a second meeting to twist the knife she'd planted in Annie's back. Just how obsessed was this woman? Stumbling into bad relations with the local police was one of the worst things she could do, and Scott would have to take Kate's side if he really wanted to marry the woman. The reasons kept stacking up to cut her ties and go, but she would leave the area with her integrity intact. Kate wouldn't rob her of that.

'What made Jennifer recommend me? Did you ask her for a PI?'

Nicole shook her head. 'I wanted her to get something official done about Brittany Booth. I didn't know there'd really been a complaint. But Jennifer said she couldn't do anything. The cow hadn't broken any law. In the end she told me it would have to be a private investigator or nothing.'

'Have you known her long?'

'Yeah, Jennifer and I go way back.'

Annie suspected that Jennifer's recommendation had come when her own discreet enquiries had uncovered Donna's role. There was a streak of garrulousness in Nicole that spelt danger in the wrong hands. Jennifer would have foreseen Nicole's loose tongue betraying her own unauthorized digging. Far better to let Annie do the deed.

'I could easily persuade Charlotte we should go elsewhere. You're not the only firm in the area, you know.'

Annie nodded her acknowledgement, but wondered if anyone else would take Nicole on.

'PC Ronsen recommended someone.'

'Yeah? Who's that?'

'A guy called Vincent Sleeman.'

Annie struggled to feign indifference as she felt a flush of anger creep up her neck. In the half light of evening, she could only hope Nicole wouldn't notice. Vince Sleeman had enough of a hold over the firm already, without handing him Nicole who would go to him with a burning sense of injustice and a tale of unethical behaviour. And it would be the worse for Nicole if Vince agreed to take her on. He wouldn't get out of bed for the sort of money she and Charlotte had to offer. He would clean them out of every cent they'd earmarked for their business and probably a bit more besides. But there was no way to warn Nicole that wouldn't sound like sour grapes.

'It's your decision, but just check with Jennifer before you commit to anything. She knows the area. Kate Ronsen hasn't been here five minutes.'

CHAPTER NINETEEN

Annie sat on into the darkening evening after Nicole had drained her glass and left. A gust of wind plucked an empty crisp packet from a small boy's hands as he went to push it into the bin. He chased after it, laughing, trying to stamp his foot on it as it eddied round the tables.

There was unfinished business within reach and this was too good an opportunity to miss. A clump of trees across the main road bowed their branches towards her. Annie watched and made calculations. The wind blew off the estuary and with enough force that the rustling of the leaves was audible here in the shelter of the pub garden. Closer to the water, it would be louder.

She ran the idea through her head. A stiff breeze to orchestrate the flapping canvas of the marquee, and in the right direction to keep her downwind of the dogs as long they weren't loose. It was the perfect opportunity to close the Longs' case once and for all.

The shadows lengthened around her as she dawdled over her lemonade. They served a nice looking lasagne here. That and a cup of coffee would insulate her against the night air. After ordering at the bar, she wandered out to the car to check she had everything she needed.

Her long-sleeved black T-shirt was scrunched in a corner of the boot. It badly needed a wash, but she'd learnt on a long-ago surveillance-and-tracking course that dogs were less likely to raise the alarm at the scent of unwashed bodies than clean ones. Thin dark gloves... balaclava... slim torch that would shine a discreet but sharp pencil beam. Picklocks masquerading as a key fob and the camera on her phone completed the kit. She returned to her table to wait.

Her food came and she ate hungrily. Her plate and glass were cleared away, and she waited as night closed in. Down in the rural wilds by the estuary, there would be a cloying darkness to provide a cloak of invisibility.

She sat and waited until it was time to leave

Annie drove as close as she dared to the Morgans, then killed the car's headlights and inched forward on sidelights only. A couple of hundred metres from her target, she pulled up on to the verge and prepared to make the rest of the journey on foot.

The wind blew in her face, whistling across from the sea, making her scrunch her eyes against the sting of the salt-laden air. She trod carefully, even though the gusts blew hard enough to mask the sound of her footsteps. Reaching the gate, she rested her gloved hand on top of it and rattled it gently. If the dogs had access to the yard, it was best to know now before being inside there with them.

Nothing.

A stout padlocked chain secured the gate. She felt the way the links were looped over and through the metal bars. Not too hard to pick, she judged, but in the darkness, there was a real danger of it noisily clanking free. Chances were that the Morgans had fastened this gate exactly the same way every night for years. It would be hard to ensure the same alignment if she tried to re-do it from the outside when she left, and her plan was to avoid leaving any trace behind her.

She pictured Sheryl Long on her spindly heels contemplating this gate and knew she need have no lingering doubt about whether or not the woman had been in here.

The breeze cut through the undergrowth in a muted roar that underlay the sharper sounds of something banging rhythmically against a wall, and the rapid-fire crack-crack-crack of the canvas from the far side of the yard. Annie rattled the gate again, louder, wanting to be sure before she climbed inside.

The house remained a grey silhouette, but any one of the ink-black shadows could conceal the dogs. The darkness painted strange dancing shapes at the edge of her vision.

She reached out with both hands to get a firm grip on the gate, braced herself and jumped up, rolling sideways over the top and landing as gently as she could on the gravel.

For a minute, she stayed very still.

No lights. No sound other than the wind in the undergrowth and the rhythmic crack of the canvas.

She picked her way across the yard, through the darkness, not risking the torch beam yet. When she gained the tall shed, she eased the latch and pulled. It stood firm against her. Now she must risk the torch and turned her back to the house to shield the pencil-beam as she inspected the door. It was fastened with an old double-lever lock, sturdy and hard-wearing but no trouble to work open with the crudest of picklocks. She flicked off the torch and slipped it back in her pocket.

Within moments, the lock tumblers snapped back. Annie eased the door just wide enough to squeeze inside and pulled it shut behind her. At once, the air stilled, the noise of the wind became muted. She played the torch beam carefully, knowing there might be cracks in the fabric of the barn that would let light glint through.

Praying not to illuminate the shining eyes of a waking dog, she began a structured sweep around the space.

A car.

Large round straw bales piled high.

A forklift truck.

Dirt and detritus in the corners, garden tools, hay forks, over-sized sweeping brushes.

More canvas, but not the white of the wedding canvas, this was blue with sturdy ropes threaded through metal reinforced holes.

She took a picture of the uneven mound, then pulled aside the blue sheet, which crackled as it slid off what looked like a heap of engine parts. She shone the torch down into the tangle of oily metal and photographed it to show what had been hidden.

After moving the canvas back into place, she moved outward scanning every square metre. If Sheryl stuck to her story of having been in here, despite that gate and locked door, Annie would not leave her with any opening to say the search hadn't been thorough enough. She shone the torch along the edges and through the cracks of the great mound of bales as she moved to the back of the shed.

It was here she came across the wheelbarrow, its handles showing from beneath another canvas mound. It surprised her, as apparent confirmation of Sheryl's story, but was in keeping with the motley collection the Morgans kept in here. The pictures would be useful.

'Here's the wheelbarrow. Look, nothing in it.'

What would Sheryl say to that?

Annie held the torch in her mouth to free both hands to lift the stretch of blue canvas, and as the shape became clear, she felt her eyes widen in surprise. She looked at the heaped sacking and imagined Sheryl, nervy and frightened, seeing it as a slumped human form. It was plain this was what she'd mistaken for a body. Annie reconstructed the tale as she lifted the blue cover free enough to be able to take a picture of the whole thing. Sheryl couldn't have been in here. She had seen the Morgans pushing the wheelbarrow into the shed. Her imagination had made up the rest.

Whatever the truth of it, here was the root of the story.

Annie took pictures of the curled sacking from different angles, then held the torch between her teeth as she began to unpick the wrapping. It wasn't the stout material of the canvas sheeting and she had to concentrate not to tear it. She took it slowly so as to be able to rewrap it, determined to leave no trace of her visit.

Reaching under the cloth, she eased the handle of some kind of tool so that she could slide the material free. The torch, between her teeth, wouldn't stay steady and played distracting patterns across the sacking. She stopped to put it in her pocket, and carried on by touch in the darkness.

As it came loose, the small tines of what felt like a miniature leaf-rake dug into her forearm.

She worked the cloth free, keeping careful hold of the thin handle not wanting a metallic clatter of cascading tools on to the floor. With her other hand, she aimed the camera lens.

But instead of a momentary flash searing the darkness, the click of the button beneath her finger exploded the whole barn into a blaze of light.

Shock coursed through her in a prickle of retreating blood.

Blazing, blinding light. How? Where? What had she done?

Her eyes began to focus as the scene hit. Every aspect of it together.

The rush of the breeze from the open doorway... the silhouetted figures...

Tim Morgan, features indistinct in the glare, but outline unmistakable... a shotgun over his arm. The form of a woman beside him, hand grasping a spade or shovel, its blade catching the light.

Instinct immobilized Annie. She saw at once that they too struggled in the light that seared down from industrial-strength ceiling tubes. Tim's silhouetted form showed his free hand shading his eyes as he squinted into the big barn.

They'd heard something... seen something... but they hadn't yet seen her at the back of the barn, partly hidden by the straw bales.

She let her knees soften and bend, lowering herself towards the concrete floor.

As she did so, the barrow and its contents were beside her, inches from her face. Her hand still grasped the thin shaft.

A second shock reignited the fire across on her skin... curled her insides... turned her legs to jelly. She could barely swallow the whimper that rushed to her lips.

The gaping sockets of a skull stared outward, a deep gash displaying its violent end.

Annie's gloved hand held a long grey bone that ended in curled digits digging into the flesh of her forearm. Desperately fighting an urge to yank her hand free, she eased it back silently.

No time to react to the horror of touching it... no time to take in that Sheryl had been here... really been here... had told the truth...

All her attention must be tuned to hear the Morgans' footsteps, to know which way to creep round the space to keep hidden from them.

But the thing at her side was too close to ignore. A snake poised to strike. Her eyes were drawn to where the sacking now hung free and the lights had exposed the secret it had covered.

The skull with its gaping sockets stared away from her but the deep gash was clear. One massive fatal blow.

They bludgeon them...

My God, Sheryl, you were right.

Her gaze snapped back to the high mound of straw bales that hid her from the doorway.

Two images burnt themselves on to her mind's eye.

The glint of light from the blade in Tracey's hand: the gaping wound that had killed the body beside her.

Her mind made the match as she eased herself silently lower and sideways.

No point trying to kid herself the Morgans had come to the barn at this hour for any reason other than to guard the secret they kept here. And for all its disorder and dark corners, there was no way to remain hidden once they accustomed their eyes to the light and came in to investigate.

'Wait here.'

Annie heard Tim Morgan set his wife with her deadly blade to block the barn's only exit. Then came the crunch of his footfalls on the concrete floor as he moved towards the back of the barn.

CHAPTER TWENTY

A thirty-mile stretch of coastline to the east of the once busy ports of Hedon and Hull has see-sawed from solid earth to open sea and back again over the centuries; its last metamorphosis a well-documented reclamation of land a brief 200 years ago, when a small island a mile offshore was embraced into the mainland. Further east and helping to protect this reclaimed salt-marsh, conscious human effort holds tight to the spit of land that is Spurn Point while debates flare and ebb over whether the sea should be allowed to reclaim it, and what it would mean to the industries that rely on the Humber as a navigable passage for shipping; or to the people whose homes stand where the tides used to flow. The clay and silt of Holderness clutches its history in cloying mud, but without the promise of riches to unleash or the resource to explore, it gives up its treasures unpredictably, and often to unwilling recipients.

Annie sat at the stout wooden table in the Morgans' kitchen, her hands wrapped round a steaming cup of tea. She wasn't fond of tea, but Tracey had insisted.

'It'll warm you. You've had a shock.'

It was true; she shivered more than the chill of the night air warranted. But then she'd shocked them too. Her dark, balaclavaed form coming at them like an apparition from next to their guilty secret.

She'd moved so quickly, it had been the Morgans who had stepped back alarmed.

The gun had stayed over Tim Morgan's arm as though he'd forgotten it was there. Annie knew the rules. If you saw the end of the barrel, you gave in, at once and unconditionally. But if you could get in close before the gun was raised, take your opponent by surprise, get the gun out of the picture long enough to get away...

In the fraction of a second it had taken to pull herself out of the horror of the secret laid bare beside her, she had planned the whole move in her head. A rush over the top of the canvas mound covering the old engine. It was solid enough to take her weight. Jump down on him sideways, spinning him round, putting his body between her and Tracey, flinging the gun back into the cobwebby depths if she could wrench it free, tipping him off-balance, and in the same movement, diving past them and out of the door, sprinting for safety.

It was Tracey who stopped her.

'No!' the woman had shrieked. 'It's not what you think!'

And Tim had jumped back, surrendering to her before she was on him, never making a move to raise the gun.

They'd all stopped, a frozen tableau by the door, Annie aware only that she was in the most vulnerable position she could be, yet all that eddied around the barn with the inrush of night air, was fear. Her own and theirs. No menace.

For a moment, they'd stared at Annie as she swung her gaze from one to the other of them.

Then Tim leant towards her, eyes screwed up to make out her features under the woollen mask. 'My God, it's you,' he'd gasped.

They sat in the big kitchen, drinking tea. Sleeping dogs flopped in a variety of wicker baskets, or draped themselves over a moth-eaten settee. Even the small yappy ones had done no more than dart in Annie's direction in a token gesture before returning to their cushions.

Between them, Tim and Tracey told Annie how they'd had to rush to organize the big wedding their daughter had sprung on them. Family connections provided the marquee, and to keep the cost down, they levelled the ground themselves. It was whilst digging into the side of a slope that they'd unearthed the skeleton.

'I thought I'd hit a stone,' Tracey said, with a shudder. 'I was trying to pull it out by hand when I realized what it was.'

Annie nodded. The shock of finding herself handling human remains was fresh in her mind. She'd been right about the wound to the skull. It was recent and inflicted by Tracey's spade.

'Imagine what would have happened if we'd reported it,' Tim said. 'We could see it was old, hundreds of years old. We know we should have called the police out and not moved it. We talked it over. We couldn't delay the wedding and the cost of holding it somewhere else at short notice... we looked into it, but you wouldn't believe how much it would be.'

Annie knew she shouldn't condone what they'd done, but it was hard not to sympathize.

'But why didn't you cover it over again and leave it till afterwards?'

'We thought of that.' They both nodded vigorously, and told her how they'd explained to Tracey's brother-in-law that they would foreshorten the marquee, and leave the slope untouched.

'That made it worse,' Tracey said. 'He wouldn't listen. He said he'd send a couple of guys to dig it out for us. He thought we couldn't manage, said he wouldn't charge us. They were going to come round the next morning.'

'We had no choice then,' Tim put in. 'We went out that night. We dug it all out, the whole way, further than we needed, but we had to be sure there wouldn't be any more of them. We were knackered, weren't we, Trace? We hid it away in that shed.'

And that was the night Ron and Sheryl Long had chosen to watch the farm. Everything Sheryl said she'd seen was true. The Morgans with the wheelbarrow... the body in the shed. She hadn't mentioned the Longs to the Morgans, but said now, 'Have you always kept the gate chained at night and that barn locked?'

'No, never before. We didn't even think to lock it that first night. But then we thought, better safe than sorry.'

So that one night when the secret lay freshly wrapped, there had been no locked gates for Sheryl to negotiate. Annie reflected on the effects of bad timing, bad luck... of not looking after the details.

'We never thought for a moment it was recent,' Tim said. 'You believe us, don't you? If we'd been in any doubt, we'd not have hesitated. No one's touched that land in centuries. It's a wonder it wasn't washed away over the years.'

'Maybe it was,' Annie said. 'Maybe it never started here. With all the shifting currents, who knows? I guess the archaeologists will date it eventually.'

'Will we have to go to the police now?'

Annie looked at Tracey, then at Tim. After she'd heard the story, she'd asked to go back for a proper look. For once, she could have used Barbara, who had studied archaeology, though Annie wasn't sure whether or not that qualified her to put an age to a skeleton. Certainly to her untutored eye it looked ancient.

The only marks that looked recent, other than the gash to the skull, were teeth marks at the top end of one of the arm bones. Annie asked the question and saw Tim look shamefaced.

'We didn't cover it over well enough that first afternoon. We came back in here for a cuppa to get our heads straight while we talked about it, and when we went out again, one of the dogs had got that bit free.'

'We knew then we had to dig it right out,' Tracey added. 'I threatened the dogs within an inch of their lives not to go into the marquee, but can you imagine, in all the fuss of it all, if they'd started digging and pulling bones out. It's not what you want at a wedding.'

For Annie, the penny dropped. 'So that's why they're not loose in the yard. Did they used to run free?'

They both nodded. 'We shut them in the kitchen here that first night, and we don't let them out unless one of us is with them. We don't want them digging out anything else, not until we've the christening done with, anyway.'

'He's a smashing little lad,' Tracey put in. 'And waited to the day after the wedding to be born. Good as gold.'

Annie sipped her tea and looked around the big kitchen. The space felt full with canine snores and snuffles. Dog hairs danced in the air. One lay across the surface of the liquid in her cup. The uncurtained window showed a smudge of dark sky, with a hint of scudding clouds. The yard below was in darkness.

'How did you know I was there?'

'Bel saw you from the window. She woke us.' Tracey pointed to a small, tan pool of fur in a basket. 'She and Sweep sleep upstairs with us. They cause havoc down here. We weren't sure. We couldn't see anything at first, but then there was just a small flash of light from by the barn so we knew we had to go and check.'

Annie nodded. She looked up at the high mantelpiece and recognized a couple of the photographs from the Facebook page.

'When's the christening?' she asked.

They told her. It wasn't long and she couldn't see that any particular good would come of disrupting it.

'Officially, I should advise you to go straight to the police. You know that. But on the other hand, officially, I haven't been here tonight, so I can't give you any advice. However...'

She watched the Morgans hang on her words and hoped this was a conversation Jen would never hear about.

'Get the christening done with and then get that skeleton wrapped and in your car, and take it to the museum in Hull. Tell them when and where you found it. Don't lie about it. You'll be in trouble with the police, but I doubt it'll be more than a severe telling off for not calling them out at once. Just stick like glue to the fact you knew it was hundreds of years old right from the start.'

'Won't we be in more trouble for taking it away from where we found it?'

'You've already done that. If you call anyone out to a skeleton on your property, you'll end up with police and forensic teams, and the whole caboodle cordoned off. They'll probably take the marquee to pieces bit by bit.'

'Oh, we don't want that.' Tracey looked worried and Annie saw concern for family favours already stretched too far.

'No guarantees,' Annie said, as she stood up. 'But if a museum has confirmed it as that old, it leaves a way out for the authorities. They don't want the paraphernalia and hassle of a potential murder hunt. They'll give you a good dressing down, but they'll be secretly relieved you've saved them the bother. Not that you've had any of that from me.'

'Thanks.' Tim smiled. 'I'll turn the yard lights on so you can see your way out.'

As Annie headed towards her car, it was the Longs who were uppermost in her mind. This should settle the case, but somehow it didn't. There was something she'd missed. Her mind couldn't grasp hold and she wouldn't try to force it. She was tired.

And after all, it was Michael Walker who sat on her tightest deadline. The Longs could wait. She would get back to them in her own good time.

Chapter Twenty One

Next morning, Annie strolled towards the office, casting her gaze across to the building opposite, wondering about the woman who'd clocked Barbara's late-night visits. No sign of life there at the moment. Once inside, she went mechanically around the space, turning on the computers, checking the phone for messages. Brittany Booth was due in this afternoon. Annie might dangle the bait of the elusive witness in front of her if she were difficult, but wouldn't give her Donna. That would just cause trouble.

She tapped Susan Gow's number into the phone and idly whilst waiting for an answer, typed *Jawbone Gang* into Google. It gave her an old reference to the whaling industry.

Susan Gow spoke with the same calm voice as before. 'Yes, the Jawbone Gang,' she said with a laugh, when Annie told her what she'd uncovered. 'I'd forgotten all about that. Written on the inside and painted in gold.'

'There's no trace of gold, but the words are scratched into the timber. What did it mean?'

'My grandfather was a member of a jawbone gang. He worked on the whalers going out of Hull. But why Mother wrote it on the box, I've no idea.'

'You'd think she might have wanted you to have it, to keep it in the family.'

'No, no. We were never sentimental that way. It was only an old box. To tell you the truth it almost felt wrong to open it after we found it. It had been mother's locked box for all those years. I wasn't allowed to look in it. One of the few times I saw inside, I was struck by that beautiful lettering. My hand was never as neat as my mother's, though she tried to teach me time and again. I remember her snapping it shut and giving me such a look.'

'What did she keep in there?'

'Bills, I imagine. We went through some hard times. Later on, I don't know. Maybe by then she just kept it locked through habit.'

'You never saw what was inside?'

'No, the few times I saw it open, I always tried to sneak a look at those beautiful golden letters. You didn't see much gold in those days. I'd completely forgotten till you mentioned it, though thinking about it, it was handwritten pages, not printed bills. I suppose you'll have Mrs Lambit sacked?'

Annie's enquiry, as far as Susan Gow was concerned, was to do with the care agency and Donna's role. 'Uh... it's not for me to say. It wouldn't be my decision, that sort of thing.'

'No, of course. I wasn't impressed by what I saw of her. There'll be no tears from me if she loses her job.'

Annie wondered if there were ever tears from Susan Gow for anyone.

Feeling as though clutching at straws, Annie asked about the man who had pulled the box from under the stairs; and if there could have been papers hidden elsewhere.

'No, I went through everything. Mother hadn't many material needs in her last few years. The locked box was the only item in the house that didn't have a use.'

'Any idea when she hid it under the stairs? Her carer mentioned seeing it soon after her eightieth birthday, but not since.'

'Then it wasn't Mother who hid it away. She was beyond getting under the stairs at that stage. She must have asked someone to do it.'

'One of her carers maybe?'

'Maybe, but that sort of thing's supposed to be logged.'

Annie thought of the sheets of handwritten records. There must be hundreds of them for May Gow after all those years of four visits a day. She began to mull over ideas for getting into the care agency's files.

'Mrs Lambit said she saw your mother showing it to one of her friends. Any idea who that might have been?'

'If that's true, I can only think of Eliza Ellis. I found her as a surprise for Mother's eightieth. She was one of mother's oldest friends but they'd lost touch. Eliza was the only one of her old ambulance pals I was able to track down.'

'Ambulance pals?' Annie queried.

'They drove ambulances together in the war. A horrific time in Hull by all accounts. The city was flattened.'

'I suppose you aren't still in contact with Eliza Ellis. I'd like to speak to her.'

'Yes, I have her in my address book. Give me a moment and I'll get it now. She's in a residential home.'

After she put the phone down, Annie pulled the keyboard towards her and typed in the address Susan Gow had given her.

She studied the pictures and read the slightly overblown prose with which the home was described. A couple of relatives of residents had added comments to an online guest book. It didn't look too bad a place. Somewhere May might have been happier to spend her last days than in her own home with Donna Lambit circling.

Annie rang and introduced herself as a friend of a friend of Eliza Ellis. The man who answered the phone was unsuspicious and, by showering him with questions about the area, the best way to find the home and the likelihood of a sudden change in the weather, she managed to end the conversation without giving her name, but with a firm commitment to call in tomorrow.

She wondered who had hidden the box under the stairs and why? Had May handed it over full? And had it been empty by the time it had been stashed? Before she made serious plans to break into the care agency's records, she would see what Eliza had to say.

She picked up the phone and clicked out Jennifer's number. It rang half-a-dozen times then went to answer-phone.

'Hi, Jen. It's me, Annie. Are you free later, or over the weekend? Give me a call.'

And that was that until Jennifer got back to her. Maybe Nicole had already told her about Annie's supposed treachery, but Jen was fair-minded. She would wait to hear Annie's side.

It reminded her she had another call to make. That blasted fancy-dress competition; the letter she'd shoved in a drawer back at the flat. Two or three times a year the invitations landed, and she just ignored them, but this one was different, inviting her to be more than a spectator and carrying a presupposition that she would jump at the chance to judge the competition, as though she was the one in receipt of the favour. She should get in touch and make things clear. Maybe it would be better to bite the bullet and go out there, see the woman face to face, leave her in no doubt that she had no interest in horsey events. She didn't want to take polo lessons no matter how hefty the discounted special offer. She had no intention of joining a healthy sponsored outdoor trek for adult beginners no matter how worthy the cause. And most certainly she did not want to judge a mythical warriors fancy-dress competition.

The click of the latch sounded from downstairs. Annie, who had been listening out for it, grabbed her jacket and bag and dived for the door on to the landing, knowing that Barbara's lumbering gait would allow plenty of time for her to hide at the end of the top corridor.

Curiously, she listened to Barbara's progress. Sure enough, it was silent but for the creak of the stairs.

The door to the office scraped open and Annie heard what sounded like a tut of irritation as Barbara disappeared inside.

'Annie?' She heard Barbara's voice call.

Annie tiptoed to the stairs and crept down. As she reached the bottom, Barbara's voice reached her.

'You know what that girl's done again? Only waltzed off out leaving the office wide open.'

Damn it.

Annie found herself poised, undecided. In her rush to avoid Barbara, she hadn't thought how the unlocked door would look. And Barbara had said 'again', because of course this wasn't the first time she'd played this trick. As she turned to head back upstairs, to make clear she hadn't abandoned the office at all, she heard a phone start to ring, and Barbara's voice say, 'Got to go. Someone on the other line.'

It would be ridiculous to stand about waiting for Barbara to finish her call, just to tell her no, she hadn't left but was about to. Instead, she marched out on to the street and slammed the door behind her. Let Barbara wonder about that.

Chapter Twenty Two

By the time she returned for her appointment with Brittany Booth, Annie had dismissed Barbara from her mind. She harboured a hope that Brittany would not be so prickly this time, but when the buzzer sounded ten minutes early, the woman stalked in, aloof and hostile.

'Have you found my proof?' she barked out, with a toss of her head that folded her hair over her shoulder in a heavy black wave.

'I'm getting there.'

'Getting there? What does that mean? I've paid you to find proof.'

'You paid us to find the truth,' Annie corrected, and saw a rush of fear sweep across Brittany's features.

'What have you found? What lies are you trying to make up?'

'Sit down.' Annie pushed a chair forward. 'Take your coat off. Would you like a coffee?'

'No, I don't want anything. I just want to know what you've found.'

Annie waited until Brittany had slumped into the chair.

'As I said, I'm getting there, but I have no proof yet, either way. I need to ask you some questions.'

'What do you mean, either way? Look, they could sentence Joshua any time.'

Brittany's obvious vulnerability made Annie feel a little more sympathy for her. She must have allowed in the possibility her idol was wrong, but she didn't want to hear anyone say it.

'I need to know more about Joshua's own investigations about the complaint that was made six years ago. I know he won't talk to me, but would he talk to you?'

'I told you, he wants to protect me. He doesn't want me involved.'

'In that case, I need you to look through his papers, or better still bring them to me so I can look through them.'

'I don't have his papers. The police took everything.'

'Maybe they missed something. You still have access to his place, right?'

Brittany's lips pursed. 'No, I don't. Why would I? We respected each other's privacy.'

'You didn't live together then?'

'It was a mutual decision. We had important work to do. It would have meant distractions. Joshua wanted what was best for me... spiritually.'

Annie read the defensive tone. So Yates had spurned Brittany's advances but kept her on a leash made of promises of being his soul mate and better things to come. Without any discernible reason, the idea came to her that Brittany didn't even know where Joshua Yates had lived. Nonetheless, Annie knew she had access to some of Yates's effects.

'Last week, you gave me a copy of a letter that had been sent to the police six years ago. You told me you'd found it in Joshua's things.'

Brittany threw her an outraged glare, but for a moment was lost for words.

You're not as good as you'd like to think you are, thought Annie. I've caught you out, now just admit it and let's make some progress. We're supposed to be on the same side.

'He happened to leave some bags round at my place, that's all. What's wrong with that?'

'Nothing,' said Annie, unable to suppress a heavy sigh. All this defensiveness was wearing. 'But this is important. This could be the key to finding the truth. I really need to see this stuff.'

Annie sat back, feeling pleased despite the frustration of dealing with the prickly woman in front of her. The other strand to her enquiries felt about to peter out with Eliza Ellis, but here was a whole new avenue opening up. For form's sake and because it was important to clarify the details, she asked

Brittany when Yates had left the bags. Sure enough, it fitted the timetable she'd already surmised. These were things Yates had decided to dump on Brittany just before he went to murder Michael Walker; things he hadn't wanted the police to find. This was exactly the paperwork she wanted.

Why hadn't the police been to Brittany's to find this stuff? But then why would they? Yates had a number of hangers-on. His guilt was never going to be hard to prove even if he'd tried to deny the killing, which he hadn't. Brittany never stood out from the crowd until she began her one-woman crusade to get him vindicated.

'I don't know,' said Brittany. 'You've found nothing so far. You're so slow. I trusted Mr Sleeman when he recommended you, but now I'm not so sure. You're not the only people I could go to.'

The words rang alarm bells. Annie had heard them before.

'It's only been a week. We're good, but we're not miracle workers.'

'If you must know, I've been talking to a detective. A real one.'

Annie felt the drop in her insides. She shouldn't be surprised. If Kate had targeted Nicole, why not Brittany, too? 'Who's that?' she asked.

'I don't think I want to tell you, but she had some pretty telling things to say. I came here to see what you'd found and to close the case. As it goes, you've found nothing, so don't think I'm throwing good money after bad. Joshua told me to stop you and I'm going to him tomorrow to tell him I've done just that. He needn't know that I'm going back to Mr Sleeman.'

This speech was made with an air of gloating satisfaction, as though to pay Annie back for catching her out earlier. Annie knew she should fight for the case, for all sorts of reasons, but a part of her rejoiced that this might be the last time she had to deal with the petulance of the ever more unstable Brittany Booth.

Would this be where all strands were snipped off? The dissatisfaction of leaving loose ends would rankle, but there seemed little point fighting to keep alive a case that was dying on its feet.

Then a new angle struck her, the realization hitting hard in a huge rush of dismay. Jennifer!

In her mind's eye, she saw Vince Sleeman taking in Brittany's defection. She thought of how the woman's fanatic adherence to her cause would come out as a rant against Annie and by association, Jennifer. Now that Kate had blabbed, one session with either Nicole or Brittany would give him enough to ferret out the core of it. And then he'd know that Jennifer strait-laced Flanagan, the incorruptible copper, had been digging where she shouldn't, prying into files that weren't her business and passing information on to Annie. In the grand scheme of things, what Jennifer had done wasn't that bad, but for it to become known would be devastating to her. Vince would know just how valuable a nugget he'd found and he wouldn't hesitate to use it.

She could be pretty sure that between them, Charlotte and Jennifer would stop Nicole going to Vince. Now she had to do a mental about-turn and keep hold of Brittany, who was already getting to her feet and reaching for her jacket.

'Go where you like,' she said carelessly as she, too, started to rise. 'A pity, though. Another couple of days and I'd have had your witness.'

'What!' Brittany spun to face her.

'The woman Joshua called to come forward. I think I've found her.'

'Where? Who is she? I'll kill her.'

'That won't help Joshua.'

'Tell me who she is.'

'For one, I'm not on the case any more. And two, I won't tell you anything until I'm sure. Like I said, I need another few days. But if you don't want me to carry on, fine. We'll call it quits right now.'

'You're bluffing. You haven't found her.'

'Oh, I have. Like I say, another few days.'

Brittany hesitated. Annie watched her for a while, then said, 'When you see him tomorrow, tell Joshua I know what was in the box. And tell him I'm going to get it and give it to you to pass on to him. That is, unless you've decided to call a halt.'

Again that outraged glare. Brittany didn't know how to deal with being bettered. And yet, thought Annie, she must have had a lot of it to deal with. She was nowhere near as clever as she fancied herself to be.

'It'll be down to Joshua,' Brittany said. 'I'll do whatever he wants.'

Remembering Yates's apparent vehemence against Brittany for calling in a private detective in the first place, Annie wasn't too hopeful the case would still be hers after tomorrow. But maybe he'd stop Brittany going anywhere else. Or he might take her bait and agree to see her.

On her own after Brittany had left, Annie paced the floor. Maybe by tomorrow she would know what had been in the box. She had to hope Eliza Ellis would not take against her and have her thrown out. A place like that wouldn't hesitate to call in the authorities. Again, the spectre of Kate loomed large.

She reached for the phone and called the Longs.

You have reached the voice mail of...

She opened her mouth to speak, but then stopped. The words she bit back were that she had finished work on his case, and was ready to report back. Suddenly, she wanted extra time to think this through, so clicked the phone off before the recorded message had finished.

CHAPTER TWENTY THREE

The residential home sat in the curve of a main road on the outskirts of the city. A substantial Victorian mansion, probably built by a successful merchant. Its front aspect was functional, windows with blinds not curtains; easier to keep clean, the outside space tarmacked to provide a small car-park. A path down the side led on to a lawned area, pleasant enough, maybe where the residents sat on sunny days.

A heavy front door with impenetrable frosted glass barred her way. She rang the bell. After a minute, the door swung open to reveal a large woman in a pale blue uniform that strained at the seams.

'I'm here to see Eliza Ellis. I rang yesterday.'

The woman opened the door wider to let her in. 'You been before?'

'No, this is my first visit.' Annie held on to her smile, though it made no dent on the uniformed woman who appeared neither welcoming nor hostile, just uninterested. She stepped inside, bracing herself for the smell of age or the clinical aroma of a hospital ward, but it was a spacious hallway that smelt of nothing much and looked clean and bright. Apart from the woman's uniform and the outsize proportions of the dwelling, it could have been an ordinary house.

'Sign in.'

Annie turned to a big book resting on the hall table. It was all handwritten, the pages divided out into columns. Date – Name – Visiting – Time in – Time out. Annie filled it in, making Eliza's name just legible and her own not quite. She took the time from the clock on the wall. 10.15 a.m.

As the woman led her to the back of the house, they passed a closed door with the sounds of a television quiz show seeping through, then an open door where a tiny, wrinkled man lay back on a bed, his eyes open but unseeing, the only sign of life an incessant twitch of his clawed hand that lay outside the sheets. Further on, they passed an office where desks high with paper framed a wall-mounted box that held small lights labelled with numbers. Round a corner in the corridor, Annie breathed in a hint of well-boiled vegetables and caught a glimpse of stainless steel cooking pots.

Then the woman said, 'Visitor for you, Eliza,' as she knocked at a door and opened it in one move. Annie was struck by the change in her tone. Less robotic, warmer, as though liking the residents was part of the job, but interacting with visitors would be unpaid overtime.

Annie entered the room expecting Eliza to be frail and comatose like the old man in the bed. In contrast, she found a woman fully alert, dressed in a smart brick-red suit, and sitting in a high-backed chair. The only obvious concession to her age, apart from her being a resident here, was a magnifying glass on the book at her side. And when Eliza turned to Annie, her eyes looked dull, as though obscured by frosted lenses.

'Who are you? Did May have a grandchild after all?'

'Uh... no.' Annie paused and turned to the uniformed woman. 'Thanks.' She gave the woman a nod and a smile, hoping she would take the hint and leave.

'You OK, Eliza pet?'

'Yes, yes. Don't fuss.' Eliza flapped her hand dismissively.

The woman looked from one to the other of them, seemed satisfied, and left the room without another word.

'I never knew May,' Annie said. 'Her daughter told me where I could find you. I was asked to look through some of her things, to find out more... um... about her life.'

'An imposter or a busybody, then. I thought as much. Still, you're here now. I don't get many visitors. But if it's May you want to know about, Susan would know more than me. I didn't see much of May over the years.'

'Susan told me you were at May's eightieth birthday party.'

'That's right, I was.' Eliza's gaze wandered away from Annie and she smiled. 'It was a surprise to have Susan call round. I was in my own home back then, of course. May and I lost touch years ago.'

'She must have been pleased to see you.'

'Yes, I think she was.'

'You'll have had a lot to talk about.'

'Hmm, yes, we talked, of course. It was all very jolly. You know the thing. All false. Young people bouncing about, wondering how soon they'll be burying the old girl. I remember the smell of the flowers. A bit overpowering to tell the truth. Susan didn't expect her mother to last the year out, I could see that. That's why she made the effort. But May was tough. She always was.'

'What did you talk about?'

'Old times, you know. What else was there? Sunday-school. When we worked together.'

'Reliving the good times?'

Eliza laughed. 'There weren't many of those for such as us. Not in those days. School. I loved school. May didn't. She was glad to leave. I wanted to stay on. The teacher went to see my parents, but it did no good. There was war talk in the air. They wanted my wage coming in. I had to leave when I was thirteen.'

'Did May leave at the same time?'

'The same age, not the same time. There's a decade between us. May left when she was thirteen, too. Ten years before I did. May wasn't sorry to leave school, but she wanted to enrol at the hospital. Only her mother didn't think it was quite the thing for a young girl. And when the church offered her a position, her mother made her take it. It was the only thing she ever stood firm on, and May never forgave her, to her dying day.'

Annie ran through a quick mental calculation. 'Then you can't have been at school together at all.'

'Of course not.'

'I thought you said you'd talked about school... old times.'

'Sunday-school. All ages went together. Our parents made us go, of course. May was one of the eldest. She was a helper.'

'So she enjoyed that more than regular school?'

'Oh, I wouldn't say so.' Eliza's gaze strayed to the window, although Annie wasn't sure how much she could see.

'You say you worked with May, too?'

'Yes, May drove ambulances in the war. She used to let us come along. We weren't supposed to. We were just there to skivvy at the hospital, but we wanted to go out. You'd have shaded headlamps, you know, not to show from the sky. We had our noses glued to the windscreen, peering out, telling May, this way and that. No streetlights, of course. And you couldn't go by memory even. They weren't the same streets two nights in a row what with all the bombs.'

'But you enjoyed working with her?' Annie asked the question at random, not sure yet how to bring the conversation round to where she needed it, but wanting Eliza to keep talking.

'You didn't enjoy things in those days. You just got on with it. May did, anyway. I'll give her that. She didn't fuss. It was dreadful sweeping out the back of the ambulance some nights. Sweeping the blood out, you know. And the smell was dreadful. Some of the women were silly little cats. Ooh, I can't do this... I can't do that. Like that, you know.' Eliza puckered her nose disdainfully. 'Silly fools!' Her decades-old irritation burned bright.

'Not everyone can cope with those things,' Annie said.

'Cope? Of course they can cope. You have to cope. What do you do when you've a dead baby in the van? All that silliness and superstition. What harm can a dead baby do you? Poor little mite. It was May and I had to climb in there and wrap its little body.'

Annie's notebook lay empty in her lap. This wasn't what she was here for, but she felt it a necessary lead-in. The story would unwind gradually and bring her to Eliza's last meeting with May, when the locked box had been brought out. Eliza talked on, clearly starved of visitors and happy to have an audience for her memories. There were few books in the room and all large print despite the magnifier. Bulky tomes that looked too heavy for Eliza's skinny arms.

She understood May letting the friendship lapse. Eliza had probably felt the same. If these were the memories they had to share, then best leave them to fade. During a pause where Eliza looked as though she might drop off, Annie said, 'May had an old box, didn't she? She called it her locked box.'

Eliza's eyes snapped open and the milky whiteness of the lenses turned to Annie. 'What of it?'

Definitely touched a nerve of some sort, but Annie knew she must tread carefully. She had no real right to be here at all.

'I would have expected her to leave it to her daughter, that's all. With her having had it so long.'

'It was only an old box. Our generation wasn't sentimental over possessions. We couldn't be. We had none. And those we had went up in flames in the war.'

'It's just that I understood May left it to one of her carer's daughters. I wondered why she would have done that.'

'I didn't know that. Her mind was going, you know. She was probably confused.'

Annie sensed minor puzzlement, but no wariness. Maybe she'd imagined it before.

'Did the box ever belong to May's father?'

'No, it was May's always.'

'Her father was in the whaling industry I believe?'

'That's right. He was killed in an accident on the dock when May was thirteen. All our fathers went to sea. In peacetime. And those that could went out in the war, too. They didn't all come back, not by a long chalk.'

'Did your father work with May's father?'

'Yes, for a time, on the whalers, you know.'

'Uh... the Jawbone Gang?'

Annie watched closely for a reaction, but Eliza just said, 'That's right. They were both in a jawbone gang. Who told you that?'

'I just guessed from something I saw.'

Annie paused, feeling frustration well up. She knew she was close to something, but she must be careful. If she upset Eliza she might be thrown out and the uniformed carers would become guards who would bar her way back. Eliza mentioned the Jawbone Gang with no hint of unease, but that was as expected. The Jawbone Gang was from a different age.

To keep things rolling, Annie asked, 'What is a jawbone gang, anyway?'

She only half listened as Eliza talked about stories her father had told of life aboard the old whalers... the size of the animals... the need for a gang to deal with just its jaw.

The key question formed in Annie's mind.

'That's interesting,' she said. 'I know next to nothing about the whaling industry, but it must have been big in Hull back then. Only it isn't that jawbone gang I really want to know about. It's the Jawbone Gang that was to do with May's locked box.'

'I don't know what you mean.' The words shot out too quickly. Eliza's beady eyes did their best to lock with Annie's, but couldn't focus.

Annie saw Eliza's bent fingers clutch at the chair arms, but she suppressed a rush of triumph. It was an achievement to have found someone alive who held the key to May's secret, but she reminded herself that knowing Eliza had the information was a long step from getting her to tell. And even if she did, there was no reason to think May's old secret had anything to do with Michael Walker or Joshua Yates.

'Some tea!' Eliza shouted suddenly, making Annie jump. As she spoke the words, Eliza reached to the table at her side and banged her hand on a bell push.

Annie imagined the light flashing in the office down the corridor. She must make a split second decision whether to push hard now or whether to retreat and try to secure a later visit.

'Uh... I... what can I bring you next time I come?' She gabbled the words out, wanting to divert Eliza from having her barred from visiting again. 'Something to read, audio books, maybe? I could find you an old player if you don't have one. Not so heavy to lift.'

Eliza chuckled. 'I know you're trouble. I sensed it the moment you arrived. I wasn't born on an apple cart, you know. But I will let you come again. You're to bring me a packet of Hamlet cigars and something good to drink. I like brandy and water. A good brandy, mind. None of this modern cheap stuff.'

The door clicked open and two women bustled in, both throwing suspicious glances Annie's way.

'How you doing, Eliza, pet?'

'My visitor's going,' said Eliza. 'I can't remember her name. I can't be bothered with names these days. She's coming again, though, and she might take me on a trip out. We haven't decided yet.'

'Well, that'll be nice for you.' They turned friendlier faces to Annie. 'That'll be nice for her.'

'Yes,' said Annie. 'I'm coming back this afternoon.' Seeing Eliza pull a face at this, she added, 'It has to be. I'm short of time.'

'I've rung for a cup of tea,' Eliza said. 'And the girl's going now. She's tired me. I'll have a cup of tea, then I'll take a nap.' She lifted a crooked finger to point at Annie. 'Bring one of those big bottles of spring water. Don't stint. Ice and lemon, too. And don't forget...' She raised her hand to her mouth and mimed the action of smoking.

CHAPTER TWENTY FOUR

Annie hadn't been back at the office for more than a couple of minutes before the phone rang. It was Ron Long asking for a report on his case.

'I can't talk just now,' she improvised. 'I'll get back to you.'

'You're with someone, are you? Well, how soon? Time's pressing, and Sheryl won't budge until she has your verdict. We can come in this afternoon.'

'Sorry, I have no time at all this weekend. Early next week. Can you come in on Tuesday?'

'Make it Monday.'

'OK, but I can't give you a time right now. I'll ring you back later today or tomorrow.'

'And you'll have a result for us?'

'Yes.'

'I'll be waiting for your call.'

Annie put the phone down knowing this was a loose end she must tie carefully. It wasn't her job to wrap felons in neat parcels and hand them on to the police when she hadn't a scrap of solid evidence against them. Furthermore, she must allow people their own agendas without prying. But there was a line she wouldn't cross when it came to turning a blind eye and she'd yet to determine just where this line lay with the Longs.

She returned the file to its drawer. There were a couple of days to think it through.

A pile of messages lay on the desk. Annie flicked through them. Most were for Pat, but one had her name on it.

'Oh hell,' she murmured, as she read Barbara's scrawl.

Horse woman rang to confirm fancy-dress comp.
Told her you'd be there.

Now she would have to get in touch and grovel a bit, but not now.

More immediately problematic was Eliza Ellis. Without much hope, she pulled out the petty cash tin. The cash book showed a positive balance of £50, and a scrawled handwritten note fluttered out that said, 'IOU 30 quid. Barb'. At the bottom of the tin, a solitary 50p rolled about.

That would barely buy matches, let alone good brandy. Annie let out a sigh. It would mean risking her credit card and fighting out the claim later.

Brandy? Do me a favour!

As she set off, she wondered where to find ice and how she could transport it.

Three hours had passed since her first visit when Annie arrived back at the residential home.

It was a stranger who opened the door to her, still with no particular acknowledgement or curiosity. It was as though she'd been ringing this bell to be let in twice a day for years. This time she could answer yes when asked if she knew the way to Eliza's room.

She knocked and hesitated, but when there was no sound from inside, she opened the door and found Eliza in the same chair as this morning, but now bundled in a thick coat with matching hat and gloves in her lap.

'Is that you?' Eliza greeted her, squinting her eyes in an effort to make out who had come in.

'Yes, it's me, Annie. I'm here to talk some more about May.'

'Let me see what you have.'

Annie opened her carrier bag and lifted out the brandy which Eliza peered at from close range before pronouncing it to be 'Not the stuff I remember, but good enough. Put it back in the bag for later.'

She looked over the two-litre bottle of spring water as Annie held it for her to read the label. It was too heavy for Eliza to lift.

'It'll do,' was the verdict. She turned the packet of Hamlet cigars in her hand. 'It's a good many years since I had one of these. Did you bring matches?'

Annie handed across a disposable lighter and threw a glance towards the door. Smoking couldn't possibly be allowed in here. Presumably that explained the coat. She wondered where Eliza wanted to go.

'What's wrong with matches? I don't know what it is with youngsters today. Everything throwaway and poor quality. Does it work?'

Annie took the lighter from her and flicked it to a tongue of blue flame. 'It's fine. I've matches in the boot of the car if need be.'

'I'm not ready to go anywhere yet,' Eliza said. 'We need to talk first.'

Annie felt a ripple of apprehension that took her right back to school days and smuggling forbidden substances on to the premises. 'We'll have to go out if you want to smoke.'

Eliza sniffed. 'We can go in the garden for that. They're stuffy in here. It's the law, apparently. You can't do as you please in your own home these days. I don't suppose you bothered with the ice.'

'Yes, it's here.' Annie patted the bag. The thermos flask she'd borrowed from her upstairs neighbour and filled with ice cubes from his freezer stood upright next to the brandy bottle.

Eliza seemed surprised. 'I expected you to forget that. Then we can have a drink later if we want to. There's no law says we can't do that. And a lemon too. Now did you bring a knife to slice it? No? I thought you'd forget something. You couldn't cut butter with the knives they give you in here.'

'I've a sharp penknife in the car.'

'You keep quite a kit in that car of yours.'

Annie wondered what Eliza would say if she were to show her the balaclava, the picklocks, the whole motley collection. She asked, 'Do you want a drink now?'

Eliza shook her head. 'No. I need you to do something for me. If you agree, we're going out. It's something I promised May, but I left it too late. You don't think you'll end up reliant on others like this. It creeps up on you.'

'I'll help if I can.'

Eliza turned to her and seemed to weigh her words. 'I'll make up my mind in a while. Tell me what you want.'

Annie opened her mouth on a set speech about wanting to know about May's life, about her eightieth birthday, but then she paused. She thought about the way Eliza's carers talked to her, as though she were a child not quite old enough to make her own decisions. Eliza's physical frailties were obvious, but Annie detected no chink in her mental capacity. Why not be open? Or anyway, fairly open. Apart from anything else, Eliza had no one to tell.

'I'm a private investigator,' she began. 'I've been working on something that concerns a recent court case. Someone was murdered, and one of May's carers popped up as being involved. A woman called Donna Lambit.' She watched Eliza as she spoke Donna's name, but saw no hint of recognition. 'The murdered man was a Michael Walker.'

'Michael Walker?' Eliza murmured. 'I can't remember names. Would it have been in the papers? We have people come in and read the papers to us.'

'Yes, the case has been all over the local Press. May's carer, Donna Lambit, claims she and May discussed Michael Walker six years ago, but she either can't or won't remember the detail. If May were alive, I would ask her.'

Eliza gave a wintry smile. 'You wouldn't get an answer. May's mind was going even then. So she knew these people, did she? Poor May.'

'I don't know... I'm not sure about any of this. May might have known Michael Walker, or maybe his family. Joshua Yates accused Michael Walker of some terrible crimes. There wasn't a scrap of evidence, but it turns out it wasn't the first time he'd been accused. He was reported to the police six years ago.'

'By the man who killed him?'

'No, by Donna Lambit, May's carer. She claims to have had her evidence from May.'

Eliza turned her clouded gaze to Annie and tried to focus. 'May's mind was going. The woman's a fool if she's believed anything May said.'

'Frankly, it's hard to know what to believe. But she's not saying May told her. She claims she saw documents.'

'What documents?' Eliza's tone was sharp.

'From the locked box.'

'So that's why you asked me about the Jawbone Gang. You saw the writing inside the box.'

Annie nodded, and watched as Eliza's claw of a hand reached shakily across to the table at her side to feel for the outline of the water glass, which she clutched and lifted to her lips. After taking a drink, she held the glass in her lap, both hands around it, resting it on top of the hat and gloves that nestled there. Her gaze swung round again, not quite to Annie's face but somewhere close, making Annie wonder if she could see better in her peripheral vision than directly.

'So this woman took documents from May?'

'She would have done, but she couldn't find the box. It didn't come to light again till after May died, and it was empty then. At least, that's what Susan told me.'

Eliza nodded. 'What did this woman say these documents were?'

'She didn't know.'

Eliza barked out a short laugh. 'She doesn't sound very bright. But tell me, how did May know this man, the one who was murdered? What was his name again?'

'Michael Walker. I don't know how May knew him. I haven't been able to verify that she did.'

Eliza eased herself upright in her chair as though marshalling her thoughts. She licked her lips before speaking. 'You want to know what was in May's locked box?'

'Yes, can you tell me?'

'I can.' Eliza smiled. 'But I didn't keep in touch with May after the war. I know what was in that box when May was a girl, but how it is going to help you to know what May wrote back then?'

It was a good question. If there had been anything relevant in that box, it must have been more recent. The documents Eliza referred to would be from decades before Michael Walker was born.

Eliza sat up and raised a crooked finger to point at Annie. 'That's what you came for, isn't it? You wanted to know about the Jawbone Gang and what was in May's locked box.'

'Yes, it is,' Annie admitted with a sigh. She'd semi-promised to do something for Eliza if Eliza gave her the information she wanted. It looked as though she might be committed to it on the back of a wild goose chase. She glanced at the brandy bottle and hoped the rest of the bribe would not be as expensive. 'So what is it you want me to do?'

'Good,' said Eliza, 'I thought you'd forgotten. I need you to complete the job May entrusted me with.'

'Which is what?'

'Ah no, you don't catch me out so easily. I'll tell you what it is once I know you'll do it.' Eliza took another sip of water and then began. 'The Jawbone Gang. May picked up the term when she was small. Her father would come back from sea with all manner of tales. He was a big romancer by all accounts, made life on the whalers sound like tremendous fun. I don't remember him, of course, but all our fathers were the same with their stories. May was a big child. Clumsy, you know, and quite chubby. A bit of a bully, but only because she got it from the older girls.'

Eliza's bent finger shot out. 'Pull your chair round so you're facing me. I don't like to keep turning my head.'

Annie did as she was told, and Eliza went on, 'May's Jawbone Gang was something I grew up with. There were all manner of gangs then. The boys all had to be in gangs, of course. The girls' gangs were different somehow. Not that there was much time for play in those days, but I used to see May's Jawbone Gang all sitting round this tiny hedge in Tommy Ferens's garden. He was a bigwig in Hull back then. He had a lovely big garden when all we had were shared yards. It wasn't open house, but he'd let some of the children play in there. The ones that didn't go wild and mess things up. Our attic overlooked a corner of that garden. He left it to the people of Hull when he died, you know. They made a park of it.'

Annie noted a half smile of reminiscence on Eliza's face and took a surreptitious glance at her watch.

'Were you one of May's gang?'

'No, I was never a member of that gang. I was too young, but she was kind to me. I remember watching them sitting round that hedge, May with her paper, scribbling away. I longed to be a part of it, but you have to remember, May was ten years older than me.

'Yes, that pen never stopped. May was slow at writing but she loved to do it. Handwriting now, that was one thing she could do, but what she really wanted was to get the words on the paper, to tell the story. But she was so slow. She couldn't have recorded half of what they talked about. Not that it mattered to May. It was all a game and what she wanted was the pieces of paper filled with words to go in her locked box. No one but the Jawbone Gang was ever allowed to look.'

Annie noted and squirrelled away the discrepancy that Eliza, *never a member of that gang*, knew what was in the box.

'What did she write? Minutes of the meetings?'

Eliza laughed. 'Not as anyone would have recognized them, but yes, essentially that. She wanted to see words on paper. They were important to her. You see, she'd been allowed to attend meetings at the church from being quite small and she'd seen the minute-taking, seen how important it was, how powerful a tool words on paper could be. She was after the power. That was May.'

'And the Jawbone Gang?'

'May stopped bothering with it soon before the war. But you want to know what was in the locked box? Reach behind you to the bed.'

Annie looked round, surprised.

'That's right,' Eliza went on. 'Look under the bottom of the counterpane.'

Annie lifted the cover and pulled out a handful of lined sheets of paper.

'There.' Eliza looked smug. 'I had them all ready for you. You can take a proper look.'

Annie shot the old woman a glance, then turned her attention to the papers in her hand. They were pages torn from an old exercise book. The paper itself was stiff with age. Annie had to turn it to catch the light because the words were so faded. She made out a date, *Thursday 5th March 1931*, written in the same immaculate lettering she'd found inside the box, followed by the words:

We seven met today. The sun shone brightly.

The page was closely written. Her eye scanned down the text. Each new date began a new line. Otherwise, every inch of the surface, front and back, was used.

Clouds were in the sky... Today there had been rain...

She read a couple of the pages word by word and scanned the rest. Then she looked at Eliza who shrugged an I-told-you-so.

'Is it all like this? How much is there?'

'Oh, there's a lot. The box was crammed full. I know what you're thinking. You're thinking what could anyone have taken out of here about that man... what did you say his name was?'

'Michael Walker.'

'Yes, well, I have an idea about that. Go to the last page.'

Annie turned to the last of the half-dozen pages. There she read,

Mother is a cow. She is a Jezebel. Why should I do everything? Why cannot she work, not just beat me?

'You see?' said Eliza. 'May wrote all sorts. That's where it says her mother beat her, isn't it? I looked out that bit specially, just to show you what she was like. If there was ever a hand raised in May's house after her father went, it was May's against her mother, not the other way about. Someone has read something she's written and taken it the wrong way.'

Annie flicked through the pages again, but said nothing. Eliza's theory took her back to where she'd started. The one story that made the rest hang together was that Yates had targeted the wrong man. Could this be the basis of some spurious evidence on which he'd done it? Surely not. There had to be more to it than this.

She stared across at Eliza. Looked that bit out specially, had she? And with her failing sight. The old woman knew these papers intimately.

'Are you saying May could have written stuff about Michael Walker?'

'Who knows what May might have written? She had an imagination on her.'

Annie looked again at the pages in her hand. 'What was the most recent entry? Did May keep on writing this all her life?'

'No, no. Just the Jawbone Gang years. I wonder sometimes if she ever had that box open from when she was fifteen to when she was eighty. I think it just sat in a cupboard. A box of bad memories rotting away.'

Annie did the calculation. 'So the papers in the box went up to when? The 1930s?'

'1934.' The answer came surprisingly easily to Eliza's lips.

That put paid to any written tales about Michael Walker. But then Eliza and May had been out of touch for years. Who was to say what was in the box when Donna saw it? Or maybe there was another Michael Walker. She asked Eliza, who shook her head.

'Michael who? Oh, the murderer, you mean?'

'No, the victim. The one who was murdered.'

Eliza shrugged a negative. It was all the same to her. The names of people attached to recent events were not lodged securely in her mind. She pushed Eliza for her own theories of how Donna might have gleaned the wrong information, but Eliza had no ideas.

'Where are the rest of the papers?' she asked.

'I have them all safe.'

'Can I see them?'

'I'll let you take a bit of a look, but there's nothing to see. Just more like that. Now, May would understand why I've let you see those notes, but she'd hate anyone to know what she wrote about her mother. She wouldn't have wanted anyone reading it through in detail. I only looked that page out because I wanted you to see she could write some bad things. Oh yes, she could be a bad 'un, could May, but then she had a lot to put up with.'

'OK,' said Annie, cautiously. 'I'd like to see them, all the same.'

'Then I'll need your promise that you'll finish the job I started for May. I promised her I would take the papers and burn them, so no one would ever know what she'd written. She was housebound by then and had no one to trust. She'd started on burning them once, but you know how paper can float once it's alight, and she singed the carpet. She was lucky the whole house didn't go up. They stopped her having open fires then. She insisted they be done bit by bit. Put a whole wad of paper on a fire and it doesn't always burn all through. You'll help me to do it, once and for all, won't you? And none of this taking them away to put on the fire or putting them in the bin for recycling. I want to see them burnt. I promised May.'

Annie gathered from this that she wasn't the first to be asked, but she could see the old woman's point of view. If she'd made this promise to a friend, it would weigh on her mind that she was no longer physically capable of carrying it out.

'Yes, I'll do it, but I want to see them first.'

'You'll be forever if you want to read them all through, and I don't want you doing that. I promised May they'd be burnt. They're all the same as the ones I showed you. There's nothing you could be interested in.'

'I just want to flick through and check the dates. If there's nothing more recent that the 1930s then it's of no interest to me anyway.'

'All right, you can do that. Now do you promise me that you'll help to burn them?'

'Yes, I promise.'

Annie switched her concentration from the age of the papers to what had happened to them more recently.

'This happened at May's eightieth birthday party, didn't it? Is that when she asked you to take the papers? And why not the whole box?'

'Don't be daft. We didn't talk about anything like this with people around.'

Annie thought back to what Donna had said. It hadn't been the day of May's birthday party. It had been some days later. Eliza was the 'some old cow' Donna had overheard talking with May. What had she heard? And what had she seen? Whatever it was, she had assumed it came from the locked box, but maybe it hadn't.

'When you went to visit May the second time, a few days after her birthday, was anyone else there?'

'No, just the two of us. Who else would there be?'

'Not May's carer or anyone like that?'

'There was someone in and out. The post came, I remember that.' Eliza lay back in the chair, closed her eyes and held out one hand towards Annie. 'I'm tired,' she said. 'You tire me out with all your questions. You'll have to leave. I'm too tired to go out now. You'll have to come back some other time, maybe next weekend. Give me those papers back.'

Annie placed the papers into Eliza's hand and watched the bony claw close round them. She had no intention of waiting until next weekend, but this wasn't the moment to say so to Eliza. This was the moment to sit back quietly and wait.

Eliza's hands closed round the papers in her lap, scrunching them up. Her eyes remained closed. Annie sat still as she pictured the scene six years ago. May, housebound, entrusting her old friend with the task of burning her childhood diaries. Eliza, still mobile then, but of slight build. Of course, she couldn't have taken the whole box. She would never have managed it. The papers must have been stuffed into a carrier bag or similar. And maybe Eliza had shoved the empty box under the stairs. She could ask now. No reason not to tell her the truth. But she said nothing as she watched the elderly woman sink lower in her chair.

As Eliza's breathing settled to gentle snores, Annie reached forward and moved the bell-push just enough out of place that an instinctive lunge for it would miss. At her age, Eliza wouldn't sleep deeply and probably not for long. But there was little furniture to check. If she were careful, it would take only minutes to find the rest of the papers and have them tucked away in her bag. She would return them tomorrow to be burnt as she'd promised. Eliza might accuse her of theft, but she would swear that Eliza had allowed her to take them. And the carers would believe her because she was young and Eliza was old and physically frail.

She slid smoothly out of the chair and down, out of Eliza's line of sight. A flash of movement might be enough to wake her.

Once behind the chair, Annie moved quickly, easing open the drawers in the 3-drawer chest and feeling through the contents. Her search found only clothes. A pad of paper on top held notes from Eliza. Annie skimmed through them – a complaint about a dripping tap; a shopping list. Eliza's writing was spidery and frail, but very neat, trained from childhood just like May's. She moved on to the large old-fashioned wardrobe, but it yielded nothing of interest. She crept right to Eliza's side on hands and knees to feel through the chair's capacious pockets. Then she stood behind, hanging over the sleeping woman, looking for any sign the papers were somehow tucked in the chair with her. Finally, she turned her attention to the bed. An unlikely hidey-hole, but it was where Eliza had stashed the few pages she had seen. Nothing under the mattress; nothing between the covers. Frustrated, Annie stood in the middle of the room, at a loss. Other than ripping open the upholstery or taking up the carpet, she had run out of places to check.

Then footsteps sounded from the corridor outside. Quickly, she slid the bell push back into place and resumed her seat.

As the door opened and two women walked in, Eliza woke with a start.

'Ready for tea, Eliza pet? Did you not go out, after all?'

'No,' Annie replied. 'We decided to stay in and chat, today. We're going out tomorrow, instead.'

'Not tomorrow,' said Eliza. 'You tire me with all your talk. Come next weekend. I'm not used to all these visits.'

Annie stood up and bent over Eliza's chair as though to kiss her goodbye. With their faces only inches apart, she hissed, 'Tomorrow. And have May's papers ready. I'll do as I said. You'll see them burn.'

She quelled a moment's unease at confirming her promise. There could be a lot of paperwork to digest, but she had confidence in her ability to speed read and retain anything of interest.

As Eliza went to protest, she murmured, 'Tomorrow or never.'

As Annie made her way back across town towards her flat, she reflected that it didn't seem like a Saturday night. She had nowhere lined up to go. There would be options on her answer-phone, but her head was full of her cases. Then it occurred to her that it was like a Saturday night after all – a Saturday night of a few years ago, when all three of them were up to their ears in work and barely had time to surface to take a breath. But no, it had been different back then. There had been an optimistic feel of work queuing; of riding a wave. This Saturday was just a glitch. A few bits of cases with tight deadlines that happened to coincide.

She had promised to get back to Ron Long to give him an appointment time for Monday, but she wanted more time to think through how she would deal with him and his wife. She would ring tomorrow. There was no real chance that she'd forget, but just in case her subconscious tried to duck her out of it, she lifted down the outsize red pin from the top of the cork board and pinned up a scrap of paper on which she scrawled Ron Long's name. Red-pinned. No chance of forgetting him now.

As she turned to fill the kettle, she remembered the fancy-dress competition, the letter she'd rammed in the drawer. Eliza was rock solid on childhood memories, but shaky on more recent events. Annie's mind seemed to operate on the opposite track, yet for some reason, she couldn't keep the blasted horse competition thing in her mind. It was so completely irrelevant to anything else in her life, but she must be in touch. Saturday afternoon would have been perfect. Everyone would have been out in the yard or the fields. The house would have been deserted. Too late now. Still, Sunday afternoon would be just as good.

She considered red-pinning the woman's letter along with Ron Long, but it went against the grain to red-pin more than one thing at a time. It would feel like a concession to failing powers, and Annie was determined that not only was she in her prime, she was on the verge of striking out in a whole new direction. The blasted horse woman and her nagging would be something she'd be pleased to leave behind.

CHAPTER TWENTY FIVE

Annie woke early. The pale morning light streamed in through the windows, crisp and clear, a reminder that May and Eliza's wartime traumas had played out under this same sky. They might have driven down this street in the wartime blackout, May at the wheel, Eliza with her nose pressed to the windscreen.

Annie slipped out of bed, determined to be at the residential home as early as was compatible with Sunday morning visiting. If Eliza had anything for her, she must find it before the day was out. Whether or not she unearthed anything useful, there was a frisson to knowing that she would uncover secrets today. She would burn May's childhood scribblings and take the weight of the promise from Eliza's shoulders, but as she burnt the pages, she would scan them and find out what all the fuss was about. Over the years she had perfected the art of speed reading small type, smudged print, scrawled handwriting, whilst pretending to look elsewhere. Once, she had unearthed key information by reading text backwards through a mirror. May's neat, round hand would be child's play and Eliza need never know.

How bad could May's secrets be? Presumably Eliza hadn't shown her the worst that was in there, though she'd pulled out something she considered bad enough that Annie would understand. May's adolescent outbursts would seem worse to someone Eliza's age.

Eliza's memory for recent events was bad, but with just the right prompting, the story would come out, piece by piece. That passing mention of the post arriving was something she would explore. And maybe Eliza would recall something, an odd comment, an anomaly about one of the letters. Annie would tease the information out of Eliza's mind and learn what it was that Donna had seen.

The woman who opened the door greeted Annie with, 'Eliza's all ready to go. She's been wondering where you'd got to.'

Eliza was not only in her hat and coat as before, she was in a wheelchair with a patterned woollen blanket tucked round her legs. The woman carer bustled in behind Annie with a man in a white tunic.

'We'll help you out down the back way,' she told Annie. 'There's a step.'

They took charge of the wheelchair and manoeuvred Eliza out of the room. As Annie followed them into the corridor, she heard Eliza say, 'Stop at the office. I want my attaché case from the safe.'

'Your attaché case, Eliza? Are you sure? Why would you want that out in the garden?'

Annie allowed herself a smile as she recalled her futile search.

'Never you mind what I want it for,' Eliza snapped. 'You just go and get it. And you... the girl. Bring that carrier bag from by the washstand.'

Annie spun round and returned to Eliza's room where she picked up the bag containing the brandy, the water, the lemon and the thermos flask. She wondered if the ice would have remained solid.

Once they were outside, the carers withdrew and left Annie and Eliza alone. The grounds at the back of the home were more extensive than Annie expected. Half an acre or so of hilly lawns and bushes rambled back towards a line of trees.

Annie pushed the chair down towards a small wooden summerhouse that the carers had pointed out as a pleasant place to sit, but when they reached it, Eliza said, 'Carry on down that path. There's a gardener's hut.'

The corner Eliza led her to was the hidden engine room of the garden. A rotting heap of detritus smouldered gently. Just the other side of a chain-link fence, half-a-dozen large bins stood in line. Annie wrinkled her nose at the sickly sweet odour of decay that mixed with the tang of the smoke.

'This is where we need to be,' Eliza said.

Annie looked curiously at the locked attaché case that had been slung over the handles of the wheelchair.

She stopped at a low stone wall where she could sit.

The hidden corner heightened the feel of wrongdoing; of schoolchildren sneaking forbidden substances on to school grounds, scared that a teacher would appear and confiscate their things, but that was absurd, echoes of early memories. These were grown men and women who had every right to do as they pleased with their lives. Maybe more so now they were on the final stretch.

Annie thought back to the things Eliza has said about May's gang. A childhood venture, disbanded after a few years. She wondered at it being so precious to May that she'd kept its mementos her whole life.

'This gang of May's, why did she disband it in 1934? What happened?'

'She said they were a useless bunch. Silly little cats, the lot of them. She had a point. And of course, there was war talk in the air.'

Again that anomaly that Eliza referred to them as though she hadn't been a part of it, yet her knowledge of May's notes had felt to Annie like a well-embedded memory not the patchwork recall of something more recent.

'Now, I want you to get a fire going in that metal cage thing. There's a lot to get through.'

Annie stood up and inspected the structure. It was a tall box fashioned from stout metal mesh, blackened and charred. Its purpose was clearly to contain burning material, leaves maybe. She dragged it upright, checking the direction of the breeze and making sure the structure was stable on a flat area of bare earth.

'Push my chair nearer,' said Eliza, 'so I can drop the papers in.'

'No,' said Annie sharply. 'You agreed I could glance at the dates so I can see they're all from the 1930s.'

'Oh yes, I remember.' Eliza barely pretended to be convincing. 'I promised May, you know.'

'And I promised you I'd burn the papers.'

Annie lifted the attaché case from the back of the chair and helped Eliza to balance it on her knee. 'Now let's get started. Give me some papers and I'll get the fire started.'

'I want you to start the fire first. There's some wood over there. And some twigs for kindling.'

As Annie began to pull the bits of wood together, she asked, 'When did you join May's gang?'

'I was too young to be a member of the Jawbone Gang. I told you.'

There was something behind the words, just as there had been before. Eliza had opened the case now and was riffling through the papers. Annie stood up and glanced across.

Eliza caught the movement and quickly pushed the papers together. May's writing was familiar to her from the pages she'd read yesterday, but Eliza had uncovered a sheaf of papers in a different hand altogether. Yet still familiar. It took a moment to place the memory. Yesterday. The pad on top of the chest. It was Eliza's writing. It had been the briefest of glimpses but the paper looked no different from May's diary pages.

How many times had Eliza claimed not to have been in May's gang? A few too many. Annie thought back to the way Eliza had formed her answers.

'So you were never a member of May's gang?'

'I told you, I was too young. May disbanded her Jawbone Gang. I had nothing to do with it.'

Annie looked closely at Eliza as she said, 'Not May's Jawbone Gang. May's other gang.'

Eliza's eyes opened in a flare of surprise and Annie knew she'd found what the old woman had been trying to hide from her.

Eliza recovered quickly and gave a small shrug.

'Tell me about the other gang.'

'You said the Jawbone Gang. That was the agreement. If I told you about the Jawbone Gang, you'd burn the papers.' Eliza clutched the attaché case to her.

'I will,' Annie reassured her. 'I said I would and I will, but I still want to know.'

'Get that fire started then.'

'I need some paper. I can't get the twigs to catch.'

Eliza tutted. 'What do you think the brandy's for? Douse the wood and get it going before some busybody comes out making trouble.'

Annie pulled the bottle out of its bag. 'I wish you'd said. I could have brought paraffin. And at least give me the pages I read yesterday to help get it going.'

She wasn't sure brandy would burn hot enough to allow the wood to catch, but she crumpled the half-dozen pages Eliza passed to her and dribbled some of the spirit on to them before setting them beneath the twigs and lighting them from underneath the mesh.

She watched the flames flare up and die down, but they caught hold without needing further help. Then she looked at Eliza. The Jawbone Gang was a red-herring the old woman used to avoid taking about the real secret, whatever it was. She'd used it to explain her last conversation with May. Probably they'd talked about the old Jawbone Gang, but they'd talked about something else too. And been through some other paperwork. Donna had both seen and heard them.

Eliza might once have been a match for her, but age and lack of mental stimulation had taken her edge. Annie would play her gently until the full story came out. And if the incriminating papers still existed and Eliza tried to slip them in amongst May's old diaries, they would not escape Annie's eagle eye.

The wood was fully alight now. The bottom of the metal cage glowed red and embers dropped down on to the earth below. Somewhere close, a church bell chimed rhythmically. Apart from the crackle of the flames, there was little noise. Just the occasional rustle of a light breeze high in the trees.

Eliza handed Annie sheaves of pages half-a-dozen at the time. Annie scrunched each one in her hand, reading it as she did so and then tossing it into the flames. Eliza seemed to be going in order. The dates, starting in September 1930, paraded in front of Annie's eyes.

Thursday, 4th September 1930, Saturday, 6th September 1930. Thursday... Saturday... Thursday... Saturday... There was an occasional break in the pattern, but the comments attached to the dates remained banal:

We met at the tree... Just 4 of us today... It is church later.

Now and again, the tone changed as the adolescent fury in May burst forth:

I hate them all... I wish I was an orphan like the boy... Die. Die. Die.

Now and then, Annie's gaze strayed to the curve in the path that led back to the house, sure the curl of smoke must be visible from there. Would anyone come to investigate? She wished Eliza would speed up and either pass more papers at once or pass them quicker. It would take all day at this rate.

'It's quite chilly sitting still out here,' Eliza said.

'Then let me have the case. I can get them burnt far more quickly.' Annie was determined not to let Eliza talk her way back inside before the job was done.

'No, I want to do it this way.'

As she spoke, Annie saw Eliza's hand move to her chest. For a second, she thought the old woman might be ill, then saw that she held a plastic disk that was on a chain round her neck. Eliza had brought an alarm with her. Annie was glad she'd spotted it, but pretended not to have noticed. It meant Eliza could summon help.

It was time to bring her back to her last conversation with May. In all likelihood, the information Annie wanted was completely unimportant to Eliza; so unimportant that no trace of it might be left in her memory. She scanned the paper in her hand. The dates had crept into the spring of 1931.

'You remember the last time you saw May – it would have been a few days after her eightieth birthday party – can you tell me again what you talked about?'

'I've told you already. You seem to want everything again and again. Wheel me nearer to the fire so I can feel the heat.'

Annie did as she was asked and Eliza passed her another bundle of paper.

'Can you remember who else was there that second time?'

'No one. I had to let myself in. I was there a good while. One or two people came in and out as I remember. The post came. Someone made us a cup of tea. Whoever it was made sandwiches for May. I remember that. I thought that's not much for lunch, sandwiches, but they might have made some for me, all the same.'

'What happened when the post came?'

'It came through the door. Or... no, did I have to answer the door to someone? There might have been a parcel too big to go through the door. I really can't remember. We had that cup of tea soon afterwards, I think, because I moved an envelope out of the way.'

This felt promising. The post arrived when they were on their own. Then someone, surely Donna, made tea. Annie would like to bet that May and Eliza had discussed something that had come in the post. Donna had overheard them, maybe read over their shoulders when bringing the tea, but she'd seen them with the locked box and made the wrong assumption.

'Did you talk about anything that came in the post?'

'I can't remember that we did. She was asking me to burn the papers. I wasn't thinking about anything else. She would insist on reading from them. She couldn't see well enough, you know, but she read from them all the same. Can you imagine? And I don't think that box had been opened in years. I was worrying about how much there was and how long it would take me to get it all on the fire.'

Eliza stopped abruptly and looked at the papers Annie was scrunching and tossing into the fire. Annie deliberately speeded up, in case Eliza suspected that she was reading the papers more fully than had been intended.

'It's cold,' Eliza said. 'Give me some brandy.'

Annie pulled a cup from the carrier bag and poured in some spirit. 'Water?'

'No, no. Neat. Fill it up, girl. I'm not a child.'

Annie handed over the brimming cup. The old woman took a sip and, apparently satisfied, passed over the next batch of papers.

'Will you turn the chair so I get the heat on this side? I'm chilly down my back, but I'll catch alight on my legs if I'm not careful.'

Annie jumped up and manoeuvred the chair as Eliza wanted. As she did so, Eliza said, 'There isn't anyone coming from the house, is there? They don't like residents setting fires.'

As Annie turned to look back down the path, there was a sudden movement from the chair.

Her heart lurched.

A whumph... a spray of sparks... Had Eliza thrown herself into the flames?

Before she could gasp in a breath, Eliza slumped back in the chair, breathing hard.

'What the...?'

A thick wad of paper sat in the bottom of the metal cage, flames beginning to lick its edges. In the fraction of a second it took Annie to turn, Eliza hurled her cup into the heart of the fire. A burst of purple flame mushroomed upwards.

Annie sprang at the old woman, grabbed the chain at her neck in both hands, pulling it apart with a snap and flinging it on to the grass.

She kicked the cage on to its side, gasping and leaping back as a river of purple fire snaked across the grass. Red embers spilt from the mesh. Tiny fires flared in the grass. As the cage fell, the wad of papers fanned out. Small tongues of flame began to curl their edges.

Turning her head away, Annie took in a deep breath and grabbed them out of the fire, throwing them on to the ground and stamping out the flames. She turned to the grass and trod down on the scorched line of the brandy fire.

Once sure it was no longer alight, she rubbed her hands and pulled the plastic bottle out of the carrier bag to tip water on to her wrist where the flame had bitten. With a stout stick, she hooked the cage upright again and kicked at the grass where the spillage had blackened it.

This would have convinced her, if she hadn't already been sure, that Eliza's knowledge of the papers was not recently acquired. She knew them intimately and knew exactly which ones she wanted to hide.

Annie picked up the alarm with its broken chain but did not hand it back to Eliza as she manoeuvred the wheelchair away from the fire.

'You promised!' Eliza spat out.

'So did you. You promised I could scan the papers, see the dates. I'll keep my promise if you keep yours.'

CHAPTER TWENTY SIX

Annie sat down again on the low wall with the partly scorched papers in her lap and began to flick through them. These were in Eliza's hand; the same spidery writing she'd seen yesterday but without the frailty. The words were robust and clear; the comments longer.

> *Thursday, 15th February 1934. The Jawbone Gang met today and we talked about what we liked.*

'The Jawbone Gang?' Annie queried. 'You said you weren't part of it.'

'That was the new Jawbone Gang,' said Eliza. 'May wrote that on the box when she started the first one. That's the one you asked about.'

Annie glared at the old woman. She'd tried to cheat on her promise by using a long-ago distinction between two gangs that Annie couldn't possibly have known about. She carried on looking through the papers, making no secret now that she was reading them, but she kept to her side of the bargain and tossed them into the fire. The comments were longer; the sentences better formed, but there was nothing of interest. Eliza, as minute-taker, made a better job, leaving more to be checked.

> *We must all go to the Day Out, even if we do not wish to go...*

As the diary made its way into June, an entry read:

> *We two have made a pledge. We used the knife and swore to it in blood. It is agreed that we shall meet every Thursday.*

Annie stifled a yawn. She had scanned entries for almost every Thursday and Saturday since 1930. Why this pronouncement now? She had a moment's hope that the Saturday meetings might have been dropped, but they carried on just as before. *Thursday... Saturday... Thursday...*

Except that...

For the first time since she'd started on this, she unfolded a page she had already scrunched in readiness for the fire, and read it through again, aware all the time of Eliza's resentful gaze.

We two have pledged... We two...

'You and May met without the others, didn't you? Saturdays, you and May. Thursdays, all five of you. Why?'

Eliza's answer was a shrug.

Annie retained the papers in her lap now.

'You promised,' Eliza growled.

'Yes, and I will. I— Oh my God!' Annie stared at the page in front of her.

'This is what he does,' she read out.

'For pity's sake,' Eliza shouted. 'Don't read it aloud. It's bad enough that it's there. I had enough of a job stopping May from reading it. That's why I promised to take them all away.'

Annie gaped at the diary entry. *That was the start of his unspeakable degradations...* It went on to describe how *he* first *forced his unwelcome attentions* on to *her*. The acts described were the touching of hands and a foot moving to rub against an ankle. It wasn't these that horrified Annie. It was the phraseology. *That was the start of his unspeakable degradations... the forcing of his unwelcome attentions...*

These were exactly the arcane phrases used by Yates in his tirades against Michael Walker.

Quickly, Annie flipped forward through the pages. She barely had to scan them to find what she wanted. The passages describing the abuse of the anonymous *her* by the anonymous *he* were easy to spot, because they were back in the original handwriting.

'May wrote these bits,' she said.

No doubts now. This was what Donna had heard. This was what Yates had quoted back in court. But how... why?

Eliza said nothing.

'What was it? Why did she write this? What's it about?'

'Go back to the Saturday before the first one,' Eliza said. 'If you haven't burnt it.'

'*May put forward a plan of action*,' Annie read aloud. '*But the Jawbone Gang decided against it.* What plan of action? What does...? Oh, just you and May? May wanted to do something. You disagreed. What did she want you to do?'

'I wrote the notes, but she kept the box. When we met, she would give me the box and I'd open it. When I had the box back from her that next time, she'd written that, and it was there on the top. I couldn't have missed it. No, don't for pity's sake read it aloud. It was to convince me we had to act. Of course, we could never have spoken openly about that kind of thing.'

'But who was he?'

'His name was William Digby. Mr Digby we had to call him. He was in charge at the Sunday-school. Young girls aplenty and forced to attend by their parents.'

'But how long did this go on? Who were his victims?'

'Mainly May. She walked out on him when she was thirteen, said she'd never go back, but then she was offered a job by the church. That must have been Digby's doing.'

'Yes, you mentioned that before. May wanted to work at the hospital.'

'Her mother made her work for the church. She never forgave her for that. Not to her dying day.'

'But didn't she tell her mother?'

'Of course not. The shame of it. It would have been the worse for May if she had.'

'But surely if he really did...' Annie's voice tailed away. She hadn't read beyond the first few of May's entries, but she recalled the allegations Yates had made against Walker.

'Don't say it!' Eliza's lips pursed, as though she'd bitten into a lemon.

'What did she want you to do?'

'She had a plan for revenge. It couldn't ever have worked, but it helped her just to plot and plan. She wanted me to tell the rest of them about it – the new Jawbone Gang – so they could help.'

'And you wouldn't?'

'Oh, I did, eventually, when she told me enough of what he'd done. I was very young then. I didn't understand.'

'What was the plan?'

'Childish stuff. May wasn't very bright.'

'But what was it?'

When Eliza didn't answer, Annie turned back to the sheets of paper still in her lap.

'Oh, all right,' said Eliza. 'It's all in there. May had a plan to kill Mr Digby.'

Annie felt her eyes snap open wide. 'You killed him?'

Eliza's lip curled. 'We were children. All we could do was plot and plan. It made us feel better while we were doing it.' She threw Annie a look of exasperation. 'Just look. A dozen pages on. My writing. May dictated: I wrote.'

Annie riffled through the pages and sure enough found a heading, *The Plan*, underlined twice. It was set out like a recipe. A list of items included a blanket, a pen and a wash bowl. There followed numbered steps in the process beginning with:

1: We five arrive at the room by the back of the hall.

And ending:

20: We five return to our homes in good time for supper.

Annie had half expected to see a blueprint for the frenzied knife attack on Michael Walker, but it bore no relation.

It was hard to work out what May's plan actually meant.

T hands to L the red crested vase and opens the chest for the shoes. T says, now for the books, be quick, and L takes the red crested vase and M tells E for her turn with the pen.

Eliza shook her head. 'T was code for Digby. You can see he had a speaking part in the plan. She had it all scripted. We rehearsed it, the five of us.' Eliza paused and laughed coldly. 'We had some fun with it, back and forth. May would make one of the others play Digby with his lines and his moves. She had us rehearsing till we were bored with it.'

'But what happened in the end?'

'We walked away from it one day. All five of us. I think that the plotting gave May the strength to break free. And we all followed where May led. We never went back to the church.'

'What happened to him? What about the other children who stayed?'

'It must have scared him, the way we all left. Brought it home to him, you know. He won't have done anything to anyone else after that.'

Annie said nothing. It was a dreadful memory to have raked up after all these decades. She supposed this Digby person had carried on abusing the girls in his care, unless he'd been caught in later years. She could understand why Eliza, and probably May, made themselves believe their actions had stopped him. She might do a bit of digging and see if he had been caught and sent down. That would be something for Eliza.

And as to Donna Lambit and Michael Walker, how on earth had things untangled the way they had? There was no doubt that Joshua Yates had been quoting May's diary when he'd spouted his poison about Michael Walker, but how had Donna come to make such a catastrophic error?

'When you went to see May that last time, you told me she read from the diary. Did she read all of those bits?'

'She couldn't see well enough to read it, but she knew it by heart. I tried to shush her, but she would go on. She wanted to make me promise to burn the papers. Well, of course, I said I would. My handwriting was in that box. I should have done it straight away. I should never have left it, but I put it off. Things drift. They were locked away in the attaché case. Safe enough, I thought. Then one thing led to another and I ended up in here. Oh, they're all right in here, but your life's not your own. What are you going to do with them? You promised me, you know.'

Annie considered. Logically, she should take the papers away with her, use them to show that Yates had his story upside down, that Michael Walker was innocent of all allegations. And yet, no one was saying any differently apart from Brittany Booth and Donna Lambit. Annie would face both women with the truth and they would have to swallow it. She could see in Eliza's face how much it would mean to her to have the old secret gone forever.

'I'll burn them like I said I would. But this is what I've been after: it was Digby's crimes that were quoted in court.'

Eliza looked up sharply. 'What do you mean?'

So Annie told her everything. About Michael's murder, Yates's allegations, about Nicole and Brittany.

'The puzzle remains,' she ended, 'why May wanted to leave the box to Donna's daughter.'

'But are you sure she did? Her mind was going.'

'May's daughter, Susan, confirmed it. She remembered her mother being insistent about it.'

'What was this woman's daughter called?'

'Charlotte.'

'Oh.'

Annie looked sharply across at the tone of the exclamation. Eliza sat immobile, her hands clasping the chair arms as though to make herself rise up. Her face, pale at the best of times, was translucent with shock. Annie felt a bolt of fear that she would witness Eliza's death right this moment.

'What? What is it?' she found herself whispering, and repeated the words louder so Eliza could hear.

'Charlotte,' said Eliza, her voice barely a whisper. 'After all these years I'd forgotten about Charlotte.'

'Who was she?'

'May was getting old at fifteen. He was looking for a new girl to take her place. Charlotte was new to the church. A youngster. From a family of toffs. I didn't like her, stuck up little madam and younger than all of us. But May took to this newcomer like anything. Wanted to take her under her wing, you know, look after her. But the little madam wouldn't look twice at the likes of us. I doubt she had a thought for May, but May looked out for her just the same.'

'And Digby was grooming Charlotte to take May's place?'

'Is that what you call it? I think that's when May started on her plan. She'd stand it for herself, but she wasn't going to see young Charlotte go the same way.'

'What happened?'

Eliza tipped her head in a don't-know gesture. 'I've neither seen nor heard a word of Charlotte since I walked out of that church and swore never to go back.'

'Did May still keep an eye out for her?'

'No, we none of us had anything to do with any of them again. We never spoke his name, nor hers. Not until that day I visited May and took the papers away. I don't recall that she mentioned Mr Digby by name, even then, but she talked about Charlotte. She'd never forgotten.'

Annie sat back. It wasn't quite a complete story yet, but it appeared to be the link between May Gow and Donna's daughter. She looked across at Eliza. 'Do you want a drink?'

Eliza shrugged neither a yes nor a no, so Annie reached for her cup and tipped the brandy bottle.

'Not so much,' Eliza rapped out. 'I don't want to be drunk. And I'll have water with it.'

CHAPTER TWENTY SEVEN

That evening, Annie strolled down to the Whalebone. It was quiet, too early for the Sunday regulars. The city's history adorned the yellowed walls; Hull's glory days on the rugby field, past triumphs more numerous than recent ones, faced her. She knew without turning that men in the sturdy oilskins that bespoke life aboard the whalers looked down on her from behind. For decades, the fabric of this room had been steeped in the fog of a thousand cigars, pipes and cigarettes. She imagined William Digby, stinking of stale tobacco, coming in here, an oily obsequious presence in amongst the men who sent their daughters to his Sunday-school. A group of people came in chatting and threaded their way to the bar, but what Annie saw in front of her were scenes that had played out elsewhere. Scott and Kate could have brushed past and she wouldn't have noticed.

The real scenario had been the one that had occurred to her right at the start. Joshua Yates had simply been wrong. The evidence was plain. Annie had stayed with Eliza until the whole story was out. Yates had been hugely wrong. He'd targeted Michael Walker for crimes committed by a stranger six decades ago. A man... a monster... called William Digby.

There was no link. May's path had never crossed Michael Walker's, nor his family's. Yates had taken Donna's word and never checked. Donna had jumped to conclusions because she was already boiling with resentment against her daughter's partner. She'd heard references to what was being planned for Charlotte and made the absurd assumption May and Eliza were talking about her daughter.

Annie knew now how circumstances had come together to pander to Donna's prejudices. It was something she must spell out when she reported back to Nicole, but not to Brittany. She would not hand Brittany another cause to latch on to. It was a relief that she could report back to Nicole and not Charlotte, who was bound to be devastated to learn how needlessly her man had died.

As to Brittany Booth, Annie couldn't guess which way she would take the news. Would she break down, upset? Would she bluster and refuse to believe it?

If she were to meet incredulity, the evidence in the old diaries would have been a useful persuader. It would have been easy to take the incriminating pages either behind Eliza's back or openly. What would Eliza have done? She couldn't demand help from the carers without drawing attention to the secrets she wanted to hide. Indeed, she couldn't call for help at all until Annie returned her alarm.

But Annie hadn't kept anything. It wasn't her place to throw a spotlight on a dead woman's secret shame. She felt sadness that May had seen it that way her whole life. Eliza, too, but there was nothing she could do to change that. The fact was that the tiny wave of interest Brittany Booth had generated had begun to wane almost before Annie took on either side of this case. No one had ever taken Yates's accusations seriously; nor Brittany Booth's. Yates would be sentenced next week. Brittany would start a new life without him if she had an ounce of sense. Nicole and Charlotte would get their business up and running. Donna must live with what she'd done.

Everyone had childhood secrets, Annie supposed. It was up to them to bring them to light, not other people, not without far better reason than she had found.

Donna had always been blinded by her prejudice. At a stretch, Annie could see where she'd snatched at this chance to discredit her precious daughter's lover. But how on earth had Yates listened to the words quoted to him and not questioned their provenance?

In the end, Annie had given the specific sheets back to Eliza, because otherwise Eliza would never know for sure whether Annie had destroyed them or not. There were nine in all, the pages on which May had written the detail of the abuse she'd suffered.

Much of what May had written had been beyond her comprehension. Her style, abbreviated and mired in misunderstanding, made her descriptions more horrific than if she'd had the insight and vocabulary to be graphic.

Once she had the whole story and understood Donna's part in it, she had looked out the pages and handed them to Eliza.

'Are these all of them? There are nine.'

Eliza had clutched her bent fingers round them and flicked through one by one, counting.

'My glass is in the pocket of the chair.'

Annie had handed across the magnifying glass and Eliza had scrutinized each page.

'Give me the one with the plan.'

Annie searched out the page where Digby was scripted to co-operate in his own killing and scanned swiftly across the words as she handed it across.

We five arrive... the red crested vase... now for the books... her turn with the pen... we five return in good time for supper.

Then she moved the wheelchair close to the wire basket, and left it to Eliza to reach out with her shaky hands to drop in each of the last ten pages.

After the last one had fallen into the flames, Annie had retrieved the brandy bottle. 'There's enough left for one each.'

Eliza had squinted at the fire for a long time before finally saying, 'Yes, and I'll have a cigar, but douse that fire first. It's all burnt, isn't it? The smoke's getting on my chest.'

Annie had pulled the bag towards her and splashed water from the bottle carefully on to the red embers.

The ice in the flask had been watery, but with a few lumps still intact. Annie had scooped them out into Eliza's cup and splashed brandy on top. The old woman sat back in her wheelchair and drew deeply on the cigar. She'd coughed, but it had been with a contented smile she'd raised the cup to her lips.

Sitting here now in the pub with the bustle of evening life beginning to grow and the history of the old whaling industry looking down from the walls, Annie wondered if she'd been right to carry out Eliza's wishes. Almost a century ago, May's father might have sat where she sat now. Eliza's too. Their faces could be amongst those smiling out from the old photographs. She could almost hear the shouts and commotion of the whalers docking just across the way; feel the jostling crowd and bonhomie of the men bringing in a boat with a good catch; the tight-knit jawbone gang celebrating its safe homecoming with a glass of ale at the Whalebone, then breaking up to stride home to waiting families.

Something about the weight of the secret had got to her. May had carried it all her life, finding Eliza again at almost the final hour. What had made Eliza hold on to the papers, beyond her vague mention of 'not getting round to it'? Whatever it was, Eliza must have been tormented by thoughts she would go to her grave and leave it for others to find.

Annie thought back to how she'd moved about, clearing the remains of the fire, putting things back in the bag, carrying out a makeshift repair to the chain that held the alarm, knowing that as far as Eliza was concerned at that point, she wasn't even there. She recalled the look on Eliza's face as she'd savoured the good brandy and pulled in the smoke from the cigar. It had been contentment: a woman relaxing into the comfort of a promise fulfilled.

Too late for regrets, though she wasn't sure she had any. The papers were fragments of ash melting into the fabric of that big garden.

Just one thing she would like to confirm. She pulled out her phone and clicked in Donna's number.

'Sorry to call so late,' she said, with no attempt to inject sincerity into her apology. 'I want you to tell me what happened when you told May you had to have her locked box.'

She listened to Donna's attempt to bluster, but cut her short.

'Oh yes, you can remember. Now, listen to me carefully. You were alone with May in the house; you'd searched for the box and it was gone.' Annie hardened her tone. 'I have no doubt you threatened her, Mrs Lambit, but right now I don't care about that. What I want to know is what May said back to you. Her exact words.'

The phone remained silent, but Annie knew Donna wouldn't cut her off. After a moment, she heard a throat-clearing and then the answer to her question. 'She said, "The box is for Charlotte."'

'And those were her exact words? You're absolutely sure? Repeat the conversation to me.'

Annie felt the fear leak down the phone as Donna's assurances tumbled out. But she didn't need them. She was satisfied Donna had told her the truth.

She ended the call, allowed herself a deep sigh that was a mix of exasperation and anger, then she stood up and tipped the remains of her beer down her throat.

As she left the pub, she cradled her phone in her hand. Ron Long was due a call too, though she had still to work out what line to take. To force herself into a decision, she rang him. The call was answered at once.

'At last! What have you got for me?'

'Come to the office on Monday morning. Ten-ish. I can't talk now.'

'We'll be there, but just tell me—'

She clicked the phone off with a sudden stab of annoyance that wasn't aimed at Ron Long but at herself. The blasted horse woman needed a call too, but this was the worst time to try. She would almost certainly be in. The minute she arrived home, Annie determined to red-pin that letter to the cork board.

CHAPTER TWENTY EIGHT

The next morning, Annie climbed the stairs to the office, turning over in her mind what line to take with Ron Long. Either she disrupted his plans to come to the area, or she reported him officially. The latter went against the grain, not quite malpractice, but not the way to operate, a bit like the tightrope of running with both Nicole Perks and Brittany Booth.

Barbara was at the desk, her face screwed up in concentration as she peered at the screen in front of her and pecked at the keyboard. She paused to give Annie a hard stare. Then, jerking her thumb over her shoulder indicating the back office, she said, 'Visitor for you.'

'The Longs? They're not due for an hour.'

'No, the law.'

Puzzled, Annie pushed open the door to the back room to see Scott, oblivious to her presence, rapt in some paperwork on top of one of the filing cabinets. He jumped round as she spoke his name. Her gaze darted across to see what he'd been reading. Trust Barbara to leave him in here unattended.

She relaxed a little when she saw he'd been engrossed in an article in *PI Magazine*. It would embarrass him to be caught reading that.

He wore jeans, so it wasn't an official call.

She looked him over. He was nice enough and they'd had some fun over the years, but how much better if he'd never been more than a useful work contact? Too late for those sorts of thoughts.

'What can I do for you?'

'Annie, we have to get things straight between us.'

For a second, Annie felt irritation that he should think her the one needing to get things straight. Then it dawned on her. 'Let me guess,' she said. 'You've been told to choose between me and Kate. And you've come to tell me you've chosen Kate.'

'Kate and I had a long talk.' Scott's tone was snappish. It had been tactless to imply he was under orders.

'Scott, this really isn't a problem. We gave each other up a long time ago. What happened the other night was just... well, we should probably avoid being alone together when we've been drinking. But it didn't mean anything. You know it didn't. I hope it works out for you and Kate. I really do.'

'We've worked together well over the years, Annie. I don't want to give that up.'

'I don't have a problem with keeping it on a professional basis, but are you sure Kate can live with that?'

His gaze flicked away, and Annie assumed he'd had an earful about discussing Kate with her. She pointed to the article he'd been reading when she came in; an interview with an investigator who'd relocated from London to New Jersey. 'Interesting ideas there. What did you think?'

She saw him waver on the edge of pretending not to know what she was talking about, but then he shrugged and said, 'Have you ever thought of working in the US?'

'It would be a whole different ball game.' She almost confided that she was leaving Pat and Barbara, leaving the area, just as soon as she'd tied a few loose ends. How much easier would that make things for him with Kate? But it was the thought of Kate that stopped her. She could trust Scott not to say anything to the sisters, but he would tell Kate, and Annie didn't trust Kate not to come hotfoot to the office to make things as uncomfortable as she possibly could.

Annie wondered what else he'd come to say, but knew better than to ask outright. They chatted for a while, going over old ground, safe ground. Theories of how and when state investigation should interact with private... the differing perceptions of each profession in different countries.

Scott glanced at his watch. 'I should be going.'

As Annie moved towards the door, he added, 'Just one other thing.'

She turned back to hear what he'd really come for.

'You know, what we came to ask about the other day. Guy new in the area... rumoured to have gone to a private investigator?'

Ah, so that was it. He'd come to try a softly-softly approach to counter Kate's bulldozer tactics. 'What would this guy have gone to a PI for?' she asked him.

'Sorry, I don't know. Probably nothing to interest us. It's him we're looking for.'

'Do you have a name?'

'No. We have very little to suggest he exists at all, but...'

Annie heard the sentence fade. It was too soon to hand him Ron Long, and all she had was speculation. It wasn't her business. She needed to know more.

'Do you mean new to the area and here to stay, or just on a flying visit?'

Scott watched her closely now. 'Oh, if he's for real, then it's a flying visit.'

'OK, so what would happen if – just for sake of argument – the person who might not exist just faded away as though he really didn't exist? What would be the effect of that?'

Scott spoke slowly. Annie could feel the intensity of his gaze. 'That would be useful. Very useful. It would drive a coach and horses through certain other parties' plans.'

'Thanks. I'll keep all that in mind.'

'Annie, listen, do you know anything that I should know?'

The Longs had first come to her just ten days ago, with their absurd tale of checking out a holiday home, and desperate to stay below the official radar. She had nothing on them, just an instinctive certainty that they were the ones Scott was after.

She thought of Yates with his sharpened knife and his certainty about Michael Walker.

Looking Scott in the eye, she said, 'Not yet.'

The Longs were due within the hour. She needed the time between now and when they arrived to get some paperwork ready. Scott had crystallized in her mind what her strategy would be. Would she need him? It depended on how Ron Long reacted.

'If I'm going to have anything for you,' she told Scott. 'It's going to be soon.' She looked him up and down. Trainers, jeans, T-shirt, casual jacket. He wasn't on his way to work. 'Which might mean within the hour, but you're not on duty.'

'I'll be around if you need me.'

CHAPTER TWENTY NINE

After Scott had left, Annie settled herself in the big office at one of the PCs. She and Barbara ignored each other as they clicked at their keyboards. Annie assumed Barbara was working on the Mellors' case, and if she couldn't make something big out of the information she'd had on a plate last Friday, there was no hope for her.

She turned her mind to her own case as she pulled up on the screen the thumbnails of the photographs she'd taken at the Morgans' and picked out the ones she wanted. They didn't need much work. She didn't bother with Photoshop, just clicked on the crop tool and trimmed the edges, making sure that the set she readied for printing showed the bits she wanted them to show and nothing else.

Barbara left after half an hour. They hadn't spoken since the brief exchange when Annie arrived.

The Longs turned up ten minutes early, but Annie was ready. 'Hello. Come in. Take a seat.'

Sheryl looked drawn and tired; Ron irritable. He wanted Annie's verdict so he could get on with his plans. Neither of them doubted that Annie would say what Ron wanted to hear. She waited until they were settled in their chairs.

'You need a change of plan,' she said to Ron. 'Your wife was nearer the mark than you realized.'

Ron laughed; his tone a mix of incredulity and uncertainty. 'What are you talking about, change of plan?'

'You need to holiday somewhere else.'

'Oh thank God! Ron, listen to her. I knew—'

'Shut up,' he barked at his wife. Then to Annie, 'What are you talking about? Are you mad?'

Annie slipped a photograph across the desk. 'Does that look familiar?'

'Yes!' Sheryl pounced on it. 'Look, Ron. That's the wheelbarrow we saw. It is, isn't it, Ron? You can't deny it.'

'I'm not denying it,' he snapped, throwing a glance at the photograph that showed the lower half of the barrow: wheels, handles, enough of the tray to show its battered paintwork. 'I'm not changing my plans for a goddamned wheelbarrow.' He glared at Annie. 'All right, what was in it?'

Annie pushed the next photograph across.

Sheryl gasped in a breath and clapped her hand to her mouth. Even Ron blanched and drew back.

She had cut away the part of the picture that showed the crumbling limbs and gave clues to the great age of the remains. The gash to the back of skull caused by Tracey Morgan's shovel gaped up starkly from the print.

'But what...? How...?'

'Don't worry. I've done all I need to do. No one can have a peaceful holiday in an area crawling with police and forensics teams.' The words themselves, if analysed as separate sentences, weren't quite a lie. The implication behind them was. She saw Ron Long draw the inference she intended.

'But this will ruin everything,' he blurted out.

'Ruin what?' asked Annie. 'You can holiday somewhere else.'

'No, you see—'

'Shut up, Sheryl.'

As the Longs glared at each other, Annie, her phone held below the level of the desk, sent a text to Scott.

Arrive now, routine visit.

'This is all your doing, Sheryl,' Ron scolded his wife. 'If you hadn't made such a fuss and insisted we come here...'

'That's not fair, Ron. We could have been murdered in our beds.'

Ron swung round to Annie. 'Are you saying those people committed murder? But why? Who are they? Who did they kill?'

'I'm afraid I can't say.'

'Dammit, woman, I've paid you to say. I want a full report on this job.'

'You wanted to know if your wife's fears were groundless or not. I'm afraid we made no commitment to divulge any further information.'

'I suppose it's more money you're after.' He heaved an exaggerated sigh and reached for the pocket inside his jacket.

Annie allowed her expression to become a little more steely. 'You realize that if one of our cases becomes a police investigation, we have to back off. More than that, they expect us to hand over our files.'

Ron held her gaze, his expression unchanging, but in her peripheral vision Annie saw Sheryl's eyes widen in alarm.

'And do you?' Ron said.

Annie heard the click of the outer door downstairs. Perfect timing. She answered Ron Long. 'Not always. Not everything.'

Footsteps sounded up the stairs, but not Scott's. And that quick, light tread certainly wasn't one of the sisters.

The door opened and Kate Ronsen walked in.

Annie's heart sank. She struggled not to show her feelings. Oh, Scott, she thought, did you have to use this one to prove yourself to her? Kate would go in heavy handed for sure. For a moment Annie considered just handing her the Longs on a plate. After all, what did she care? She was out of here soon anyway.

But she did care. It was important to deal with things properly. She had no option but to play the situation just as she would if it were Scott who had walked in.

She smiled up at Kate. 'DC Ronsen, this is a surprise. I wasn't expecting you.'

'Routine visit,' Kate rapped out, as her gaze flicked briefly to Sheryl's nails, then snapped across to look Ron Long up and down. Annie felt her fists clench as she willed Kate to get it right. Kate's eyes narrowed with suspicion, but she said, 'If you're busy, I can wait.'

Annie blew out a breath. Scott had rehearsed her in her lines.

'Oh, is it the prison thing?' she responded, with a smile. 'I think we were about finished here.' She looked Ron in the eye. 'Did you want to make an appointment to come back?'

Neither Ron nor Sheryl moved, but the tension was palpable. After a pause, he said, 'I don't think there's anything you can do for us. Come on... it's time we were on our way.'

Annie clocked the slight trip in his words where he avoided calling Sheryl by name.

'Then I won't open a file,' she said. 'And that'll be the end of it.'

She opened the door for them to hurry out, and watched as they clattered down the stairs, her gaze tracking Sheryl's fingers down the handrail. Too memorable, Sheryl, she wanted to shout after her. It's the little things that catch people out in the end. She returned to the office.

Relieved of the presence of the Longs, Annie looked at Kate properly. She wore a severe red suit, dressed for battle, but then she had stuck to the script, however little she'd enjoyed doing it.

'Thanks,' Annie said. 'I'm sure that's the last either of us will see of them.'

'But who were they? What did they want with you? Where's your file? How much do you have on them?'

Completely off script now, but Annie had allowed for this in her parting shot to the Longs.

'You heard me. I said I wouldn't open a file. We don't until the punter signs up. We can't do business unless we're sure of paying customers. It's not like being in your game.' Again, Annie formed sentences that could stand alone as the absolute truth. Not her fault if Kate put them together and assumed this was the Longs' first visit.

'But you got their names?'

'If people don't volunteer stuff about themselves, we don't insist on it, not until we sign them up.'

'Then how are we to find them? I should have arrested him while he was here.'

'What for? What's he involved in?'

'That's not your business. But thanks to you, he's still going to cause us trouble.'

'Is he? All I know is that you don't want this guy in the area, so I've made sure he isn't going to stay. I'm not here to package people up and hand them over. That's not my job. How much business do you think we'd get if we worked like that? I have no evidence he's involved in criminal activity.'

'We have!'

'Then maybe you should have arrested him.'

Kate gave an annoyed shake of her head and Annie knew she didn't have a thing on Ron Long. From the bits and pieces she'd gleaned from Scott and Jen, she surmised that Ron was a key part of someone's plan, presumably to do with this high profile gaolbreak she'd heard about, but he'd done nothing yet. Hell, they didn't even know who he was. Until now, they hadn't been certain he existed. But with her hints about police crawling all over the area that he was so interested in, he would be off. If she were to put money on his whereabouts at this moment, she would guess him and his wife to be in their van westbound along the Clive Sullivan Way heading for the M62.

Annie didn't want to antagonize Kate, but Kate seemed determined to be antagonized by Annie. There was nothing she could do about that. She took in a breath.

'Thank you for turning up so promptly,' she said, holding out her hand. 'I'm sure it's for the best. Whoever he is, he's on his way and he won't be back.'

Kate looked surprised, but after a moment she reached out to share a brief handshake with Annie. Another pause, but whatever Kate had been going to say, she thought better of it. With a curt nod, she turned and left.

Annie smiled and pulled the Longs' file from the desk drawer. Case closed. Good result. As she went to file the papers, she visualized Kate's battle dress. It had been a very bright shade of red.

'Ha!' Just the same red as the red pin on her cork board at home, currently pinning the letter from the blasted horse women. Now was as good a time as any. She looked out the number and picked up the phone. As she listened to the ring tone, a door slammed and the stairs creaked their protest at the heavy tread that began to ascend.

With a rush of relief, Annie heard the answer phone cut in. 'Hi, Annie Raymond here. About the show on Saturday. No way I can get out to you. Hope it won't cause a problem. I've had a new case come in. Bye.'

Annie sat back with the feeling of a good job done, as the door opened and Barbara came in.

'Oh, so you got the message, did you?' she shot at Annie. 'It's a new case, is it? She said she just wanted to talk to you.'

'What message? Who wants to talk to me? I was just making excuses to get out of something.'

'Oh... well. That weird woman called for you. The one working for the insurance fraud people. We were going to tell you when you'd done with your clients. The one with the gender-change name. Richard-Louise... Thomas-Martha... I can't remember. Something like that.'

Surprise opened Annie's eyes wide. So Pieternel had been in touch and the sisters had kept it from her. 'You know full well it's not that,' she snapped at Barbara. 'It's a perfectly ordinary name, just not a very common one.'

'Oh, don't get your knickers in such a twist. What's it to you, anyway?'

'You can be so bloody parochial at times.'

Barbara just laughed and turned to the desk. Annie glared at her back, but only out of habit. There was something far more interesting on the table than squabbling with Barbara.

'What did she want?'

'She wanted to talk to you, but she said it wasn't important.'

'Did you get a number?'

Barbara shook her head without turning round. Annie thought back over the past couple of weeks. She remembered the feel of a conversation cut off abruptly as she'd walked in on them. And the times just recently when Pat had been at the edge of telling her something. How long had Pieternel been trying to get in touch? No point in asking. She would look out the contact details later and ring back when neither of the sisters was about.

She slung her jacket over her shoulder and headed for the door.

'I won't be long,' she said, neither expecting nor waiting for a response.

CHAPTER THIRTY

The street was uncharacteristically busy. A background rumble of conversation hung in the air with the tang of unburnt diesel. Annie found it hard to get a rhythm into her stride. Walking fast was a way to clear her head, to see the way through a tricky situation, but she didn't want to dwell on Pieternel's call, or that the sisters had hidden it from her. Her priority was clear. Wrap up her cases and get ready to leave.

The Michael Walker case was at the point she'd always known she'd reach. Good news for one side; bad for the other. All she need do was get it over. Ring them, have them in one by one, tell them, and write it up for the records.

Who was she kidding? This needed thought. She had to report back to two women, at least one of whom would fight to disbelieve her. She couldn't make bad news into good, but part of her role was to convince clients who didn't get what they wanted, that they'd had a good job done, nonetheless.

She rehearsed conversations in her head; felt her way around the awkward edges of the story she had to tell. At the same time, she felt the tug of new ideas, new ventures.

She bought a cheese and tomato sandwich from the shop at the corner and walked back chewing on it as she rehearsed what to say to Nicole and Brittany; made guesses at how they would react. Nicole would be the easier interview for sure. She'd do her first as a practice run.

The office lay empty, but Barbara's things cluttered the desk top, so Annie knew she hadn't gone far. She reached for the phone and tapped in Nicole's number.

'Can you come in at two o'clock today?' Annie said. 'I'm ready to report back on your case.'

'Oh my God! It's bad news. I can hear it in your voice.'

'No, Nicole. It's actually good news.'

'It's not that good, is it?' Nicole's tone was flat. 'It won't bring Michael back. Yes, I'll come in.'

After she ended the call, Annie flicked through the file for Brittany Booth's number, and took in a deep breath before picking up the phone again. Quarter of an hour would be ample to close things with Nicole.

She had expected the call to Nicole to buoy her up, but for a moment had forgotten the reality that Michael Walker had been a real person, a friend to Nicole. And suddenly she couldn't face Brittany Booth's arrogant bluster.

She returned the phone to its base unit, her call unmade, and turned to the PC where she typed out an e-mail to Brittany.

> *I'm ready to report back on your case. If it's convenient, could you come in at three o'clock.*

She paused, wondering if she could put Brittany off to another day. She felt exhausted just at the thought of the high stress, high maintenance discussion she would have to have, with Brittany talking through her, raising her voice, challenging every point. But no, the best thing was to get it all over with.

> *If that's not convenient,* she ended the e-mail, *ring the office to arrange an alternative time.*

Annie put her head round the door and heard the murmur of voices from downstairs. It sounded like Barbara was down there for a gossip. She should wait until both sisters were well away from the office, but was impatient to know what Pieternel had wanted, so went back and picked up the phone.

A man's voice answered and, when she asked for Pieternel, he said, 'Sorry, she hasn't worked here for months.'

'Do you have a number I can get her on?'

'Sorry, no.'

Annie ended the call and sat back. There was nothing she

could do but wait and hope Pieternel would ring again.

The door buzzer sounded bang on time for Nicole's appointment. Annie clicked the phone to silent as she listened to the guy downstairs let her in.

'Visitors for upstairs,' he shouted.

Visitors, plural? Annie went to the head of the stairs to see Nicole and Jennifer on their way up. Jennifer was in civvies; in the garish, too fussy clothes she wore out of uniform.

'Nicole asked me to sit in with her. Is that OK?'

'Sure.' Annie pulled forward an extra chair.

'Before I start,' Annie said, 'I have to tell you that I don't have any tangible evidence; nothing you can take away and give to the Press or anything like that. But I said I'd get the truth and I have. I know the whole story now and I know Michael was wrongly targeted. Joshua Yates went for the wrong man.'

'But we knew that!' wailed Nicole.

'Is there a right man?' Jennifer broke in. 'Have you handed on what you know? It'll be a police matter now.'

'There is, but he's dead,' said Annie. 'He died a long time ago.' She injected confidence into her tone, but at the same time wondered if the man who had abused May could still be alive. She'd never checked, but he must have been at least ten years older than May, probably more. She kept any hint of doubt out of her voice as she went on. 'You know that Charlotte's mother works as a carer. Well, one of her clients had witnessed the abuse, the things Yates talked about in court, when she was a small child. Donna overheard her talking about it with one of her old friends and managed to jump to the conclusion it was Michael they were talking about.'

'But it can't just be that – an overheard conversation. Surely she wouldn't have acted just on that?'

'It got complicated. There was someone called Charlotte involved.'

Annie went through the story of May's diary; of how Donna had overheard May reading to a friend from it. She avoided mentioning Eliza's name, or letting slip that Eliza was still alive and lived nearby. She didn't mention Digby's name either. There was a story here that the Press could make a lot of, and it would get back to Eliza. The diaries were gone. The secret mustn't come out another way, so she made sure the version she told Nicole had insufficient substance for her to use it elsewhere.

Nicole, who needed no convincing about Michael Walker's innocence, didn't press for hard evidence. Brittany Booth would be a different challenge.

'Donna unlocked the memory,' she told them, 'by telling May she had to have the box for Charlotte's sake. May's mind was going, but she'd kept that box all those years for a different Charlotte. May must have been frightened, but Donna couldn't move her. The thing is, she didn't know where the box was at that point. Whether she'd managed to hide it herself and forgotten, or if she'd had someone else do it for her, I don't know. In the end, Donna settled for getting her agreement that the box would come to her when May died.'

Annie saw that Jennifer's mind was at work and wondered if she might follow up with the care agency. Probably not. Susan Gow had never made her complaint official. She told them what Donna had finally said about her conversations with May Gow.

'It was at that point that May said, "the box is for Charlotte". That had Donna adding two and two and getting five, so she asked May straight out if the box would come to her, and May said, "Yes, we must protect Charlotte at all costs". Those were her words.'

'But the old woman's mind was going,' Nicole said. 'Why would Donna take something like that on trust?'

'She's a fool. And she was so obsessed with breaking up Charlotte and Michael. Then May told her daughter, Susan Gow, that the box was for Charlotte.'

'But didn't they enquire to see if that was the Charlotte she meant? They knew she'd never met her.'

'Yes, they did, but there was no other Charlotte in May's life. She never talked to anyone about the one she'd known as a child.'

Annie thought back to the papers she'd burned; to the story Eliza had told her. May and her gang had almost certainly abandoned the young Charlotte to Digby's clutches whatever they'd tried to convince themselves about the effect of their walking away. They couldn't be blamed. They'd been in impossible circumstances. But Annie would bet that May had blamed herself all her life.

'So it wasn't ever meant to concern Charlotte Liversedge,' she said, 'but because May was insistent it was for Charlotte, and because she'd never spoken of what had happened when she was a child, everyone assumed she must mean Donna's daughter.'

Nicole sat ashen-faced as this sank in. 'It was all for nothing,' she whispered. 'He's dead because that insane idiot believed some nonsensical gossip.'

Annie nodded. She'd known from the start this was a case that would never lead to happy clients on both sides. But this outcome, in which she'd felt the professional satisfaction of being right, meant no one on either side would be happy.

Nicole looked down as though trying to digest Annie's account. Jennifer laid her hand on her friend's arm. Annie wasn't sure what else she should say; maybe nothing. She listened to the sounds of someone being let in downstairs; heard the usual call, 'Visitor', and registered footsteps pattering lightly upwards.

A second too late, her mind made the match and she leapt to her feet to divert the caller, but, as she did so, the office door opened and Brittany Booth walked in.

Annie saw Nicole glance up at the intrusion, her expression forlorn, uninterested. Then she saw realization dawn.

Nicole was on her feet, her face blotched and angry. 'You cow! You stupid murdering cow!' she screeched, leaping at Brittany. 'It wasn't him. It wasn't ever him!'

Totally unprepared for the attack, Brittany backed off, hitting a shelf, sending a cascade of pens and paperclips clattering to the floor.

'No, Nicole.' Jennifer leapt up and grabbed her now sobbing friend before Annie could reach her. 'Come on. We'll go. Any paperwork that needs sorting can be done later, OK?'

She glanced at Annie who gave her confirmation in a brief

nod, wanting more than anything to have Nicole out of the office before Brittany had recovered enough to realize who she was or the implication of what she was saying. This was not the way for Brittany to hear the result of the case.

Annie helped ease Nicole out on to the landing, mouthing, 'Thanks, speak later', to Jennifer.

Stepping back into the office, she clicked the door closed behind her and snapped at Brittany, 'You're early.'

Brittany, visibly shaken by Nicole's outburst, snapped back, 'So? He told me to come upstairs. It wouldn't matter if you had a proper office with a waiting room.'

Behind the belligerence was a hint of tears, and Annie relented. 'Sit down. I'm sorry about that. Do you want a drink?'

Brittany shook her head to the drink but sat in the chair Annie indicated. 'I just want to know what you've—' She clapped her hand to her mouth and stared up at Annie. 'Who was that woman? What was she saying?'

No option now but to dish out the tale ungarnished. 'She was a friend of Michael Walker. I'm afraid Joshua didn't bother to check his facts. He listened to an allegation from someone who had a grudge, and he believed it.'

Brittany gaped up at her, and Annie realized that Nicole's outburst had saved her a lot of time. Its raw emotion unmistakable, it had taken Brittany away from the angry disbelief that Annie was sure would have been her first reaction.

'But no, that can't be... No, I won't believe it.' Brittany tried for indignation but her voice was swamped in uncertainty. 'He told me he knew for certain... that it was absolutely certain... that there just wasn't the proof.'

'Vigilantes always say that, Brittany, because it's a lot to live with to face the fact they got it wrong.'

Brittany jumped to her feet and shouted, 'You think he's mad!'

Annie remained seated, and kept her tone neutral. 'Who am I to judge? I've never met him.'

'You think he's mad though, don't you? You think the same as they're all saying about him. You've never given him a chance.'

She fired the words as though at random, needing to stay in control while control leaked away. When Annie didn't answer, she repeated, 'Admit it. You think he's mad.'

'If I do,' said Annie, 'I'm not the only one.'

Brittany looked away, clasping her hands together. 'I know what you're saying. If he's insane, I am, too. He's wrecked my life.' She swung round to face Annie again. 'Is that what you're saying? Do you think I'm mad?'

'Of course not,' said Annie, though looking into Brittany's eyes, she was nowhere near as sure as she tried to sound. 'Be thankful you're free to walk away. Forget about him. Go and get on with your life.'

Brittany gaped down, utterly deflated, with nothing left to say. Slowly she shook her head and half opened her mouth, but no words came out. Annie realized that more by luck than good judgement, it was over. Short, sharp and painful for Brittany, but the job was done.

'Right then.' She took on a blunt no-nonsense tone, talking Brittany through the loose ends of the paperwork that would conclude the job, leaving her no opening to mount any rearguard action in support of Yates.

In a few minutes, they were done. Annie put out her hand as she said goodbye, and Brittany took it in a limp handshake as though unaware of what she was doing. Then she aimed a fierce glare at Annie, went as though to speak, but thought better of it, turned on her heel and left.

Annie stood by the door and watched as Brittany went back down the stairs, half convinced she would change her mind and come clattering back up again to harangue her about Yates. Maybe the facts, pushed in Brittany's face, had unlocked something she'd known deep within herself, something that had been glaringly obvious to the wider world all along. She would come to be thankful for her escape. But for Annie, in the end, wrapping up this case had almost been too easy.

Once sure Brittany had gone, she turned the phone back on. Its voice mail light flashed at her.

'Got your message,' yelled a robust voice, making Annie jerk the handset away from her ear. 'Shame. The kids were looking forward to showing off their ponies to you. I'll line up a stand-in judge for you, but turn up if you can.'

Annie hit the delete button.

Half an hour later, she was tidying the last of her paperwork when she heard the downstairs door followed by creaks and groans as the fabric of the building matched the grunts of effort of the person climbing the stairs.

She smiled and went to pour a fresh cup of coffee.

'Thanks, kid.' Pat took the coffee from her and sank into a chair.

'So, what's new?' Annie asked. 'You doing anything in particular at the moment?'

'No, I just popped in to sort stuff for tomorrow. Why, what do you want?' Pat spoke with a hint of wariness that Annie read as preparing her defence if challenged about hiding Pieternel's call.

'I've wrapped up a few cases. I just wanted to run them by you.'

Annie saw Pat relax, and then told her about the Longs, about the suspicions she couldn't ground, and about her text to Scott that had brought Kate to the office.

'There's a turn up,' said Pat. 'Is young Ronsen going to toe the line from now on, then?'

'I wouldn't go that far, but it's a step in the right direction.'

'You said a few cases. What else?'

'The vigilante murder. The innocent victim really was innocent. Yates heard half a story and didn't bother to check.'

'Standard vigilante stuff then.'

Annie nodded. 'Yates is clearly off his head. With luck they'll put him away forever.'

'What was the real story? How did it happen?'

Annie told Pat about May and Susan Gow, the eightieth birthday party and the locked box, Eliza Ellis and the hidden diaries. She detailed her visits to the home, taking care to mention at one stage that, 'Eliza insisted on good brandy.

Nothing else would do, and without it she wasn't going to give me anything.'

Pat's eyes narrowed, as though recognizing an expenses claim defended in advance, but she didn't comment so Annie went on with the story.

When she came to burning the diaries, Pat's eyes opened wide. 'You destroyed the evidence? Well, you've been lucky if the clients have accepted your version without it. What on earth made you do that? That story should have been out in the open, for Michael Walker's sake if nothing else.'

'I thought about it, of course I did. But it would have been pointless. There was just enough to spark off a whole new round of gossip and speculation. That wouldn't have done anyone any good. Eliza was appalled at having to reveal May's childhood shame, that's the way she saw it. And without her to interpret and fill in the gaps it made no sense.'

'Well, she could have done that.'

'Not a chance.' Annie shook her head. 'The deal was that she would tell me once and that I'd see to it that no one could ever ask her to tell the story again.'

Pat raised her eyebrows, clearly not convinced, but letting it go. Then she sat forward and looked Annie in the eye. 'So, what else is bothering you?'

The question took Annie unawares. She said, 'Nothing, why?' but heard the defensiveness in her tone as she spoke.

'There is. I can tell. That blasted instinct of yours. What have you a feeling about now?'

'No, really, nothing like that.' Yet Pat was right. She was uncomfortable over the way the case had panned out. 'I guess I'm just peed off that a monster like Digby almost certainly lived his life out and never had to account for what he'd done. And an ordinary guy like Michael Walker gets to pay for his crimes. And I couldn't bring Digby to book even if he were still alive. It would be too much for Eliza.'

'Could he still be alive?'

'No... well... no, surely not. I've no idea what age he'd be now. To Eliza, he was just a grown-up... old. But, I wonder. Maybe I'll look him up. I'd like to know for sure.'

Pat smiled and heaved herself to her feet. 'You did a good job.'
This rare praise tugged at something inside Annie. Pat knew how good she was. It would be hard to cut the ties between them. They could work so well together. But she knew she must. She'd made her mind up and wasn't going to change it. The only question was when.

CHAPTER THIRTY ONE

That evening, Annie walked home briskly clearing her head of the day's clutter. The streets were quiet. The late sun reflected bursts of light from window panes and gave the road edges a sheen as though they had been painted in translucent silver. There was a lot to think about. Notice on the flat, the car to sell or scrap.

She walked into her flat and slung her bag over a chair, but had barely shaped her thoughts on what to do first... shower... coffee... eat... when someone knocked at her door. It had to be her upstairs neighbour. His excuse would be to have his flask back, but his real reason would be to share a hot drink and hear a dramatized account of how it had been used. Perfect company to wipe away the hassles of the day. She felt her mouth curve to a smile of greeting as she opened the door.

'Hello,' said Nicole Perks. 'Sorry to drop in unannounced. I wanted a word.'

Annie held on to her smile, but asked, 'How did you get in?'

'There was someone just coming out as I arrived.'

'Right.' Annie made a mental note that it was time for the core of sensible residents to go round all the flats and put the fear of God into the newcomers and more careless tenants. Their only robust line of defence was the stout outer door. None of the internal doors was properly secure. The cheap rents came at a price and the tenants had evolved strict rules about letting in strangers.

There was nothing to do other than usher Nicole in, but this would be a lesson to her, too, about being careless with clients.

A folder that Nicole shouldn't see was lying out in plain view on a chair.

'Take a seat,' she snapped, more tersely than she intended, as she snatched up the papers and took them to the drawer where they belonged.

As she bent forward to open the drawer, the red pin from the cork board almost speared into her eye.

'Oh, for fuck's sake!' She jerked back, aware that Nicole jumped at her outburst.

She yanked the pin free and shoved it on top of the board, then put the horse woman's letter along with the papers, back in the drawer. None of this was Nicole's fault. She shouldn't take it out on her. It was she, Annie, who had given out her address, who had left papers out that she thought she'd put away. And she, too, who had put that blasted red pin in at the wrong angle. That was something she hadn't done for years. She must have been more tired than she realized last night.

'Sorry,' she said to Nicole. 'Ignore me. I'm just annoyed with myself for putting that pin so low on the board. It nearly had my eye out. I'll make some coffee.'

'No, no. It's me who should apologize.' Nicole leapt to her feet and followed Annie to the kitchen. 'I shouldn't have stormed off like I did. You've done a great job. Michael's reputation is safe.'

'Oh right. Great. I mean... uh... I wasn't sure if anything had been said publicly.'

'No, there won't be any big public pronouncement. We talked it through, me and Charlotte. All it would do is stir up interest again. Brittany Booth has withdrawn her campaign and distanced herself from Yates.'

'Really?' This was welcome news to Annie who hadn't expected Brittany to concede so quickly.

'Yes, she came and apologized to me, said she was sorry for the hurt she'd caused.'

'Well, that's good,' said Annie, surprised. 'But why you? I mean, if she was going to apologize, why not to Charlotte?'

'It was me who hired you, not Charlotte.'

There was amusement behind Nicole's words that Annie had missed the obvious. Annie smiled in response, but said nothing. Brittany shouldn't have been able to trace Nicole, despite the explosive confrontation in the office. In the woman's first flush of rage, Annie could expect that she'd gone to Vince. But even Vince wouldn't give one client the name of another, would he? And he didn't know about Nicole anyway.

Then she realized: Kate Ronsen. The woman had been obsessed with raking up trouble for Annie. She'd told Nicole about Brittany, so why not the other way round? Annie could stir up real trouble for Kate over this, but maybe she would hold fire. She had diverted the results of Kate's efforts, and shipped no real damage. Given recent events with the Longs and that Annie would soon be gone, she could leave this to Kate's own conscience. The woman must know how close she'd sailed to the wind and how lucky she was to get away with it. Perhaps when she had the leash firmly round Scott's neck and saw that he was content to be tied down, as Annie was sure he would be, she'd settle down and not be so foolish again.

'What's the latest with the business?' she asked Nicole.

'Oh that. No, we're not doing it. I couldn't go in with Charlotte now, not after all this.'

'But it all looked so promising,' Annie bit down an urge to try to persuade Nicole to change her mind. It was nothing to do with her.

'No, I couldn't.' Nicole looked down, her voice slightly edgy with a hint of tears not too far away.

And then it clicked with Annie. Nicole, not Charlotte, coming to her in the first place. Charlotte's comments about Nicole. *She's more upset than I am.* The whole mood and tenor of her conversations with both women.

She watched Nicole closely, as she said, 'You and Michael...?'

'Yes... yes.' Nicole lay back in the chair and put her hands over her face. The hint of tears was gone. Annie heard only a resigned hopelessness in her voice.

'Were you having an affair? Did Charlotte know?'

'Oh no.' Nicole looked surprised. 'Nothing like that. We wouldn't have done that to Charlotte. We'd been together before he and Charlotte met. A few years before. We were together for several months but we broke it off for stupid reasons. I suppose we didn't realize it, not until he and Charlotte were living together. We both knew we had to be with each other, but he was going to end it with Charlotte first.'

'Did Jennifer know all this?'

'Oh yes. I knew Jen back when I was with Michael first time round.'

So Jennifer had actually known Michael Walker some years ago. She'd kept that quiet. Old friends with Nicole; acquainted with Michal Walker. That explained her being prepared to overstep the boundaries in digging up information. She did a swift mental calculation. Michael and Charlotte had been together six years.

'So you knew him at the time of Donna's first allegations?'

'No, I wasn't around then. I knew nothing about it until it all came out just recently. Michael and I had been together a couple of years before that. But after we split up, we saw nothing of each other until I got back in touch with Charlotte – we were at school together – and found out who she was with.'

Annie didn't comment but worked out that Nicole's fling with Michael Walker must have been when she was sixteen or seventeen. She was surprised, and disappointed, that Jen hadn't trusted her enough to confide these details. She'd thought them on a firmer footing than that.

As soon as Nicole had drunk her coffee, Annie kindly but firmly eased her out, then came back into the flat with the feeling of business undone. It had been a jolt to learn that Jennifer had not trusted her with the whole story. Yet she felt surprise that it should bother her so much.

The following morning, Annie was up and out of the flat soon after six. Memories of the conversation with Nicole jangled in her head. But why should it get to her like this? Jennifer had always been careful. They were careful with each other, notwithstanding that they'd become friends over the years.

The office phone started to ring the moment she was through the door. She reached for it whilst slipping out of her jacket and, as soon as she heard the voice at the other end, she grinned.

'Hi, Pieternel. Barbara told me you'd rung. Why didn't you try my mobile?'

'I wanted to know for sure where you were. I thought I'd catch you at this time if you were still working in that hell hole.'

Annie laughed. 'Yes, still here.'

'Well settled? Much work on?'

Annie was cautious in her replies as she listened to Pieternel probe for information. She couldn't openly trash the sisters and their business methods, nor did she want to come clean about her intention to find a new berth, not until she knew what this was about. It had to be a prelude to an offer of sorts, but what? Maybe Pieternel wanted Annie's help on a specific job and probed to see if she would work on her own behind Pat's back, and maybe it was more than that.

'I notice you've disappeared,' Annie commented.

'How d'you mean?'

'No online footprint for several months.'

'You've checked, have you?' Pieternel laughed. 'I wanted to duck out of sight for a while.'

'You must show me one day how you do that.'

'Yeah, I will.'

After a few minutes of circling each other along these lines, Pieternel's tone changed. Annie heard the note of caution disappear into a sudden decisiveness as the voice in her ear said, 'Right then. Let's see.'

She felt herself tense as she waited to hear what it was all about. The words when they came were not what she expected.

'Have to dash now, Annie. Look out for an e-mail tomorrow.'

The line went dead. Annie stared at the handset, nonplussed, then dialled 1471.

You were called today at... the caller did not leave a number.

For several minutes, she drummed her fingers on the desk trying to second guess what Pieternel's e-mail would say. Then she pulled out the files for her cases and began to go through them.

CHAPTER THIRTY TWO

After an hour or so, Annie felt the building wake up around her with the sounds of footsteps and doors banging. When she heard the post arrive, it was a welcome excuse to leave her desk.

She peered into the downstairs office, hoping someone might wave her in for a chat, but it was a bustle of people darting about, probably chasing a deadline. Regretfully, she took the mail back upstairs. Some routine invoices she put aside for Pat; obvious junk mail she opened and binned. There was one envelope addressed to Barbara and marked as confidential. Annie didn't need to open it to know what was inside.

Following her advice a week last Friday, Barbara had written a demand for disclosure of a specific document – the letter she had sneaked into the post tray in the small hours, almost catching Annie and Scott in the office. And this looked like it. Annie wondered at it arriving so soon. This document would put the skids right under their opponent's case. Her fingers itched to rip it open and see it for herself, but that would wind Barbara up for no good reason, so she put it on the desk unopened and went back to her files.

By the time she heard the familiar grunts and groans of Pat's arrival, the sun was high enough to spear light through the glass panels of the door downstairs, half-blinding her as she peeped out to see if Pat was alone. She was.

'Hi,' she greeted her. 'That document's come for Barbara. The Mellors' case.'

The reply was a grunt, but after she'd hung her coat over a chair and sat down, Pat reached for the phone and rang her sister.

'Babs? Letter for you. Shall I open—? Oh, all right, don't get shirty. And get a move on.'

Annie smiled. Pat was itching to get a look at it too.

'You about done there?' Pat asked, surprising Annie who was used to Pat as a monosyllabic companion before midday.

'Uh... yeah, just about.'

'So that weird woman from down south's been in touch. What did she want?'

It was way too soon to confide any details. 'Barbara said no message; just that she wanted to speak to me.'

'Hmm. Well, not to worry. And did you look up that Digby guy?'

'No, I haven't. Not yet. But I will.'

'What if you find him? Will you tell the old lady?'

Annie considered for a moment. 'Depends what I find,' she said.

They relapsed into silence and Annie finished what she was doing. She made a half-hearted attempt at looking up William Digby, but it was too common a name and she had insufficient data to pin him down. It needed focus and she couldn't give her whole mind to it while that letter sat in her peripheral vision. Pat, too, didn't seem able to settle and twice looked at her watch, then towards the door with an irritable, 'Where's she got to?'

When at last the click of the downstairs door was followed by the creaks and groans of the staircase, both Annie and Pat sat up, alert, their stares homing in on the door, which swung open as Barbara walked in.

Barbara gave them each an expansive smile, said 'Nice morning,' and shrugged out of her coat. 'Right then.' She rubbed her hands together as if in anticipation of a treat and turned towards the back of the office. 'Who's for coffee?'

Annie felt her fists ball.

'Bugger coffee, Babs,' Pat growled. 'Get this damned letter open and let's see what's in it.'

Annie watched Barbara slit the top of the envelope and slide the letter out. Pat peered over her sister's shoulder, and Annie had a glimpse of a block of text. Very short. Far shorter than she remembered. That must be the cover letter.

'Oh hell,' breathed Pat. 'You were wrong, Babs. This isn't what you thought.'

'What!' Annie leapt across to stare at the letter. This was impossible.

'You idiot,' Barbara yelled at Annie. 'Why did I listen to you? I must have been mad, and now look what you've done.'

'What's Annie to do with it?' Pat looked from one to the other of them.

That's right, thought Annie. Give me the credit now it looks to be going pear-shaped.

'Listen,' she said, 'this isn't right. I thought they'd been a bit too prompt sending you a copy. It looks to me like they really thought ahead. They wouldn't dare forge it. I bet they did two versions at the time, in case the client got wind of it and demanded to see what they'd done.'

'Rubbish,' Barbara snapped. 'You misread the blasted thing in the first place. I've always been against these dodgy methods of yours, reading over people's shoulders, it's no way to run a business.'

'Be fair, Babs. She's been right more than she's been wrong. She's got the instinct.'

'Instinct nothing! I'm the one who's going to look a proper Charlie now. Oh that's right, walk off. Look at her, turning her back on her responsibilities. Leave me to carry the can, why don't you?'

Annie held on to her temper as she headed for the back office. She'd show them who was right and who was wrong.

The sound of the phone cut across the tension.

'That'll be the client,' said Barbara with a groan. 'I left a message when you told me the document had arrived.' She heaved a theatrical sigh. 'I'll just have to see what I can salvage out of this mess.'

Annie spun on her heel. Barbara was about to throw in the towel. This was their reputation down the tubes for sure.

'No, Barbara, wait!'

They both leapt for the phone. Annie, at a slightly greater distance was a fraction of a second ahead as Barbara struggled to get her bulk into motion. Annie clutched the handset as Barbara fell on top of her; her senior colleague's ten stone weight advantage pinning them both to the desk. Annie could only gasp for air and hold tight against Barbara's scrabbling hands, praying for the ringing to stop, signalling the call through to voice mail.

When the handset fell silent, Annie blew out a breath as she felt Barbara relax her grip. Barbara struggled to pull herself upright, and Annie squirmed free.

Barbara's face was blotchy red. Annie watched her panting hard; saw the struggle for breath to vent her fury, was aware of the alarm in Pat's eyes as she looked at her sister.

Inside Annie, something broke. 'You stupid cow!' she shouted. 'I have a copy. I wasn't making it up. I'm not wrong. When have I ever been wrong?'

She marched to the cabinet in the back office, yanked open the bottom drawer and fished out a piece of paper, which she flung down in front of Pat before she stormed out.

A furious power-walk took Annie into the centre of town in minutes. Her mind raged with imagined arguments. She knew if she'd stayed, she'd have slapped Barbara. That would have been the end of things and that wasn't how she intended the end to be.

Barbara never admitted to being in the wrong, even when the smoking gun was in plain sight in her hand, and Annie knew just what the woman's tactic would have been had she stayed to argue. It would have been to harangue Annie for her clandestine copying of the document in the first place; an iffy act for sure, but one that would pull a spectacular result out of this case.

Almost without conscious decision, her footsteps took her to the library. She needed to calm down, to immerse herself in something that would take all her concentration. For her own peace of mind, if not Eliza's, she would find William Digby.

It took a long time. Not all the relevant news reports had been digitized and she had to squint through reams of microfiche files. No easy search facility here. But she found him, and was astonished as the story unfolded.

The biggest surprise was to find that Digby had died soon after the Jawbone Gang had walked out on him. But in talking to Annie, Eliza had been clear she'd neither seen nor heard of him from that day on. Was it credible she never knew; that none of them ever knew? Annie sat back and considered.

They were all young. The newspapers were full of impending war. Maybe they didn't read the papers themselves, certainly that could be true of Eliza, the youngest of them all. Their parents surely noted the death of the Sunday-school supervisor, but maybe they kept it from their daughters. That was what you did in those days, kept children in ignorance of what they were deemed too young to know.

As the story unravelled, Annie's eyes widened further. Yes, this would have been kept from the young Eliza, and maybe Digby hadn't got away with it after all.

Annie became aware of a movement as a figure slumped into a chair next to hers.

'Thought I'd find you here,' said Pat.

Annie acknowledged her with a nod, but said nothing.

'So, has she offered you a job? Is that why she rang?'

Annie looked at Pat and shrugged. 'I don't know what she wants. I'm waiting to hear back.'

'But if it's a job offer, you'll take it, won't you?'

There was no point in avoiding the truth. 'Very likely, yes.'

'When will you go?'

'I'll work my notice if that's what you want. I'll tie up the current cases. They're all but done, anyway.'

Annie had to look away. Pat was going to be fine about it. She wouldn't make things awkward or try to stop her. Probably she'd wish her luck when it came to it. It might have been easier to leave on the back of a blazing row.

'I won't hold you to a full notice period,' Pat said. 'But I'd like the loose ends tied up. I know what you are for leaving the paperwork.'

Annie smiled. The rebuke was justified.

'So what are you after here?' Pat's tone changed as she looked at the screen in front of Annie.

'William Digby. I'm going back to Eliza Ellis with this. Whatever she thought at the time, she must have gone through her life assuming Digby carried on his nasty little ways.'

'And didn't he?'

'No, he died. It happened very soon after they walked out on him, but I don't think they ever knew. Certainly Eliza didn't. Imagine the chaos of a war starting, people joining the forces, being called up, whatever... And Hull was one of the big ports. The whole place must have changed. Digby's death just got lost.'

'It was reported in the papers though, wasn't it?'

'Yes, but Eliza was really young, only ten or eleven. May might have known. I hope she did. She and Eliza met up again a couple of years into the war, but they never talked about what had happened, not until Susan put them back in touch when May was eighty.'

'How did he die?'

'He was murdered.'

'You don't mean those kids killed him, after all?'

'Hell, no. It wasn't done by a couple of kids. The reports say he disturbed an attempted robbery at the church.'

Pat gave her a quizzical glance. 'But you don't buy that?'

'Maybe it was as simple as that. Who's to know after all these years? But look at this.' She ran her fingers over the keyboard to bring up an indistinct scanned document. 'Have a read of that. It was brutal.'

'That doesn't give a name.'

'No, but I've linked it through the stuff that's still on microfiche. That's Digby's murder. Now tell me, is that someone disturbed mid-robbery or is it maybe one of the girls' fathers or brothers taking the law into their own hands? You couldn't report stuff like that back then, not without bringing so-called shame on the kids. And there wouldn't have been any protection of their identities. No, I think someone found out and did what Yates thought he was doing. Only this one had the right target.'

Pat's lips pursed as she read the report. 'Are you sure your old woman wants to see this?'

'I'm not going to show her the detail unless she asks, but I want her to know that the kid May tried to protect never fell into Digby's clutches.'

'When are you going to see her? Now?'

'No, I'll go tomorrow morning.'

Her research into William Digby sustained Annie most of the way home, but thoughts of Barbara kept intruding and she was annoyed to find herself on the brink of slamming the outer door behind her.

She slung her jacket at the settee and headed for the kitchen, stopping as the red pin in the cork board caught her eye. She could have sworn she'd put it back on top. If she was losing it, it was all Barbara's fault. Annie had handed her a superb result with her copied document, but knew Barbara would squander the opportunities it should provide.

Chapter Thirty Three

Annie slept fitfully and although she woke as usual with the dawn, her limbs felt heavy. She washed and dressed and set straight off into the crisp morning air, promising herself a leisurely cup of coffee just as soon as she arrived.

Halfway to the office, she realized she'd left behind the copies she'd made at the library; the reports on William Digby, but she didn't go back. She could take them to Eliza any time.

Twenty minutes brisk walk energized her after her disturbed night, and she made it to the office before seven. She opened her e-mail and felt a rush of anticipation to see Pieternel's name against a mail marked as urgent.

As she'd half hoped, half expected, Pieternel had a new business venture on the go. Better than that, Pieternel was specializing in investigating insurance fraud – just the direction Annie had always wanted the sisters to take. And if Annie could come up with the financial stake, she could go in as a partner; someone who would have autonomy and a say in the running of the venture.

It would mean finding capital. Her aunt had offered to back her years ago, but she'd never taken the offer seriously. How could someone without money to spare back anyone? Now Charlotte and Nicole had opened her eyes to options she'd never considered before.

I know you'll have stuff to check, the e-mail ended, *but I need you to tell me by Friday if it's a definite no. If it is, I need to look elsewhere.*

It was tempting to reply at once, because how could it be a definite no, but she decided to give herself time to think about it.

When Pat arrived some hours later, Annie's head was full of plans she couldn't share. Not yet. She scrabbled round in her mind for a reason to leave the office, but it was Pat who gave her the excuse by saying, 'I thought you were off to see that old biddy this morning.'

Annie stood up and reached for her jacket. 'Yeah, I'm on my way now.'

She left with no intention of going to see Eliza, because that would mean a round trip to her flat to pick up the papers. She would make time at the weekend to let her know about Digby. For now, she had phone calls to make, people to contact, and there was Pieternel's story to be checked out before she made up her mind.

By the evening, Annie felt as exhausted as if she'd done a shift of close surveillance on a difficult quarry. She picked up a sandwich on the way back to the flat and looked forward to unwinding with a few hours in front of the television.

'Did that woman find you?' one of the neighbours greeted her as she went in.

Woman? He must mean Nicole the other night. 'Yeah, she did.'

In the office the next morning, Pat asked, 'How did the old biddy take it?'

'I didn't get round to going. I got sidetracked. I'll go later.'

Annie glanced at Pat, hoping not to be asked what she'd been sidetracked into, but Pat yawned and said, 'Yates is back in court for sentencing today.'

'Not before time. What do you think he'll get?'

'After what he did? Locked away in a loony bin, I should think. I mean, it's about—'

The shrill of the phone cut through Pat's words. She reached forward and answered it, passing the handset to Annie with the words, 'Donna Lambit.'

Annie kept her voice impersonal. 'Mrs Lambit. What can I do for you?'

'You said you'd tell me what you found, remember?' Donna's voice was nervy.

'I'm under no obligation to report anything back to you, but yes, I did say I would if I could.' Annie was surprised Donna had come back to her. She must know the truth by now, but Annie was not loath to take the chance to ram what she'd done down the woman's throat. 'I don't have the time to come out to you. You'll have to meet me in town.' She named the coffee bar at the far end of the street.

Donna was effusive in her thanks and promised to be there.

'Why didn't you just tell her on the phone and be done with it?' Pat said.

'I want to see her face when I spell out to her what she did.'

Annie arrived to find Donna huddled in a corner, sipping Diet Coke through a straw. She jumped up and offered to buy Annie a drink, but Annie waved her back to her seat and placed herself in the chair opposite so she could look directly into her face.

'Michael Walker was innocent, you know.'

Donna's gaze dropped and she put her head down. 'I know what I heard.' The voice was a whisper that Annie had to strain to hear.

'May was talking about someone else. Someone who died over seventy years ago.'

'But she said—'

Annie cut roughly across Donna, not letting her finish. 'It was a different Charlotte. Someone she'd known when she was young.'

At last Donna raised her eyes to meet Annie's. 'Then why would they let me have that old box?' There was defiance in her tone.

'Because you told them it was for your daughter. It wasn't. It was the Charlotte whom May had known decades ago. If you hadn't put your oar in, May's daughter might have gone to one of May's old friends and found out the truth. How could you ever have thought that May meant your Charlotte? She'd never even met her.'

Annie could see that Donna was close to breaking down, but the flash of defiance remained. The woman was not going to admit to Annie that she was in the wrong. Why was she here at all? It was obvious this wasn't news to her. Annie wondered if Donna had heard the tale from Charlotte and had come to Annie hoping to hear a different version. If so, she would be disappointed. Annie had no intention of letting her off the hook.

'How could you have thought that what you overheard was about Michael Walker?'

When Donna didn't answer, Annie allowed her anger to show. 'A man's dead because of what you did.'

'Joshua Yates is a madman,' Donna blurted out. 'I didn't know... how was I supposed to...?' She stopped on a sob.

'Heaven knows if Charlotte will ever look you in the eye again.'

At that, Donna looked up. 'I'll make it up to my Charlotte. I'm going to help her set up her business. I'll see she makes a go of it. We're going into business together.'

'You and Charlotte? Going into business together?' Annie was amazed. Then she thought of the ruthless streak she'd seen in Charlotte and could see the woman playing this situation for all it was worth. She would get what she wanted: her business off the ground; Michael out of her life; her mother subservient and compliant under the weight of what she'd done.

Annie didn't like any of the players in this case. Nicole was no better, having some sort of affair with Charlotte's partner behind her back, and planning to run off with him. How she ever saw the business venture surviving that, Annie couldn't imagine.

'She'd never have gone into it with Michael,' Donna announced. 'She was all set to leave him.'

'I know,' said Annie. 'And wasn't he planning to take up with Nicole?'

She knew she might be making trouble for Jennifer's friend by referring to this, but she couldn't bring herself to care.

Donna's mouth curved to a sly smile. 'Oh, you know about that, do you? No, he didn't want her. He was terrified of Nicole getting her claws into him again. Charlotte used to laugh about it. That's how come Nicole agreed to put so much into the business, because she thought she'd be in it with him. Michael Walker couldn't stand the doe-eyed tart. Just imagine the problems if they were all tied together and trying to keep a new business afloat.'

There was a ring of truth to Donna's words, which gave yet another layer of deceit to this web of relationships. Somehow, it was Brittany Booth now who came across as the only decent human being in the whole tangled web. Brittany at least had the excuse of extreme youth; of her infatuation with the insane Yates; and she had accepted the truth of what had happened.

Annie left Donna without any goodbyes and went out into the street to head back towards the office. Partway along, she stopped and spun round, scanning the street behind her. Nothing untoward. Plenty of people milling about. She looked for Donna's face, but didn't see it in the crowds. There was no reason why Donna should come after her, but it took the rest of the way back to throw off the feeling she was being watched.

'Have you heard about Yates?' Pat greeted her.

'No, what's happened?'

'Broadmoor. And they've thrown away the key.'

The next morning, Annie headed towards Eliza's care home. The old woman deserved to know that Digby had been stopped. The uniformed woman who opened the door to her, said, 'Eliza's not been feeling too well. She's still in bed.'

Eliza, looking frail and insubstantial against the soft white pillow, stared balefully up at Annie. 'I thought I'd seen the last of you. I've caught a chill with being kept outside too long.'

Ungrateful cow, Annie thought, but said, 'Sorry to hear that, but at least you can rest easy about your promise to May.'

Eliza acknowledged this only with a slight curl of her lip and then asked, 'What do you want?'

'It's about William Digby.'

'No! We had an agreement. You can't come back pestering for more.'

Annie jumped to reassure Eliza as she saw the old woman's hand fumble for her alarm pad.

'No, no. It isn't that. I've found out something that I thought you'd want to know.'

Eliza stared towards Annie, her eyes unable to focus, but radiating suspicion. 'What? What have you found out?'

'William Digby died. A long time ago. Quite soon after you walked out on him. Whatever he did to May. Whatever he planned to do to Charlotte, he didn't. He never had the chance. He died.'

Eliza remained silent for a moment. Then, 'He's dead. How do you know?'

'I traced it from some old newspaper reports.'

'I never saw any newspaper reports.'

'Well, you were very young. Your parents would have kept them from you, wouldn't they?'

Annie wasn't sure she understood why Eliza was so antagonistic towards her. She had, after all, allowed her to destroy the papers that had been preying on her mind. Maybe it was that Annie was now the only person left who knew what the old secret was really about and Eliza didn't want her anywhere near.

'Do you want to see them?' she asked.

'No! Of course not!' Eliza's clouded eyes opened wide in panic. 'I want nothing to do with him. Why are you pestering me still?'

'I just thought you might want to see for yourself that...' Her words tailed off. What was it that she thought Eliza might want to see? That justice had been done? There'd been no justice in any of this.

As Annie left Eliza's room, the old woman shouted after her. 'I don't want you back. Promise me you won't be back.'

'I won't, I promise,' Annie shouted back, as she headed for the front door.

CHAPTER THIRTY FOUR

Annie collected contacts the way a sick hedgehog collects fleas. She had a nose for information that might one day come in useful and she drew casual acquaintances into her network almost without conscious thought.

The real struggle was in keeping them all warm enough to be useful when she needed them. It took physical effort to be at the right leisure centre often enough to sustain a friendship; to make the rounds of the bars where people had lunch; to drop by offices at slack times when her presence would be a welcome distraction.

The inside information and knowledge she could pick up had saved her hours of hard slog over the years. Now she skipped from place to place, trying to find as many of her people as she could, to touch base, to drop words in ears that she was moving on, and that Pat Thompson was OK and could be trusted. Pat was too lazy to run any contacts network efficiently, but Annie hoped to leave her something.

It was early afternoon when she returned to the office, and as she climbed the stairs, she heard Barbara's excited tone. 'They've admitted it!'

She smiled. Her clandestine document copying had produced results. An admission by the other side made for an easy resolution and a smoother route to more business.

As she opened the office door, she saw Barbara clench her fist and give a crow of triumph. 'That's it! The conniving bastards. This is dynamite. It's—' She stopped as she saw Annie.

Annie worked on keeping her expression bland.

'Message for you,' said Pat. 'From someone at the old people's home. The old biddy wants to see the newspaper cuttings. Can you drop round with them?'

Annie gave a tut of exasperation. 'I've just come from there. She said she didn't want to see them. Or me, for that matter.'

Barbara turned to chivvy Pat. 'Come on, let's get to work.'

Annie listened as the sisters began to bicker over their next move. She decided to stay in the office and join in the debate, to make sure they set off on the right track.

Eliza could wait till tomorrow for her papers.

When she woke the next day, Annie regretted not having rushed back round to the home, because it left her with a task she could do without. It was Saturday, and she had planned to start on the serious business of wrapping up her life in Hull. Irritation rose against Eliza. Stupid woman with her antagonism and changes of mind.

But then she relented. What if it were too late? Eliza hadn't been well. How would she feel if the old woman had died in the night thinking Annie had made up the tale about Digby's death and would now never see the newspaper reports that Annie could have delivered yesterday? She picked up her phone.

'Hello. I'm enquiring after Eliza Ellis. She wasn't too well when I called in yesterday.'

'Oh, she's a lot brighter today. She's quite her old self.'

'That's good. I'll be round in about twenty minutes. I have some newspaper cuttings for her.'

A neighbour was coming in as she went out on to the street. Her nod of greeting turned into a groan of disbelief. Her car lolled down on a flat tyre, completely flat to the ground. How long had it been like that? Surely she would have noticed when she came in yesterday. Please let the spare be OK.

She stepped closer and realized the spare would not be enough. Both nearside tyres were down.

Today of all days! But how on earth—?

Heading for the boot of the car, she realized this wasn't bad luck, and knew what she'd see before she walked round to the car's offside. All four tyres flat to the ground. She looked closer to see the cuts where a knife had sliced deep into the rubber.

'Bloody hell!'

She looked up and down the road. It was quiet now, but her car had fallen prey to a gang of kids in the night.

When her phone rang, she answered absently, her mind still on the carnage in front of her.

'Hello, Ms Raymond. I wonder if I could have a word.' The voice was so calm and controlled it took Annie a moment to recognize it.

'Uh... yes, of course. It's Brittany Booth, isn't it? What can I do for you?'

'Were you in court to hear the sentence?'

'No, I wasn't, but I know about it.'

'It's not like a prison term, you know. He might never come out.'

Brittany's voice was calm but there was an underlying sadness. Clearly she still nurtured feelings for Yates. Annie had a lot to do today and wanted the woman off the phone, but she made the effort to inject sympathy into her tone.

'This way he'll get treatment. He'd have had a bad time in prison. It's the best option, really. I know it's hard after all that's happened, but you need to walk away from it.'

'Do you really think he'll get the treatment he needs?' Brittany's voice washed over her, unnaturally calm yet with an undertone that betrayed turmoil beneath the surface. 'Isn't it more likely they'll shackle him and fry his brain, or stuff him so full of drugs he doesn't know who he is anymore?'

Annie felt trapped and impatient. She didn't want to snub the woman or lie to her, but she wanted her off the phone. She had to sort out her car. The plan had been to use it this weekend to get round to everyone she had to see. She thought about insurance, about having to report it and get a crime number, about all the hassle that she just didn't need.

'Brittany, you've been reading the wrong stuff. It's not like that these days.'

There was a silence. Annie wondered if her no-nonsense tone had been convincing. For herself, she thought Brittany's account probably nearer the mark, but she had neither time nor inclination to worry over Yates's fate.

'The thing is,' Brittany said, still in that unnaturally even tone, 'this wouldn't have happened if you'd done a proper job.'

'You know that's absurd. Nothing I did made the slightest difference. No one but a handful of people even know about it. All I did was verify that Joshua Yates was wrong. Terribly wrong. A man died because of it. The court simply looked at the facts.'

Another pause, and when Brittany spoke, her voice was hard. 'You haven't a clue what it's like. Have you ever been close to anyone? I'll bet you're close to your mother, even if no one else'll touch you with a bargepole. Oh yes, this is about you. You're going to find out what it's like to lose someone close to you; to see them condemned to a living hell.'

As Annie began to speak, Brittany cut the call.

She looked at the silent phone and let out a sigh of exasperation. Brittany hadn't accepted it after all. On a sudden thought, she spun round and stared at her car. Was this Brittany's revenge? If so, she could live with it, but it was a bloody nuisance. And just in case it wasn't, or if Brittany had something else planned, she called Pat and told her what had happened.

'Annoying about the tyres, but the rest of it sounds like hot air,' said Pat. 'Any idea what she might have meant?'

'I don't know who she'd target other than you or Barbara.'

'Well, you watch your back, too. It's likely nothing but you never know.'

As Annie stood trying to gather her thoughts, a voice from behind her said, 'Dear me, what's happened here?'

She turned with a smile for her upstairs neighbour.

'I could have done without it, today,' she said.

He stepped closer and saw the cuts in the tyre walls. 'Is it to do with a case?'

Annie smiled as she opened her mouth to tell him probably just kids in the night, but then she caught the gleam of excitement in his eye and said instead, 'Yes, it's the same case that I needed your flask and the ice for.'

'Dear me,' he said, with a beam of satisfaction. 'You'll be needing more than ice to sort this out. Now, would you like to borrow my car? I shan't be needing it today.'

'Thank you,' said Annie, genuinely touched. 'That's very kind, but I'm sure I'll manage.'

After he'd disappeared into the house, Annie rang the home to let them know not to expect her and to say she would post the cuttings to Eliza.

'Yes, we'd heard. It's your car, isn't it?'

Annie felt her guts flip over as she stared at the immobilized vehicle.

'Don't worry,' the voice went on. 'Your sister's been to collect Eliza. She's bringing her to you.'

'My...? Oh my God! No! No, you have to stop her. Quick!'

'But they've already gone. What is it? What—?'

Annie cut through the bewildered tone to bark out, 'Call the police. Eliza's been kidnapped.'

She clicked the phone off. Her finger hovered over the 9 button, but then she did what she always did when it was an emergency and there wasn't time for explanations. She called Jennifer.

Everything she'd missed came back at her in a rush. The whole picture. That feeling of being followed. The woman who'd come to call. Not Nicole. Brittany.

It had always felt odd that Brittany had gone to Nicole and not Charlotte. All that pretence at remorse was a ploy to learn all she could about Annie.

Then she remembered the irritating anomalies she'd blamed on her own carelessness. The red pin, too low on the board... a document out that she was sure she'd put away. Brittany had been in her flat.

Brittany had followed her to the home.

And with a disregard for the facts that could have been Yates's own, she'd assumed Eliza was Annie's mother.

Annie remembered Nicole's words, the very first time they'd met. *The woman's insane. I mean it. You can see it in her eyes.*

At last, Jennifer's voice was in her ear.

'Jen, thank God! She's mad. Brittany Booth. She's as mad as Yates.'

'Annie, what are you talking about?'

Annie pulled in a deep breath, trying to slow the thumping of her heart. She gave Jennifer as concise an account as she could, sticking to the salient facts. Brittany Booth had kidnapped an old woman called Eliza Ellis and she meant to harm her to get back at Annie.

Jennifer absorbed the information, asked no spurious questions and promised to mobilize help.

A gentle breeze swept down the street as Annie stood breathing hard, trying to work out what to do next... which way to turn. Thank God for Jennifer and that she knew Annie well enough to take her seriously. It hadn't always been that way.

Before she could return her phone to her pocket, it buzzed a new call. Annie whipped it back to her ear.

'Yes?'

'Annie, good to catch you for once. Just wondering about that emergency business and if you'd sorted it?'

Disorientated, Annie struggled to put a name to the voice. 'Sorry, what?'

'Because if you have, there's still time to come out here. I've someone else lined up to do it, but the kids were all looking forward to having a real detective judge them. Mythical warriors, you know. They're putting on a special show as well if you can come early. They've really gone to town on the theme.'

'No, sorry, not a chance. Another emergency has just cropped up.'

'Ah well, if things calm down, come on out.'

'Of course, but I'm afraid I don't have time to chat. I must—'

'Oh, I didn't ring for that. I've a message to pass on. You've been working with some people out this way, haven't you? Name of Morgan.'

'Uh... yes, I have.'

'They've seen you on the posters, I guess. They left a message; wanted to catch you after the judging.'

Annie did a lightning mental reconstruction. Either the Morgans had had the christening, all had gone well and they wanted to thank her. Or they'd got cold feet about some aspect of it and wanted further advice. Either way, they were at the bottom of her priority list.

'OK, thanks, I'll ring them. Now I have to go. Bye.'

'And if you can—'

The woman was still talking as Annie cut her off.

As she turned back to the house, an image replayed in front of her. That red pin... too low on the board... what had it held there? Fancy-dress... mythical warriors... That message hadn't been from the Morgans at all.

At once, she was back on the phone to Jennifer. As she paced back and forth across the pavement, Annie became aware of people walking past, their glances straying to her four flat tyres, their faces betraying relief that this was someone else's problem.

'Brittany Booth thinks I'm judging a fancy-dress competition this afternoon,' she told Jennifer. 'That's where she's gone. At least I think so.' She gave Jennifer the details and explained the call she'd just taken.

'She won't get that far,' Jennifer said. 'Someone at the home had their wits about them. They saw two people arguing in the car and then going off in a shower of gravel. They got a description and a partial number and there's CCTV just down the road. We'll have her before she gets out of the city.'

'But can't you just look up her car?'

'She doesn't have one. She's borrowed or stolen one. It's a black Megane, but don't worry... Ah, hang on. We might have her. Got to go.'

'Ring me, Jennifer, the minute—'

The phone went dead. Still standing out in the street beside her useless car, Annie decided to make one more call just to be sure.

She got Tim Morgan. No, neither he nor Tracey had left any message or even tried to be in touch. When he started to tell her the latest about their skeleton, she cut him off, then stood undecided. There was no reason not to go back to her planned itinerary. Jennifer's colleagues would get Brittany. Of course they would. They might have her now.

Brittany's plan had been to head out into Holderness expecting to find Annie judging a fancy-dress competition. Annie hated the feel of Brittany's illogical thinking. Clearly, she wanted Annie at that village show, yet she'd slashed her tyres so she couldn't go and get Eliza. How did she expect her to get there? She didn't like how it felt that Brittany was irrational enough not to have thought that through. Would it occur to her at some point that she'd wrecked Annie's only obvious means of transport? Would she head back here to the flat?

Or did the woman have some insane plan to go out there in her place, to get in amongst the contestants as the substitute judge? And then what?

She tried to tell herself that Brittany was angry and upset, that was all. She would come to her senses and she wouldn't harm Eliza. She brought Brittany's face to mind. The fanatical gleam in her dark eyes; her disregard for fact or logic; the well of anger she'd seen ready to erupt when Brittany was bested. She could find no reassurance in any of the memories.

Again, she was on the phone to Jennifer. And now Jennifer was beginning to sound impatient.

'We'll have her soon, Annie, whether she heads out of the city or goes to your flat. I'll let you know.'

Annie knew she couldn't settle to routine business. She had to join in the hunt for Eliza. She headed back indoors to take up the offer of a car from her upstairs neighbour.

It was as she pulled away that a text message beeped through on her phone telling her she had voice mail. She clicked the handset to speakerphone and laid it on the dashboard.

'Where the hell are you?' screeched Pat's voice. 'Who the hell are you talking to all this time? For God's sake ring me the moment you get off the phone.'

She stopped to ring back.

'Annie, at last!' Pat's voice was urgent and breathless. 'Booth's after the old woman... thinks she's your mother. I was about to ring 999.'

'No, stop. I'm on it. I've called Jen.'

'But Booth's taken her already. We saw her.'

'I know she has. That's why—. Hang on, what do you mean you've seen her?'

'It clicked just after you'd rung. When I couldn't get you, we went straight to the care home. The Booth woman was driving her away. We tried to follow, but we lost her. Look, are you sure it's in hand?'

'Yes, Jen's on it. Did you get a number?'

'No, we were too busy trying to get after her. Flanagan can just look it up. It's all in hand, right? Because I've things to do. I haven't time to run around after madwomen.' Pat's voice became muffled as she added. 'You can leave me here.'

'Who are you talking to?'

'Babs's lass. I made her drive me. That's why we lost her. If I'd been driving...'

In the background, 'But Aunt Pat, I couldn't...'

CHAPTER THIRTY FIVE

Thirty minutes later, Annie pulled the borrowed car into the gravelled yard at the riding school. Vehicles were crammed in everywhere, the grassy verges churned to mud. She climbed out of the car and looked around.

A couple of people wove their way through the maze of cars, but the real activity was over in the big paddocks. Annie heard a public address system boom out, calling entrants to a show class. Between her and the hub of the action lay the barns and stable blocks. Built as a neat courtyard, a motley collection of lean-tos and sheds had been added over the years, their bare concrete blocks at odds with the brick and timber finish of the original.

'Annie! You made it.'

Annie turned at the shouted greeting, to see a couple of young girls running off round the barn to spread the news of her arrival.

Her memories of previous visits were overlaid by the smells of horses and mown grass, but today with all the vehicles, it was the oily aroma of petrol that hung in the air. The sickly tang held in the back of her throat as she inspected every car, looking for a black Megane or something that might have been mistaken for it; looking, too, for any sign of Eliza or Brittany in any of the empty vehicles, though not sure what sign they might have left. There was nothing to find.

She decided to head for the action and find out more about the message, but she avoided the direct route through the courtyard. Although it appeared empty, she knew how suddenly the enclosed space could fill with ponies that darted here and there dragging their tiny owners and barging into anyone in their path.

As she picked her way along the grass track that skirted the boundary of the premises, she approached from behind, working her gaze across the knots of people, looking for familiar faces.

She was aware of one or two people looking her way, pointing her out to others. The news of her arrival would spread quickly to those who had any interest in it. She strained to check every face, to be absolutely sure that neither Brittany nor Eliza were in the crowd.

The proprietor of the yard marched up to her. 'Why, Annie, you made it. Wonderful. And just in time to see the special display.' She turned away from Annie to shout, 'Girls! Come on, ring two. Look sharp. Annie's here.'

Annie allowed herself to be led across the bumpy grass, her gaze raking the crowds again and again; her attention half on the road behind them where Brittany would drive down if she were to get here at all.

The voice at her side rattled on, telling her that the fancy-dress contestants had organized a special show. 'They've worked hard... and all by themselves... worked it out... bit on the dodgy side... insurance... but still, can't keep them in cotton wool... wonderful initiative...'

For a moment, Annie allowed her attention to be drawn to where it was directed, determined not to be coerced into a judging role. 'This is a special show?' she queried. 'This isn't the fancy-dress competition?'

'No, no. Don't you worry. The fancy-dress is later as per the schedule I sent you. They'll just stand in line for you to look them over. This display was all their own idea. They wanted to put on something special after the trouble of making the costumes and getting the ponies used to them. They'll be thrilled you're here in time to see it.'

Annie fingered the phone in her pocket. Nothing yet from Jennifer, so they hadn't caught up with Brittany. 'I don't know how long I can stay. I might not be able to stay and judge. You said you'd found someone else.'

The woman laid her hand on Annie's arm and leant close. 'Well, if that's the case, why don't we get you a ringside seat for the display and you have a close look at them while they're doing their stunts? They'd much rather hear that you'd decided who the winners are. I can announce it later. Come along, we'll get you in the ring before they start.'

Her hand half raised to turn down this offer, Annie paused, her refusal unvoiced. Inside the show ring with the ponies was exactly where Brittany would expect to find her. If the woman evaded Jennifer and her cronies and turned up here, wouldn't she seek Annie out? That surely was the whole point of what she was doing.

'About this message you had for me, how did you get it?'

'The woman phoned. I don't know if she's here.'

'So you haven't met her?'

'No, she said her name was Morgan.'

Brittany must have picked that up from the Longs' file in Annie's flat. Mentally she kicked herself again for missing the signs. Not only the gaping hole in Brittany's sanity, but the misplaced red pin, the files that had moved, the instinct screaming at her that she was being followed. She'd been preoccupied with Nicole or angry with Barbara and had brushed the anomalies aside.

'Is she a friend of yours?'

'No, she isn't. Tina... Tina! Listen to me.' Annie took hold of the woman's arm to grab her attention from the ponies bouncing past. 'This is important. If she turns up, if you see any sign of her, you have to let me know at once. And she might be with an old woman.'

'I've no idea what she looks like, but if she makes herself known I'll let you know.'

Annie described Brittany and Eliza as best she could, adding, 'But if she turns up, they might not be together.'

'She's trouble, then?'

'Yes, big trouble. Just be sure and let me know. Is this where I go?'

Tina called out to a gangly youth who shambled across to join them. 'Take Annie into the ring. Show her where to stand so she isn't in the way.'

Together they made their way into the roped-off area. As he led her across the grass, he said, 'This is great, you turning up. We were gonna have some old git from the council judging the fancy-dress. What would he know about it?'

Annie resisted the obvious answer of 'more than me' and scrutinized the area all around the paddocks. The grassy expanse commanded a good view of the road where it led down to the car park entrance. She indicated a patch of slightly elevated ground. 'Can I stand on here?'

The boy nodded so she stepped up and raked her gaze once again across the crowds. No Brittany. No Eliza. Jennifer would do her job and might already have Brittany in custody and Eliza safely back at the home, but her phone remained silent so she couldn't be sure. And from here, she could see everyone who arrived.

Three ponies and riders materialized in front of her in a babble of voices.

'Hi, Annie, this is great.'

'Wait till you see this!'

'Really glad you could come early.'

A mêlée of equine bodies and flapping cloth circled her vantage point. The three ponies, clad in garish and intricate robes gazed out at her from under fake armoured helmets, whilst their riders struggled to manage handfuls of multicoloured reins and their own bizarre costumes. Just for a moment, she found herself pushing away the idea that everything had been a dream – the car tyres, the call from Brittany, the account from Pat – and now three mythical dream creatures had come to wake her up to start the day.

She shook the notion out of her head and smiled at them. 'Just three of them doing this bit?' she asked the boy. 'How many altogether in the bit I'm supposed to judge?'

'This is it,' he said, looking at her as though she'd said something silly. 'How many did you expect?'

The tannoy system boomed out, introducing the ponies and the marvels they were about to perform. Annie raked her gaze all around the area, looking at the faces in the crowds. The road remained quiet.

'Rosie, Mathilda and Moonbeam,' the boy told Annie, pointing to each pony in turn.

The pony, Rosie, advanced up the grass mound and lifted one of its front legs in a high arc, pawing the ground in front of Annie. She kept a wary eye on its iron-clad hoof and leant away from it.

'See, it's telling you welcome to the show,' the boy said. 'Now if you come down and stand here.' He indicated the ground in front of the second pony. 'Mathilda'll kiss your head. It's for the fancy-dress line-up really.'

'OK, I'll wait till then.'

'You don't need to be scared. Look, I'll show you.'

The boy stood in front of the pony and Annie watched the animal pucker its enormous lips and brush them on to his head. Standing there watching the bizarre antics of animals covered from head to tail in bits of material and card, Annie again had to shake off a feeling of unreality.

'Moonbeam'd show you how he can close gates, only there aren't any. They're gonna start now.'

Annie looked at him and then at the three ponies that now stood in line, side on to her, facing their audience. There was an air of expectation that she couldn't share. She stared at the jumble of colour. It looked as though the trio had been covered in glue and dipped in a giant vat of oddments from a handicrafts factory.

'What are they meant to be?'

The boy gabbled out something that sounded to Annie like 'Vleth, Ytraa and Goddess Fire.'

She nodded and then her gaze jerked towards the road. A car appeared over the brow and headed down the hill. She followed its progress as it swept by. It contained a man and a gaggle of children all laughing. She relaxed and glanced back at the people round the edge of the ring. Tina was talking to a youngish man, their faces were puzzled. They turned to walk away as Annie watched.

The three ponies were trotting towards the far end of the enclosure.

'What exactly are they going to do?'

'Stunt show. Jousting and charges and all that.'

She nodded again and fingered the phone in her pocket.

The three ponies began to circle, twisting and turning to their riders' commands. Annie watched the road. A collective gasp from the spectators brought her attention back to the show in front of her, where the multicoloured group went through a complex twisting manoeuvre. She felt her mouth drop open, certain she was about to witness a spectacular fall, but against gravity, as far as she could see, the ponies and riders remained on their feet. A light patter of applause rippled through the crowd.

She allowed her hands to go through the motions of appreciation but her gaze was on the road beyond the mythical warriors until the boy nudged her to pay attention to what she saw was the finale.

The pony, Rosie, from a standstill with its back to her at the far end of the field, suddenly turned and flew down the grass, its costume streaming behind it, its rider crouched low. As the thudding of the hoofs vibrated the earth beneath her, Annie saw the rider take a dive and heard her own gasp echoed from the spectators. Mathilda and Moonbeam closed in at speed as the first rider miraculously spun back from upside down to upright. At the point of inevitable collision, came a flurry of arms, legs and flowing costumes that seemed certain to end in a tangled heap. But out of the confusion, the three ponies shot apart, each with a different rider on its back. One rider clung on at an angle and another scrabbled for balance over her pony's neck, but they'd completed their move and the crowd applauded enthusiastically.

Annie found herself grinning as she clapped.

Then a chill ran across her. Why hadn't Jennifer rung? She looked again around the paddocks, out towards the road.

Nothing. Nothing at all. But if they'd found Brittany, Jennifer would have been in touch.

Abruptly, she turned and marched down off the grassy mound and headed for the break in the tape, clicking out Jennifer's number as she went.

'Don't worry, Annie,' Jennifer rapped out. 'Bit of a delay getting the CCTV but we've almost got her.'

'Get back to me, Jen, as soon as you have anything.' She disconnected the call feeling ever more uneasy. Why had she come all the way out here? She was far too far from the action. Looking around for Tina, she picked her way back across the grass.

'Ah, Tina, there you are. I have to go. Emergency cropped up.'

As she spoke she lengthened her stride towards the car park. It would be a relief to get away from the sickly tang of unburnt fuel.

'Good heavens, it's all go in your game,' said Tina, matching strides with her, but looking round as if she too were distracted. 'Where's...? Ah, well, never mind for now. Did you manage to pick out your winners for later?'

'Oh... uh... yeah. Rosie, Mathilda and Moonbeam.'

'What, first, second and third in that order?'

'No, no. Joint first. They were all as good as each other.'

Annie clambered round the edge of the ditch, and on to the gravel of the car park, as Tina's voice floated away into the distance. 'Well, I suppose... Most unusual. Do we have any spare rosettes? What shall we do about the cup?'

As Annie rushed for the car, her phone rang. The screen showed Jennifer's number.

'Annie, it's an inside job,' Jennifer's voice sounded hard, worried.

'What do you mean?'

'You must have wondered how Booth knew who to target?'

'No, she's been following me. I'm pretty sure she broke into my flat. What do you mean an inside job?'

'The car. It belongs to Barbara Caldwell's daughter.'

'What! No. Oh no. It's the wrong car. That was Pat. She

guessed what Booth was going to do and she tried to get to the home. They saw her.'

Annie reran Jennifer's words about the witness. Two people arguing. A car going off in a spray of gravel. That was Pat yelling at Barbara's daughter to get the car turned round and after Brittany. 'Get on to Pat,' she told Jennifer. 'She followed Brittany for a while, but lost her.'

Annie stood in amongst the cars, the smell of petrol seeping all around her, and as she looked back towards the paddocks, and the jumble of stables and outhouses, she felt a chill of foreboding wrap itself around her.

CHAPTER THIRTY SIX

The place was segregated into areas that were hidden from each other. The proud parents at the show rings could see nothing of Annie in the drive. The stable courtyard was hidden from all sides.

But consciousness of something was unfolding; awareness of disaster was seeping through the big yard.

Then she saw Tina, white-faced, rushing towards her, and understood before Tina opened her mouth to speak. The unnaturally strong smell of petrol.

Brittany had been here all along.

'There's a madwoman,' Tina burst out. 'She's in the big barn... thrown petrol about... burn the place down unless we fetch you. I recognize her voice... the message... she's the one who—'

'Oh my God, where? Get the police. Get them out here. They're already looking for her.'

'But who is she?'

'Her name's Brittany Booth. We must stay calm.' In her mind's eye Annie saw ponies tearing about, panicked, dragging their small charges with them. 'Can you keep the horses the other side of the courtyard? They mustn't come barging through.'

'Hellfire,' said Tina. 'There are ponies everywhere. I'll try, but some of them'll be in there already.'

'Do what you can,' Annie ordered, as she headed for the concealed courtyard.

Brittany sat on a hay bale in the arched entrance to the big barn, tossing a lighter in her hand. Eliza sat behind her on a wooden bench.

'You took your time,' said Brittany, getting to her feet.

'Come on, Brittany. What are you doing?'

'They've sent him to a secure institution. He'll be there forever. It's your doing.'

'It was nothing to do with me, Brittany. You know it wasn't. And it's certainly nothing to do with Eliza Ellis. She's not my mother. She was involved in a case. That's why I visited her.'

Brittany laughed. 'Don't think you can fool me with more of your lies. It'll only take a second, you know.' Brittany lifted the lighter and went as though to flick it.

'No!' Annie's heart flipped over in her chest.

'And if I go up with it,' Brittany said, 'what do I care? I'm going to teach you what it is to lose someone close to you.'

'But she's not—'

As she spoke, Annie realized she should never have rushed in. She should have let the woman think she hadn't arrived, or couldn't be found. Brittany had waited this long, she would have waited longer.

She looked at her face, seeing no trace of rationality, nothing she could argue with.

All she could do was play for time; try to judge what would push her over the edge and what would hold her back.

Hurry, Tina, and make that call. Hurry and get here, Jen.

Their stares remained locked for a moment until Brittany's eyes jerked wide. Annie saw confusion and suspicion flare in them.

Then horror twisted Annie's gut. Horseshoes clattered on the cobbles behind her. Metal-clad hoofs on stone. She daren't look round.

'What did you think, Annie? Weren't we good ... been practising for ages. We've—'

The excited chatter stopped on a shocked intake of breath. The scene at the barn door hit the riders' consciousness.

A weird sensation of hot breath ran shivers down the back of Annie's neck. She daren't look away. Brittany appeared in the midst of some internal struggle. Annie forced herself to be still, even when she felt the gentle touch of an enormous pair of lips. The pony, Mathilda, had delivered the kiss it had been taught to give her.

Brittany leant forward as she stared.

Annie's mind raced desperately to find a way to tell the riders behind her to back their ponies off.

What was the matter with Brittany? Had the fumes confused her? Could Annie dare to try to get closer?

What could Brittany's see? Through the haze of dust and filmy petrol fog, Vleth, Ytraa and Goddess Fire materialized behind Annie. What did it look like to someone with Brittany's slim grasp on reality?

She saw Brittany's gaze dart back and forth over the surreal scene, saw the woman's feet move her backwards into the barn where she stopped close beside Eliza as if seeking protection.

For the first time, Annie looked properly at Eliza. She saw a pen gripped convulsively in the old woman's twisted right hand. In her left lay her personal alarm – useless out here.

Annie looked again at the pen. Then at Eliza's lined face. She could see fear and anger. This wasn't the way for things to end for Eliza.

It was enough that Michael Walker had had to die. This must stop.

Again, she looked at the pen in Eliza's hand. Then at Brittany beside the chair, recovering her composure, setting herself to threaten again. She thought of a set of words she'd read that made no sense. *Your turn...*

Eliza had never given her a date. Not an actual date. All she had was the date of May's last diary entry.

Praying not to hear the whoosh of a petrol fire igniting, Annie turned her back to the madwoman in the barn.

'Keep very still,' she hissed urgently. 'Say nothing. Do nothing.' For now the ponies stood quietly, but Annie could see the rainbow curl of a line of fuel snaking out round the edge of the yard. Too close. One clash of metal-clad hoof on stone... one spark...

She took a step backwards, gauging Brittany's reaction only from the mirror of the three riders who faced her, staring horror-struck at the tableau over her shoulder. If she could just get within range before Brittany's confusion lifted...

Eliza, remember your script.

'Stop that!' Brittany screeched. 'That's it! This is for Joshua!' It was a triumphant shriek.

Annie half turned, saw Brittany's raised hand, knew she hadn't a hope of reaching her before the lighter flared.

'Eliza, your turn,' she shouted, and hurled herself at Brittany.

Her stare glued to the glinting metal in the woman's hand, knowing that any second the space between them might explode into a wall of fire.

Brittany, her focus on Annie, her eyes bright with triumph, let out a sudden 'Uhh.' Annie saw her face crumple in pain and surprise as the attack came from behind. The pen jabbed hard into her abdomen.

It was the fraction of a second Annie needed. She had Brittany's wrist in an iron grip, twisting her arm, crushing her fingers, seeing the lighter fall.

It spun in the air, Annie's heart doing back-flips with it, as it traced an arc and flew towards the ground. One spark was all it would take. It clattered on the cobbles and lay still.

Annie's teeth clenched involuntarily and, as she gasped in a breath, she became aware of the backdrop of shouting and alarm. Awareness had spread through the premises in a chaotic wave of panic.

Both Brittany's wrists were in her hands, as she forced the woman's arms up her back, pushing her to keep her off balance, to stop any fight back. She shoved and hustled her away across the yard, ignoring the screams and curses.

She shouted out to anyone who would listen, 'Get Eliza out of there. Get her out. Now! Hurry!'

Other voices joined hers.

Tina's authoritative tone roared, 'Keep those ponies back!'

'Get Eliza out,' she screamed again, never losing focus on the woman she held, who tried to writhe her way out of her grasp.

It wasn't until she was far enough away to prevent Brittany hurling anything back into the petrol-soaked yard, that she allowed herself to stop. She pushed the madwoman hard against a wall, keeping her arms locked behind her and looked round for help.

Four people ran towards her. 'We'll hold the bitch,' one of them shouted. 'The police are on their way.'

Annie allowed strong hands to take Brittany from her grasp. 'Eliza,' she panted. 'I have to make sure she's OK.'

'You go on. We'll look after her.'

'We'll lock the bitch in an empty stable till the police get here.'

Annie started to run back towards the stable block, then stopped and turned, cursing under her breath. She sprinted back towards the group, her chest now burning, 'Don't you lay a finger on her,' she yelled.

'Are you kidding? She could have burnt your mother to death back there!'

Annie felt a rage of her own well up. It burst from her in a string of curses that had even Brittany's eyes widen. Then she jabbed her index finger towards them. 'That's why we're here, for God's sake!' she screamed. 'People taking the law into their own hands. That's what's caused all this. I mean it. One step out of line and I'll see you all in court!'

By the time she found Eliza, some order had been restored. Ponies and people were threading their way to safety round the perimeter of the fields, everyone quieter now, watching, waiting for the one stray spark that would send it all sky high. Annie strained to hear the wail of approaching sirens, distant but audible under the gentle breeze.

Eliza had been put in a plastic chair at the edge of the gravelled yard and shot her a resentful glare.

'It's too much at my time of life.'

'I know. I'm sorry. I had no idea she'd do something like this. I thought she'd accepted that Yates was wrong. Are you warm enough? Can I get you anything?'

'Haven't you done enough?' Eliza spat out. 'I don't want anything from you. One of the girls has gone to get me a brandy from the house.'

They had to pause. Eliza's words were drowned in the sudden swell of a fire engine screaming its way over the rise that brought it into view. Soon the yard would bustle with officialdom.

Annie leant close. 'I was coming back with the proof about what happened to Digby, but I don't need to, do I?'

'You'll have a job turning me in. I'm a sweet old lady now who wouldn't hurt a fly, and there isn't a scrap of evidence left.'

'I've no intention of turning you in. I don't think there's much about you that's sweet, but I don't think you're a danger to anyone after all this time. So it all went to plan, did it? Just as May wanted.'

Eliza gave an incredulous shake of her head. 'Of course not. We rehearsed and we enjoyed pretending, but we'd never have done it.'

'So what happened?'

Eliza looked up as the noise and shouting increased in volume. Annie looked round, too. 'They'll be wanting to move us further away. It might still go up.'

'Then listen and I'll tell you, because I'm not having you back again. I don't ever want you back.'

'Don't worry. I'm leaving the area.'

'It was the rehearsing that was our downfall. And Digby's. One day, he started on about taking the new girl, Charlotte, on a trip. May's face was like thunder. Digby had the arrogance to think she was jealous and he laughed at her. Then he said, "Now for the books". Just like that.

'You saw it yourself in the plan. That was his opening line. Now for the books. Then he was to trip as he turned.'

'And did he?'

Eliza nodded. 'Oh, but don't get the idea he followed his script. He didn't. Truly he didn't.' She shuddered. 'But he did just enough. He said the words and then he fell. I've never been sure if he really tripped, just like the script said, or if someone put their foot out.'

Annie remembered the words she'd read in Eliza's neat handwriting. 'Then May was to say, "Your turn". That was to you, wasn't it?'

Eliza gave a half-shrug. 'We'd rehearsed it so often, we just carried on. It was the first deliberate blow, you see. Once we'd landed it, there was no going back. Imagine the trouble we'd have been in if he'd got up to tell the tale after that.'

'And yours was the first deliberate blow?'

'Unless someone really tripped him, yes. I was to jab my pen hard under his ribs, where it really hurts. Whoever tripped him, if they did, it might have been an accident, but there was no mistake about that pen. I did it fast and sharp like May taught me. I wanted to show them I was as brave as they were, for all I was the smallest.'

'And then?'

'Then we all knew we'd to go through with it. But it was so hard. The fight he put up. It was nothing like we'd imagined. Nothing. Hacking him down, bit by bit. And the mess. Blood everywhere. The state we were in afterwards. There was that much blood it was like we'd drained the last drops out of all our bodies.'

Eliza pulled in a deep breath. 'But we were young and resilient and we faced worse in the next few years.' She screwed her eyes up to peer across the yard. 'These bits of ponies,' she said. 'They're nothing. You should have seen the big dray horses they had in Hull back then at the brewery. Poor things. Not an ounce of malice in them. They found their bodies right up on top of the woolsheds. Blown there by a bomb. The brewery was too near the docks. Not that they stuck to the docks with their bombs. The whole town was flattened. Oh yes, the sights we saw, me and May, when she was on the ambulances. What was Digby, just another bloody body in amongst dozens? I was the smallest, you know, but May always said I was the pluckiest for all that. She taught me how to dig it in to the side, just below the ribs, where it really hurts. I've no strength in me now, but it still works.'

'It gave me just enough time to get to her. I'm glad you remembered.'

Eliza fixed her with a glare. 'Of course I remembered. Do you think anyone forgets something like that?' Her vehemence betrayed the earlier lie that Digby's murder had come to mean nothing.

Suddenly, her tone softened; her face took on a benevolent smile. 'Why, thank you, dear. So kind.'

Annie turned to the young girl who passed Eliza a large brandy glass with golden liquid sloshing around inside it.

'I don't drink usually,' Eliza said, in that same soft tone. 'But I've had such a nasty shock. Now do you think you could find me a cigar? How about that big chap over there? He's a smoker if ever I saw one.'

The young girl's eyes opened wide. 'You won't be allowed to smoke anywhere in the yard. Tina forbids it anyway, even without all this.'

'Then let's find someone with a car who'll drive me out on to the road. I've had a nasty shock, you know.'

Annie knew there was no point in offering to help. Eliza had dismissed her from her mind and her life. She glanced back just once as she wandered over to where she'd parked the car. Eliza was in good hands. Brittany would soon be under lock and key.

As she prepared to drive away, three ponies and riders crossed her path. Rosie, Mathilda and Moonbeam, still dressed as Vleth, Ytraa and Goddess Fire, not that Annie had any idea if she'd heard those names right. They meant nothing to her. But thank heavens for the way they'd materialized behind her, creatures from another dimension, to distort Brittany's twisted reality just too far for the woman to cope.

CHAPTER THIRTY SEVEN

Annie sat in the office on the morning of her last day. There was little for her to do, but she checked again through the leads she'd left for Pat to pick up. Silly, she thought, to have expected anything different because it was her last day. The sisters sat and sniped at each other and talked openly about the replacement labour they would buy in.

'We'll do it on a temp basis, just when we need.'

'That's all very well, Babs, but we'll need experience now and then. We might need to think about training someone up.'

'Too much bother. We can go to Vince if we need help.'

Annie winced but held her tongue.

The worst of it was that they weren't going to take full advantage of the case she'd wrapped up for them with her clandestinely copied document. Pat had left Barbara in charge of it and Barbara couldn't see a golden opportunity if it bit her on the ankle. Annie let out a sigh. It was no longer her problem. She was heading for a partnership with Pieternel that promised job satisfaction and financial security. She'd made the first moves in asking her aunt for help. It was a massive step; a way back to her family; building up a business and using that as the bridge between her and the past. A part of her longed to stay put, to avoid all the unknowns of a new life. But another part relished the thought of the challenges ahead.

'What train are you on tomorrow?' Pat asked.

As she answered, she was surprised to see Barbara, too, looking interested in the answer. She had no real regrets for her time with them both. It had been a necessary apprenticeship without which she would never have been able to take the next step.

Somehow over the years she'd clawed her way up. She'd left school in a complete mess, left her aunt's custody as soon as she could to the mutual benefit of both and she'd climbed out of the disaster she'd made of her early life, largely with Pat, the unlikeliest of allies. And now she would complete the process with Pieternel who had the gumption and vision both the sisters lacked. In a few years she would arrive on her father's doorstep as a success, a daughter to be proud of. Her debt to her aunt would diminish quickly and Annie would be in a position to help out with some financial backing the other way round. This venture would work. This venture had to work.

'We'll drive you to the station tomorrow,' Pat said.

Annie looked up, surprised both at the offer and that it included Barbara.

It was a squeeze in the car because Pat hadn't thought to empty the boot, so Annie had to sit in the back with her rucksack and holdall clutched awkwardly whilst the sisters crammed themselves in the front.

'We decided we should give you a send-off,' Pat told her. 'It's been a lively few years having you around.'

Annie felt herself smile and unexpectedly a tear pricked the back of her eye. It had been a lively few years in a lot of ways.

'Go in a proper parking spot,' Barbara said, as they pulled up outside the station. 'We'll walk her to the platform.'

They walked together into the chilly and echoing station concourse and up to the departure boards.

'London King's Cross,' said Barbara, her finger pointing at the screen. 'Platform 7. We'll leave you here.' She turned to Pat. 'How about a bite of breakfast in St Stephens?'

Pat nodded her approval and Annie realized the sticky confectionary in St Stephens, the place she'd first met Nicole Perks, was their real payback for driving her in.

'Well, well,' Pat's eyes opened wide in surprise. 'We're not the only ones who decided to see you off.'

Annie turned to see Scott and Kate walking towards them. The holdall was at her feet; the rucksack an awkward weight on her back. She hoped her last moments in Hull wouldn't be taken up with a shouting match.

'Hi,' Scott didn't quite meet her eye. 'Kate thought we should say goodbye.'

Annie's gaze shot to Kate.

'Had to be sure you were really going,' Kate said.

Scott looked alarmed, but Annie heard the effort Kate made to put a laugh behind her words. She smiled and spoke quickly, before Scott could wade in with something hopelessly inappropriate.

'Thanks. I appreciate the thought.' Yes, she and Kate could have been proper friends if it hadn't been for other baggage.

'Jen said to say goodbye. She couldn't make the time to get down.'

'No problem.' Annie had said her goodbyes to Jennifer last night on the phone. 'Well... goodbye. Good luck with the wedding. I hope it all goes OK. I'm sure it will.' She felt the awkwardness of trying to articulate what might be a final farewell to people she had let into her life in a way she'd never intended.

Kate, the newcomer amongst them, took charge and stepped forward. 'I hope the new job works out.' They exchanged a brief, formal handshake. Then Kate looked at Scott.

He stepped forward as though to do the same but then impulsively pulled her close. 'Bye Annie. Good luck.'

Annie hoped he wouldn't be in trouble for that. Probably not now she was leaving. She and the sisters watched Scott and Kate walk away.

'Right, then.' Pat rubbed her hands together and Annie could see that breakfast was uppermost in her mind.

'Thanks for the lift. I'll get myself to the platform. Be sure and call in if you're ever up in London.'

Pat laughed. 'Good luck with it all,' she said.

'Yeah, best of luck, kid,' echoed Barbara.

No word about keeping in touch. No suggestion that their final goodbye should be any more than this light raising of hands, but both sisters seemed to mean what they said. She smiled at them, raised her hand in farewell, hoisted her holdall to her shoulder and strode towards platform 7.

Ten minutes later, as the train flew along the banks of the Humber, Annie looked out across the wide stretch of water, its surface dappled with small waves. It reminded her of her arrival in Hull just a few years ago. As she watched, pensive, wondering if she would ever return, her phone rang. With a struggle she extracted it from her bag.

'Hello. Annie Raymond.'

'Hi, Annie.'

At the sound of Pieternel's voice, the past fell away. No regrets. No looking back. She felt her mouth curve to a grin as her new chapter began.

NEXT TITLE IN THE SERIES

THE DOLL MAKERS

Life looks good for insurance fraud investigator Annie Raymond or rather that's how she spins it. There's a ghost of a chance, but can she take it? Can she live with herself if she fakes evidence? Can she live with the consequences if she doesn't? Distracted, Annie takes her eye off the ball not realising she has vital evidence in a case she thought wasn't her business. And someone close is determined she will never deliver it.